'We'll Meet Again'

Author – Val Baker Addicott

Characters:

Sarah Anne known to her family as Surann; Nanna and Grancha her grandparents: Mother Annie a widow her husband killed in the war. Dewi and Emlyn – 'Em' as he is known to his family - her younger brothers; older sister Wendy married to Glyndwr a wealthy land owner.

Time set 1918

We'll Meet Again

Chapter One

    Sarah Anne was jostled from left to right as she made her way across the busy platform to where the train was already waiting to take her home.

It was Christmas Eve 1918 and after five years of bitter conflict at last the world was at peace. The world was at peace but Sarah Anne was not; her eyes searched the crowds; how she longed to catch just one glimpse of the man she loved. Surely by now word would have reached him that she was going home; going home in disgrace.

    Their last meeting had been five months ago when he had been home on leave from the front. How proud she had been to be seen walking by his side this handsome man in the uniform of an officer in the Norfolk regiment.

    The whistle blew and the guard shouted "All aboard; train now leaving platform----"The whistle blew again as she stepped up into the crowded compartment and all she heard of the information was the final words, "for Cardiff"; 'and home', she thought as doors were slammed closed and the train got up steam obliterating the view of those left on the platform. She was so near to tears; why hadn't he come? From her brother-in-law she had heard that he was home safe and sound surely he must have received her letters.

"Seat in that compartment madam," said a friendly ticket collector.

"Going home to the family for Christmas?" said an elderly lady who had made room for Sarah Anne to sit down.

"Yes", she replied trying to smile. Then she closed her eyes she didn't wish to hold a conversation with anyone she just wanted to shut out the world and with it her thoughts. The train left behind London and the scenery gradual changed to open pastures. Frost lay upon the fields where flocks of sheep and cattle grazed under a wintry sun; the scene, under different circumstances, would have given her pleasure but not today as she sat with her eyes tightly closed. If someone had looked closely they would have noticed tears escaping from beneath her closed lids. She had shut out the world but she could not shut out her thoughts.

Her thoughts were of him and their time together. What a wonderful time it had been. They had met at a summer fete at his home. She had not believed her sister Wendy when she told her that Sir Wilfred and Lady Katherine had invited them to the fete that was being held on Bank Holiday Monday to raise funds for the forces serving abroad. Wendy had volunteered to run two stalls; one of her home produced jams and chutneys and the other a cake stall that she had suggested that Sarah Anne could run.

Sarah Anne could still remember, as if it had been yesterday, how much preparation had gone into getting everything just perfect for these two stalls. The two sisters had worked long hours filling jars with jam and pickle and their faces had been red with the heat of the stove as they turned out sponges, loaf cakes, scones and the Welsh cakes that the sisters were so used to baking.

The summer of 1917 had done them proud as the weather had been exceptionally hot and the farmers were enjoying a bumper harvest and as long as the good weather lasted there would be a good season for the fruit that hung heavy in the orchards.

The two sisters felt a little more at peace after grieving over their father's death the previous year. Why hadn't he stayed at home in the valley and continued farming; why had he volunteered his services and joined the army to fight the Hun? Having two young boys to raise as well as Sarah Anne had been hard on their mother so Wendy the eldest daughter, who was happily married to a rich landowner, had suggested that Sarah Anne should go and live with them as her help would be an asset around the estate; and so that spring she had come to live at Oak Manor in the Norfolk countryside a world apart from what had been her life in the mining valley of South Wales.

She would never forget the day they had met. Her cake stall had been placed in the worst possible position as the afternoon sun had streamed in under the canvas canopy. The chocolate icing had begun to melt and cream oozed from between the Victoria Sandwich cakes; even the Welsh cakes, although under a snow white tea-towel, were beginning to dry. Her face was as red as a beetroot and her ringlets were in tangles beneath her pretty sun hat having become so hot she had constantly tried to push her hair from her face.

"May I purchase a dozen of those Welsh cakes; I hope they are as good as my dear grandmother makes?" She heard the man's voice quite clearly but didn't hurry to respond as she sipped a glass of lemonade that was beneath the counter.

"Certainly Sir," she said as she reappeared to come face to face with none other than Lady Katherine on the arm of a young man in uniform.

As she had leaned over to remove the tea towel her hair escaped from under her hat and a ringlet flopped into the cream on a plate of chocolate éclairs.

How well she could remember his smile, a smile she would never forget, and then his laughter as she tried to lick off the cream.

"Let me assist you", he had said; the sound of his voice making her blush redder than her already sunburnt face. He had taken a handkerchief from his pocket and reaching across had wiped the cream from her hair.

"Please come along John I don't wish to be kept waiting I have more duties to do the mayor will be arriving soon."

The band stuck up the familiar air of 'It's a long way to Tipperary' and paying for his purchases that she had placed in a brown paper bag he had bid her 'Good Afternoon'.

Whatever the condition of the cakes she had soon sold the lot and after passing the funds to her sister she began to stroll around the fete. The few pennies she had to spend were soon spent as she tried her luck at the 'lucky dip', a ride on the merry-go-round and the helter-skelter with only one penny left she had tried her luck at knocking down the coconuts but to no avail.

"May it be my pleasure to win you a bag of sweets," the voice was familiar and as she turned her eyes met those of the young officer who had bought her Welsh cakes. "If you'd care to finish up my Welsh cakes you may. Don't look at me like that, yes I have eaten almost all of them saving just one for you and I must say they were as good as my dear grandmother makes."

He had taken aim and at each attempt the small ball had knocked the coconut off its stand.

"I thought they were glued on", she had said with a smile when he had handed her the bag of sweets.

"Thank you," she had said again blushing crimson.

"The pleasure is mine but I make one condition that you will allow me to join you and as we walk we can talk and share the sweets. I am a glutton for all things sweet."

The way he looked at her made her blush even more; so she raised her hand and pulled her sun hat as low down on her brow as it would go.

"I suppose I should introduce myself Captain John Lloyd at your service".

She took his out stretched hand and smiling back at him said sweetly "Miss Sarah Anne Lloyd".

"That is a co-incidence having the same surname. Of course my mother likes to add her maiden name and does insist that we introduce ourselves as Lloyd-Smyth but I prefer to be plain John Lloyd. Perhaps we have distant relations in our family tree."

"I doubt it," she had smiled, "my family are just poor hill-side farmers. We have sheep, pigs and chickens and a couple of dogs."

"Ah! I knew there must be a connection we both love animals. You'll have to come and meet my favourite dog. He's getting on now but Bertie and I are such good pals."

There was nothing 'plain' about this young officer who stood by her side. He was tall, well-built and so very handsome. She had seen his dark hair when he had removed his hat to introduce himself. How could someone so handsome be escorting her around the fair? He had caught her arm when she had tripped over the rope holding up the circus tent and had continued to hold it as they walked around the fete.

"Would you care to join me at the circus this evening?" He hadn't waited for her reply but had told her that he would call for her at seven o'clock.

That had been the start of their romance and for the whole of the month of August they had spent almost every day together. Walking, taking picnics and even swimming together in the lake. She had never swum before but he had taught her how. Firstly by picking her up and laughingly throwing her into the water, that reflected as blue as the sky above. He had almost instantly been by her side and holding her he had let her float in his arms. That day had been the beginning of their romance; their first kiss, his first caress of her wet body.

"I'm falling in love with you Sarah Anne," he had said as they lay on the rug on the river bank watching the swans and ducks floating by and above them soft, white, down like clouds drifted leisurely by.

"When I return to the front I will always remember today and when I see the sky like it is today I will think of you."

How she had hated the day before he had left when they had had to say their 'goodbyes' as his mother was insisting on going with him to the station.

"Promise you will write."

"I'll write to you every day; how I wish you didn't have to leave. When will this terrible war be over?"

That had been the question on everyone's lips as the war escalated and continued into the following year.

Uttermost in her thoughts as she waited for his letters was would her prayers be enough to keep him safe; this terrible war had taken her beloved father whose memory she kept close to her heart surely now that she had found her own true love he would not be taken from her in some far off land and buried in a grave where no flowers could be placed.

Then the long awaited letter arrived the one to say that he would be home at the end of June just for a short leave.

She had been surprised to receive an invitation from Lady Katherine to join them at the Manor for tea on the day that John would be arriving home. Wendy had fussed over her as a mother hen over her chicks. "You really must look your best we are about the same size so I think you'd better wear my pale blue lawn dress and the hat that I had for last year's flower show, the cream straw and I have in my jewellery box a spray of forget-me-nots." Wendy was a size smaller than Sarah Anne and the bodice of the dress clung tightly across her bosom showing rather much of her cleavage. It had been a hot June day but she had picked up her white cotton shawl which she wore across her shoulders.

"You will not need that," Wendy had said but Sarah Anne had insisted that she felt a chill.

"Nerves, that's what it is nothing but nerves."

As she walked up the drive to the imposing building she really did feel nervous but when she saw John coming to meet her all her inhibitions left her.

She could not believe what afternoon tea meant in the circles of the upper-class; cucumber sandwiches cut so small and the cucumber so thin that in less than one bight they would have all been finished but she sat there nibbling the sandwich as she watched Lady Katherine; the cakes were nearly as small and nothing to 'write home about' as her mother would have said and she almost laughed as she thought of what her dear dad would have said about the tea that was served in the finest of bone china cups. The conversation was centred on John and only on one occasion did she question Sarah Anne as to what her future plans were? John had intervened by surprising not just his mother but herself; "Well Mother dear the reason I asked you to invite Sarah Anne to tea is that I thought it best that you be the first to know that I am asking Sarah Anne to marry me."

No-one had noticed her blushes as she had lowered her head but John's mother's response was not quite what he had expected.

"You know nothing of this young lady's background. Her sister might have married well but you must be aware that they are just farmers in a poor community. As a lawyer you will need someone who is used to society and knows how to behave."

John got to his feet as his mother rose from her chair and as lady-like as possible hurried from the room.

"Take no notice of my mother she is a snob; father I know is very fond of you. Come my dear let's take a walk in the garden."

He had picked a red rose for her and pinned it to her dress with the forget-me-not brooch.

"I have every one of your letters and when I am sad or distressed I sit and read them."

"Is it as terrible over there as the paper's say?"

"Don't let's talk about the war you haven't yet given me an answer. Will you marry me sweet Sarah Anne?"

"I want to say yes, yes, yes I love you so much but what of your mother she doesn't think I am good enough for you."

"This war should be over before the end of the year and then you and I will be married with or without her blessing. I love you and want you to be my wife."

She remembered so clearly that their time together had been all too short; it was their last day that stayed so clearly in her memory. They had picnicked down by the river and then taking a boat had gone up stream and suddenly the day changed the wind rose and the sun disappeared behind the clouds; now thinking back had it been an omen. They had taken shelter in an old boathouse and huddled together in the blanket they had finished their tea.

"Cold my darling," he had said as she had shivered. She had not been cold it had been the feeling of his body so close to hers.

"You know darling Sarah Anne how much I love you. I hate to have to leave you tomorrow and return to the front. I cannot bear to go without knowing that you are mine. I will soon be home again and then you and I will never be separated." He had kissed the back of her neck and then her throat and slowly he had undone the buttons of her blouse as he kissed her breasts she clung to him. Why had he to leave her?

She never wanted this day to end.

"Be mine now," he whispered in her ear. "I love you and want you now I cannot wait until this war is over. Give me something to remember you by. Every time I close my eyes I will remember what it was like to make love to you."

A sudden clap of thunder made her jump but her heart was already racing. She had heard her sister and her husband making love in the next bedroom to hers their moans and sighs of the pleasure of love making echoing in the stillness of the night. Should she now give John what his heart and hers desired? She lay back in his arms and closed her eyes as his hands searched beneath her skirt; she shivered with pleasure as he touched her and unable to stop herself she let him undress her and with his kisses upon her lips and his caresses on her body he entered her. She was his and for a while they lay in each other's arms as the lighting flashed between the cracks in the door and the thunder rolled across the sky.

"Now whatever they say you are mine; my little wife to have and to hold for ever and ever. Who needs a church wedding you and I are now one and I love you so very much." He had placed upon her finger a gold band set with a diamond. "Soon I will place next to it another band of gold".

Before she had time to reply he was kissing her again now more passionately than before their need for each other was great and before she realised they were again making love. This time her enjoyment of the act was so pleasurable; she cried out as he penetrated deep inside her. "I love you," she cried, "don't stop".

The storm inside and outside had subsided and evening clouds were gathering as arm in arm they left the shelter of their love nest. Tomorrow he would be gone from her but today he had been all hers and the time they had spent together they would never forget.

CHAPTER TWO

As the train drew to a halt at the General Station in Cardiff so did her memories except for the one of their last time together when she had given herself to him in love; a time that she could hardly forget as beneath her smart black coat she carried the results.

She was longing for a cup of tea but the café was packed so she sat on the railway bench and took from her bag a sandwich her sister had packed for her and a few Welsh cakes.

"My Tommy is coming home today he's been away from us for four years. Are you waiting for your husband?"

"No," she replied, "just going home for Christmas.

"Poor dear; fancy being away from him at Christmas with a little one on the way; never mind they'll all soon be home except for those poor buggers killed by the Hun. Mind you Maggie down the road from me has her husband home and he be no good to man or beast him being gassed."

Sarah Anne didn't wish to be rude but it was true the Valley people could talk; "Will you excuse me I see someone I know I'd like to wish them 'Happy Christmas'."

'Happy Christmas', she thought as putting her cakes back into her bag she wandered along the platform. She felt like Scrooge in *'The Christmas Carol'* and wanted to shout out 'bah, humbug.' These feelings were no good to her baby so she must put a smile upon her face and be glad that she would soon be home.

'Home'; home to Garth-Uchaf the place that would always be 'home' but to what; wagging tongues and the look of disgust on the Minister of Ebenezer's face surely to follow with a lecture on fornication and perhaps even banning her from chapel; she would certainly be a disgrace to her family. She knew that her mother would not let that happen and would be only too willing to go along with her story that her husband had been killed in the war. Then she would become 'poor Surann'. Why, oh why was Wendy's life a bed of roses how had she managed to find a wealthy man like Glyndwr Davies? How unfair was life.

Mother knew that she was coming as Wendy had written. What had Wendy really said? She could no longer hide from her sister her pregnancy when morning sickness continued making her lose weight. "Have you been misbehaving?"

She had tried to explain to Wendy that John would soon be home to marry her. It was just a week ago when Wendy's attitude had changed and she had suggested that she should return home before Lady Katherine found out.

"Why shouldn't Lady Katherine know after all the baby would be her first grand-child?"

"Lady Katherine does not approve of your relationship with her son and when he returns home he will become a society lawyer and will not need the likes of you around his neck."

She had burst out an angry retort, "What do you mean the likes of me? He loves me and I love him and we will be married."

"He couldn't possibly marry you now in that condition. Lady Katherine has given me a cheque for £100 pounds and she wants you on the next train home."

When she had heard that John was home and had made no attempt to see her she had submitted and packed her bags and now here she was just to board the train that would take her up the valley and home. In her purse was the cheque that Lady Katherine had given her; she had gone to tear it up but then thinking of the needs of her unborn child she had put it in her purse. It would come for a rainy day, a rainy day that was only four months away.

Would they ever meet again? What had those last month's in the trenches done to him that he could forget her and their love for each other?

As the train left behind the hustle and bustle of Cardiff the countryside began to change from meadowland to dense woodland and higher and higher the peaks of the dark mountains loomed above her. She wanted to cry out for the train to take her back to Norfolk to the open green fields, the clear rivers and to the man she loved. The train could not hear her cries and puffed and panted its way up the every increasing gradient. Here and there light shone from a distant farmhouse or the gaslight from one of the small villages that bordered the railway.

Hadn't every town got a Railway Terrace? She smiled at the thought. The valley widened out and now she could see the lights on the pithead; now she knew she was nearing home when she began to name each pit that she passed. Still the mountains rose high above; she loved the mountains they were the mountains of home where she had played with her sister and brothers when she had been a child. She still wasn't much more than a child having not yet reached twenty. What would her mother tell the family and friends? The answer to that had already been resolved it would be so easy to say that her husband had been killed in the war that is why her sister had told her to wear her black coat and hat; another of Wendy's left-offs. She turned the ring on her finger around so that the diamond was not showing. It was such a beautiful ring she believed then as she still did that he loved her but she could not find an answer or the reason that he hadn't come to see her or tried to make contact. What if he was ill? She should be with him not running away.

This was her stop everything was so familiar; nothing ever changed in the valley.

"Surann Lloyd home for Christmas are you? Happy Christmas give my regards to your mother and nana and grancha. I've got my misses cooking a lovely big turkey we 'ave one of yours each year. My marriage suits you you've grown into a real beauty."

Back again to the valley town where once again she was 'Surann'. She had known old George since she was a little girl he had been a porter then and now he was station master.

"Surann Lloyd I haven't seen you in years remember me we were in school together Betty Williams."

"Betty how nice to see you I've been staying with my sister but as my husband was killed in the last days of the war I've decided to return home. We'll have to meet up after Christmas I do hope you have a lovely time."

"Hard to make ends meet with two little ones and no work in the pit for my husband. They say things are going to get worse."

Sarah Anne refrained from wishing her a Happy Christmas as her one time friend seemed filled with doom and gloom.

Many familiar faces passed her by as she walked up the rise from the station yard and turning the corner by the drapers shop she noticed that the street was still full of Christmas shoppers.

"Happy Christmas Surann," said a young man touching his hat to her. Surely that was Morgan or 'Mog' Morgan as he was called locally. How much her childhood friend had changed; in fact he was quite handsome. What if she had remained at home would she now be married to someone like 'Mog' who would fill her belly with an annual baby and his belly with beer. She wished him a Happy Christmas and walked on turning the corner she crossed the bridge over the railway line as the train steamed underneath blowing the soot from its engine in a billow of smoke over her. In front of her was the Town Hall the clock showed the time of almost seven o'clock. It would take her a good half an hour to reach home. The air was getting colder and there was a flurry of snow. Pulling her scarf tightly around her neck she crossed the little arched bridge over the canal and walking passed the church she was joined by a group of carol singers. *'While shepherds watched their flocks by night…'* she put a penny in their box and journeyed on. She was tired and baby was restless the more it kicked the more breathless she got. Passing the town pit she entered the woods belonging to the Lord of the Manor; didn't everything belong to the Lord of the Manor? The pit, the houses even the woodland and the mountains were his. Life wasn't fair; would things ever change or were valley folk content for life to drift by day after day satisfied with the little that they had; some having very little?

Up yet another hill and finally she reached the little village that was home to her. In the hollow of the mountains sat another coal mine spewing out its coal and belching out its dust to blacken everything within its sight. The white washed cottage walls were grey, the clothes pegged on the line on washing day were grey, the people aged quickly and they too appeared grey. Was life grey for all these people in all the mining communities of the valleys? Somehow the people rose above the grey surrounding them; the women chatted over the garden wall, the men went to the local pub and supped their pint together trying to put the world to rights, the children played happily on the coal tips and on the mountain side. The people gathered in the churches and chapels to thank God for the little they had all in all valley life was a happy life where everyone knew everyone else and were ready to help anyone in need and united when tragedy fell.

She passed the school where she had been educated up to the age of eleven remembering her dear headmaster who had been killed on the Somme. Tears filled her eyes as she remembered her father what if the two had met, what if they had been killed together?

Passing the third terrace she left behind the village and began the final leg of her journey home. The higher up the mountainside lane she walked the colder it got and now the snow was falling more heavily. She met no-one; no-one would be daft enough to journey up the mountain this time of the evening and in these wintry conditions. To the left of her she caught the glimpse of a Christmas tree lit up by the gaslight of the room behind. The pit manager's house was the only big house in the village. Someone was ready to welcome Father Christmas. She knew that nana would have made the puddings and would now be busy with the mince pies and sausage rolls. Mother would have finished her tasks on the farm and would be stuffing the biggest turkey that had been specially fattened up for the Christmas Feast.

As she clicked the garden gate behind her the front door opened and young Em. came bounding down the path; just six year old he had been the last born to her mother and father they had named him Emlyn but as was the custom the Emlyn was soon changed to Em..

"Mammy, nanna it's our Surann. Dewi" he called, "come on Surann is 'ome. 'Ave you got presents for us? Grancha has sent Father Christmas a big red engine for me."

"Mammy" shouted Dewi from the doorway, "Surann is coming."

"Well go and meet her and carry her bag you daft bugger."

'Poor Dewi', thought Surann, 'he couldn't help the way he was.'

Dewi limped down the garden path throwing his arms around Surann before offering to carry her bag.

"It's heavy Dewi."

"Not too heavy for me grancha says that I'm a b-b-big strong lad I'll be t-t-ten after Christmas", he stammered. "Then he said I could join the choir with 'im."

She remembered how well he sung. He didn't read well but he knew the words of all the hymns in Welsh and English. She remembered how he used to sing to the cow as she gave birth or to the lamb that had to be bottle fed when it had lost its mother. To her he was as normal as any ten year old, up to mischief, happy and loving the only draw-back being his limp and the mark on his face that had happened at birth and the stammer in his speech but it was not there when he sang he sang like a nightingale on a summer evening.

She entered the warmth of the family home and as soon as the door closed behind her she left behind the outside world and felt enveloped in the happiness of the home.

"You've had a long journey," said nana. "I've got the kettle boiling we'll soon have a nice warm cuppa inside you."

"Come lass give your old grancha a hug and pull up the chair to the fire you must be frozen inside and out."

"Give the girl a chance to take her coat off", said mother as she took her hands from inside the turkey and wiped them on an old towel. "Come give your mother a big hug I've missed you so how I wish I'd never let you go to your sisters and then this would never have happened."

"I loved him mum and he loved me." Tears filled her eyes she was so happy to be home but how she longed for him.

"Tut, tut," said her mother wiping the tears from Sarah Anne's eyes with the corner of her apron. "You're home with us know safe and sound and we'll all take care of you," said her mother giving her one more hug.

"Why have we got to take care of Surann?" questioned Em. "Is she ill?"

"Don't be d-d-daft;" said Dewi, "she's going to have a b-b-baby like M-M-Molly the sheepdog. That's why she's got a fat b-b-belly."

The laughter that rang out was broken by Em. asking where was Surann's husband.

"He was killed in France like you dada," grancha told him.

"Will he see dada in heaven?" questioned the little one.

"Enough, enough talk to bed with you boys or Father Christmas won't come."

"I d-d-don't believe in Father Christmas," said Dewi.

"Well I do," said Surann "and if you don't hurry and get to sleep you wont have any presents."

"I've hung my stocking up already," said Em. as he climbed upon his granddad's knee to kiss him 'goodnight'. "Have you hung your stocking up grancha?"

"All my socks have got big holes in them as big as spuds."

Left alone in the warmth of the kitchen Sarah Anne tucked into cold meat and pickles followed by hot mince pies straight from the oven made with her grandmother's lightest flaky pastry and covered with fresh cream from the farm. This happy family were self-sufficient growing all their own fruit and vegetables and selling to the market their poultry and beef and lamb. Nana again filled her mug with piping hot tea, "Now lass are you going to tell us all about it?"

"I'll go and see to the chucks. I think this is going to be women's talk. You're home lass and that is all that matters; home safe and sound." The old man put on his top coat, picked up his stick and calling to old Jock the sheepdog left the warmth of the kitchen.

She related her story to her mother, omitting that which was for her thoughts only. When her tale was finished her mother said, "I'm sure when he comes to his senses he'll come looking for you but I hate to dishearten you my girl but this war has done some terrible things to our men folk you never know perhaps he's lost his memory. If God wishes it you'll meet again someday."

Early to bed, early to rise was the motto of the farming folk and after supper dishes were cleared and the boy's stockings filled and a few presents left around the Christmas tree that was bedecked with paper chains that the boy's had made they all climbed the wooden stairs to bed.

"Your same room is waiting for you just as you left it. 'Goodnight dear daughter sleep well tomorrow is Christmas Day and for the lads' sake we must put on a cheery face and forget the bad things. I sleep in the big bed that dada and I shared but how I miss him. God Bless you and Happy Christmas."

"Goodnight mammy, I love you. I love you all."

CHAPTER THREE

March came in like a lion; the turmoil that raged in Sarah Anne's heart equalled the tempest that raged outside.

Stormy weather and drifting snow did not stop the cycle of Mother Nature as the sheep gave birth to their offspring and grancha and the boys' bottle fed the lambs that had been orphaned when their dams had got stuck in the drifts and grancha hadn't been able to rescue them. They could ill afford to lose the ewes as the hard winter had played havoc with their stock.

The birds had built their nests and laid their eggs and now took their turn sitting on the eggs waiting for the first fledgling to appear. Mother and Sarah Anne were taking it in turns waiting for the cow, who was now overdue, to calve; 'the animals all had their mates', she thought as she watched Molly and Jock the sheepdogs; Molly had had Jock's pups, she had been such a good mother that it had saddened Sarah Anne when all but one had been taken from her. She sat on a bale of hay in the barn watching the farm cat teaching her kittens how to catch mice. Mother Nature was so good to the birds and animals why oh! why didn't she have someone to love her and hold her hand when she brought her baby into the world?

Her time was drawing near but at the moment all her thoughts were with the stressed cow. Well, perhaps not all her thoughts because as she sat listening to the pitiful lowing of the cow she recalled the articles she had read in the paper. The first one had been in the paper that was wrapped around the chips they had fetched from the town's chip shop. Grancha had spread the paper on the kitchen table jokingly saying that he was going to catch up with the news as nana wouldn't let him have a daily paper.

"Surann get that paper off my clean tablecloth" Nana had asked. She still didn't know why she hadn't just rolled the paper up but as her eyes had focussed on a picture she had stopped to read the article. She had just stood rooted to the spot her eyes transfixed to the spot. 'How could he', she thought. Picking up the paper, her supper of chips forgotten she had fled from the room. Her mother had followed her and seeing her in tears had put her arms around her. "What's upset you cariad? Come, come stop crying and tell mamma."

"He's married mam, he's gone and got married he's forgotten me. It was in the paper; I saw the photo he's married a Lady somebody or other, here," she had said almost throwing the paper at her mother, "Here, read it for yourself."

Her mother took the greasy paper and looked at the article her daughter had pointed too.

"It says here that he's been suffering from amnesia; something to do with shell shock".

"Very convenient for him," Sarah Anne remembered how she had sneered at her mother's words. "A good way to forget about me the girl who his mother thought wasn't good enough for an up and coming barrister; what say you?"

"It might be true dear, you know how many of our valley men have returned their spirits and minds broken by that bloody war. Perhaps your father, God rest his soul, is in the best place he wouldn't have wanted to live and be half a man." Sarah Anne could still envisage how her mother had wiped her tear filled eyes with the corner of her old sack cloth apron. "Come along my dear forget what you've read you've got the babby to think about and our chips are going cold."

"Give them to the boys I'll stay here for a while."

'Just like her mother', thought Surann, 'thinking of the baby and food in the same context.

'Why?' she thought, 'Why, after reading about John's marriage, had she asked any of the family who were going to town to bring her a paper?' She had scanned the pages for more news of the man whom she still loved; she tried to shut his memory from her mind but how could she with her belly growing bigger with his child. 'His child', she had thought, 'the child, come what may, that she would love as much as she had loved its father.'

The pitiful lowing of the cow brought her mind back to the event that was about to happen. "Grancha," she called, "I think she's ready to calf."

Her grandfather came hurrying into the barn, "get some water girl and some clean rags I'll need your help with this one we can't afford to lose her."

She obeyed her grandfather but at the same time she wondered how she could possibly help him in her condition. She tried hard to comfort the distressed cow but at the same time her thoughts were for herself and the unknown experience that lay before her. Was it going to be as bad as the 'old wives tales' made out?

"Go and get me some lard or some goose grease," shouted her grandfather.

'Lard?' she thought what would grandfather want with lard.

"Hurry girl don't stand there day-dreaming I need to turn the calf or we'll lose them both."

She didn't stop to question her grandfather but hurried from the barn across the muddy yard; in her haste she almost slipped and the heavy rain soon drenched her through to the skin. How she would have loved to have stopped in the warmth of the kitchen but nana was nowhere to be seen and she knew that her mother had gone to market with the boys. She got the lard from the cold slab in the larder and then grabbing an old coat off the peg by the door she hurried back to the barn. She stood trembling with cold as she watched her grandfather grease his hands with the lard and reaching up inside the cow he began to try to turn the calf. His face was red and his brow wet with perspiration, "Come on old girl one big push and we'll have your baby safe and sound."

On hearing grandfather's voice the cow tried wearily to raise her head; Surann sat on a bale of hay with the cows head on her lap trying hard to comfort her but her mind wasn't on the cow but on herself. She had stopped shivering and now felt quite hot, in fact, she was perspiring; was it the stench of the barn or the site of grandfather bringing the calf into the world that made her feel quite nauseated?

"Thank God," said grancha as he wiped down the calf and put it next to the cow that seemed already to have forgotten the stress of bringing her baby into the world.

"That was bloody 'ard going but well worth it we'll get a good price for a young bull."

Surann felt saddened to think that grancha was already thinking of selling the calf that was only minutes old; her eyes filled with tears at the thought of having her own baby taken from her.

"Come on lass let's go and have a nice strong cuppa."

"I can't move Grancha I've got cramp in my legs and my stomach."

"Here take my hand I'll pull you up; you've been sitting too long in those wet clothes. I'll have Annie after me if you get a chill."

As she went to take her grandfather's hand she doubled up as the pain in her stomach gripped her. "Where's nana? Go and get nana," she almost screamed but her breath was taken from her as again she doubled up in pain.

"Nana's gone visiting cousin Maud who's crippled with the old rheumatics and I don't expect your mother will be back from town for another hour. Why do you want nana won't you old grancha do? Come on lass you got to get in the house and have a nice warm bath you can't sit there until nana gets home."

"I can't get up," she sobbed, "the baby is coming isn't Jack or Dai working today?" She stopped talking and took a deep breath as another pain gripped her. "Send one of them for Maggie May the midwife."

"They're both working on the fences up in the high meadow there's no-one here but us lass surely I can help to get you indoors."

Once more she tried to move but again a pain gripped her and she felt as though the baby was already on the way as she had the urge to push. "Grancha," she cried "help me the baby is coming."

"How can I help you I'm just an old man I know nothing about babbies."

She wanted to scream out but dug her nails deep into her clenched fists. "You just helped the cow well help me; know nothing about babies it is you men who put them there in the first bloody place. God help me." She lay back on the bales of hay and closing her eyes she pulled her legs up on her chest as her grandfather lifted her skirts. 'Now he will have something to talk about,' she thought as she realised she wasn't wearing drawers. The ones she had all cut into her belly and as long as she had been about the farm she hadn't bothered wearing any; quite convenient on this occasion. She bit down on a piece of wood her grandfather had given her as the worse pain of all gripped her.

"Come on lass one more push and the baby will be here I can see the head."

Gone were any inhibitions she had about her grandfather helping her all she wanted now was to hold her baby in her arms. As she felt the pain coming again she panted away as she had read in a book and then with one final push she heard her baby's cry.

"It's a wee lass", said her grandfather as he wrapped the baby in the clean rags that they had brought for the cow and then he placed the crying child by Surann.

"Well, well who would have bloody well thought I'd deliver my own great-grandchild and a male calf in the same day. I need more than a strong cuppa after that; it will be drinks all round at the Butcher's tonight."

The very moment that the old man sat down on an upturned barrel to take a breather his wife called, "Where's everyone? As soon as my back is turned all work seems to stop. Thomas John come and help me Annie's left me with the shopping while she's in the village gossiping."

"In the barn Katie old girl we got a surprise for you."

His wife shouted that she had to take the shopping in and it was a few minutes before they heard her step across the yard. There was no sound from the baby as Surann held her to her breast and as her nana came into the barn all that was heard was the lowing of the cow and the bleating of the calf. "Thank God their both all right I thought we were going to lose them."

"It's a bull calf," said her husband trying hard to stifle his laughter, "and guess what I delivered a lass as well."

"What you mean you silly old fool," his wife laughed, "I can only see one; where's the other? Don't tell me it died?"

"It's you're the silly old fool; look here me dear and you'll see the other."

Just as her grandmother came towards them the baby stirred and began to cry.

"In the name of God what have we here?"

"I'm not such an old fool am I my dear I delivered our great-grand-daughter?"

His wife was lost for words and all she could say was "Come lass we must get you indoors."

There was great rejoicing when her mother and the boys returned to find both Surann and the baby bathed and in bed. Grandmother had even put clean white sheets upon the bed and picked some daffodils for the room. "What a good start to spring," she said as she fussed over her grand-daughter and the baby.

"Is the baby my sister?" asked Em..

"Don't be daft," said Dewi forgetting all about his stammer, "we're the baby's uncles and I'm going to look after her."

"What are you going to name her," asked her mother as she cuddled the baby.

"Merryl", said Surann half asleep. "Merryl, I know it's a name that John would have chosen."

It was the 21st March, the first day of spring a day that the family, especially her grandfather Thomas John Lloyd, would never forget.

Surann fell into a half asleep half-awake stupor and in this dreamlike world all she could think of was her John and the last day they had spent together. She had read many reports of how well he was doing and making a name for himself in the law courts. She fell into a deep sleep thinking that she could not think ill of him it was the war, the bloody war that was to blame. Would he ever remember her? Would they ever meet again? Why had there to be wars that robbed wives of their husbands and children of their fathers?

She must put John from her mind and raise her baby to think that her father was killed in the war leaving her a widow lady. She would not have the stigma of being an unmarried mother and her child a bastard.

CHAPTER FOUR

It was Monday morning and Surann was up to her elbows in soap suds; Monday was wash day and week in and week out it was the same old routine. Mother had been up at the break of day getting the fire lit under the boiler and by the time Surann had had breakfast and washed, dressed and fed the little one the washing was sorted and the water ready to start the family wash. She always did the baby's wash first and then her own; nana would be at the mangle wringing out the excess water and then whilst Surann pegged out her wash mother continued. How they prayed for a fine day because if it rained the clothes would be put on the old clothes horse and left to dry around the boiler. "It's like a Turkish bath," grancha would say and would wink at his wife when she asked how he knew what a Turkish bath was like?

Today was a special day for Surann but still the washing had to be done. She gazed out of the window under which the golden daffodils were nodding in the gentle breeze and lifting their heads towards the sunshine. It was a beautiful spring day and in the distance she could see grancha in the field with the ewes and their lambs.

This day twelve months previously was a day she would never forget; not just remembering the bad weather but it was the day her little one was born. Taking the large tablet of washing soap she rubbed it up and down on the washing board and then delving deeply into the tub she found baby's cot sheet and began to scrub away on the board her mind again drifting back to that day.

"Surann, Surann where are you?" shouted Emlyn as he raced up the garden path towards the back door. "I met the postie and he gave me a parcel for our Merryl; can I open it?"

Surann rubbed the soap suds from her arms and taking an old piece of sacking from the hook dried her hands.

"Let's go into the parlour and then Merryl can help us; after all it is her birthday I believe it must be from Auntie Wendy."

"I've got a present for her too; I made it all myself mammy said we can give her our presents at tea-time." Turning to his nana who was busy at the mangle he asked, "Are you coming too nana?"

"I'll just finish putting the sheets through and I'll be with you I think it's about time we stopped for a 'cuppa' go and give your mother a shout."

By the time Surann had undone the string the women folk had gathered around the table with Merryl sitting happily in her high chair waving her hands and gurgling away.

"Never know when that will come handy," said nana carefully folding the paper and rolling up the string.

"Can I open Merry's card?" Emlyn asked using the 'pet' name that the family had fallen into the habit of using.

"There's a letter for you sis are you going to read it?"

"Give me breathing space our Em. I'll read it after I've opened the box."

"What's in it?" said the excited lad as he climbed on a chair and seated himself on the table ignoring the look that his mother gave him but when nana said, "Tables were made for glasses and chairs were made for arses," he quickly got down but wasn't to be out done;

"I'll tell grancha you said a naughty word." Then with the next breath he asked, "Can I give Merry her present?"

Surann handed him the box from which he took a silver teething ring and rattle.

"Money would have been of more use," said nana as she returned to finish the mangling.

"What has your sister got to say for herself? Has she settled in at last? Wendy and Glyn had sold their farm a year previously and since then Surann had had no further news of John; although she still searched the newspapers and the press cuttings were mounting in the old shoe box she kept under her bed. The pain would not go away never mind how much she tried to forget him.

"She says that she now has the house in Knightsbridge just as she had planned; furnished entirely from Harrods; she goes on to say that she loves London and especially taking afternoon tea at the Savoy with her new friend Margo. They also enjoy going to the Ballet and the theatre with Margo and her husband."

"I think our Wendy has forgotten where she was raised," Annie tut-tutted. "Go on you'd better finish."

"There's not much more she just sends her love to you all. She's added a P.S. on the bottom listen to this. 'Now that I'm not living near 'you know who' why don't you and Merryl come for a holiday.' Holiday! She must be joking where does she think I get the bloody money from to go traipsing up to London? I'm going to finish pegging out the clothes keep an eye on baby Em. you've got nothing else to do I think you are well enough to be at school."

Emlyn said, "No I'm not; and began to cough to prove his point; "See I've still got a bad cough."

Ignoring his remark Surann picked up the clothes basket and returned to the garden. It wasn't her nature to stay angry for long and as she pegged the clothes on the line she thought about her sister's letter realising that if she was honest with herself it wasn't the mention of a 'holiday' that had really annoyed her, as she knew only too well that Wendy would have willingly have paid for her ticket, it was the mention of 'you know who'. How many times over the last year had she wished that her sister had been still living in Oak Manor in Norfolk then it would have been so much easier for her to see John. Their eyes would have met and he would have remembered her and their love for each other and he would have left his wife and they would have had their dream home together; the three of them and how he would have adored their child. Tears filled her eyes it was just a dream – 'a pipe dream'.

"Hello sis; did I make you jump?"

"Dewi you shouldn't go creeping up on someone like that you really startled me." Surann brushed her hand across her eyes; "Surely it isn't dinner time already."

"What are you crying for sis?"

"I'm not crying." She snapped "It's the wind in my face or perhaps I might have caught Em's cold. As you're such a strong lad pick up the basket for me and we'll go and see what's for dinner."

After dinner when the table had been cleared and the dishes washed Surann decided to take Merry for a walk; "Do you want anything from the village, Mother?"
"No dear; I think we have everything we need for tea. The jelly has set and I've done the blancmange. Nana's just finishing decorating the cake and wants to surprise us so we're banned from the kitchen."
Surann put on Merryl's new angora coat and bonnet that nana had knitted; it was such a pretty shade of lavender and really suited Merryl's colouring. As each day passed she grew to look more and more like her father. Surann sighed as she put her in the old pram wrapping her shawl tightly around her; the sun shone brightly but the light breeze of the morning now had a certain chill. She took her coat off the peg; the same old black coat that she had worn when she had returned home and pulling on her hat she shouted 'Bye' and set off for an afternoon stroll with her baby.

The old pram had seen better days but it still served its purpose as it bumped along over the stony path that led from the farm to the village below. It was a mile up hill to the next village; passed the old 'tin' chapel that was no longer in use and which had seen better days. She thought how nice it would be to live in this village; especially in one of the new houses that had been built opposite the church, with their prettily curtained windows and long back gardens where she could imagine Merryl playing happily.

Surann continued her walk through the village passed the village pub and the little row of original miners' cottages; it was hard to believe that these two up two down homes housed large families and could not be compared with the larger houses on the left with steps leading up to the front gardens. Her walk took her passed the manor house and the further she journeyed the closer she got to the mountains. The lambs were frisking gaily in the fields and everywhere the trees were 'dressed' for spring; the brook was quite full after the winter's snows and it babbled gleefully as it rippled over its stony bed.

She stood for a while listening to the blackbird singing wondering why he had time to sing when his mate was sitting on her eggs or caring for their young; how she loved the mountains and the countryside and longed to be able to enjoy such beauty every day farm life was hard; it was always the same routine early to bed and early to rise and the hard labour didn't always show a profit when the winters were bad and animals perished.

"Time for home", she said to Merryl when she saw sky clouding over; "at least down-hill will be a lot easier"

She stopped at the village shop, that was quite busy, to buy the boys some sweets and as she waited to be served she got roped into the conversation.

"Aren't you Annie's daughter? How are your mother and nana? I had heard you had a baby daughter; she is a little beauty; how old is she?"

She wasn't given the opportunity to reply as question after question was thrown at her.

"Hello Surann," she turned to see Mog's mother bending over the pram.

"Mrs. Jones was right there you are a little darling," then turning to Surann she said "she must be almost a year old."

"She's one today", replied Surann.

"Oh bless! Let's see if Auntie Maggie has a 'dicky' bit for you." She placed a shiny three penny piece in Surann's hand.

"Have you got time for a cup of tea I'm sure our Morgan will be pleased to see you."

"Mother and nana are preparing tea so it will have to be a quick one."

It was more the case of being nosy than the need for a cup of tea. Mog had told her that he had been lucky to rent one of the new houses and had on many an occasion invited her to visit.

Half way down the terrace they stopped at a house whose brass letter box and door knob shone bright and as she stepped across the doorstep it too was scrubbed and bricked whiter than all the others. The passage that led to the stairs smelt of beeswax and wherever she looked everything sparkled.

"Leave the pram there dear and bring baby into the parlour; I'll just go and call Morgan he's down the garden doing some spring planting he's already got the garden looking lovely."

Surann stood by a lace draped window and watched as Maggie went down the back steps calling to her son. A roaring fire gave out such a heat that it made Surann feel quite weary she knew Maggie wouldn't mind her taking a seat; so pulling a chair from under the table she sat down. The fringed crimson chenille table cloth matched the heavy curtains; everything was just perfect even down to the two china dogs that stood at each end of the mantelpiece and the sparkling fire irons and fender. She noticed a row of Mog's pipes by the side of the hearth and then her eyes turned to the family portraits that hung on the walls; there was one of Mog dressed in his Sunday best hanging above the fireplace 'he really was handsome' she thought.

Just as Maggie re-appeared the baby woke up.

"Here let me have her;" said Maggie holding out her arms. "Morgan is just taking off his dirty boots and once he's had a wash we'll have some tea."

"The kettle's boiling ma," shouted Mog from the kitchen.

"Well you are quite capable of brewing a pot of tea; get the best china cups from the dresser."

"Hello Surann nice to see you," said Morgan as he took two cups and saucers from the dresser.

"Can't you count boy? There are three of us for tea."

"I'm not drinking tea from these things."

"You'll do as you're told when we have guests."

"It's only Surann."

"There are some Welsh cakes in the box," said Maggie getting up and putting Merryl on her shoulder began to pat her back. "It's the nasty old wind that's upset you isn't it? Auntie Maggie will soon get it up."

Merryl soon fell asleep and was put down in her pram whilst they took afternoon tea.

"I really must be going," said Surann as she noticed the time on the grand-father clock that stood in the corner of the room.

"I'll walk half way with you," said Mog as his mother cleared the table.

"Call again soon," said Maggie as she stood on the doorstep waving to her.

As they walked down the terrace Surann felt 'eyes' peeping at them from behind the lace curtained windows.

"How do you like the house then Surann?"

"Your mother keeps it lovely."

He put his hand on top of hers as she pushed the pram; "Why don't you say 'yes' Surann then it could all be yours."

Suddenly, having left the village behind, a cold wind blew along the open fields making her shiver.

"It's too soon Mog," was all she said.

"But he's been dead now for nearly two years."

"I'm not sure if he is dead as all they said was 'that he was missing'.

"Baby needs a dad and you need someone to look after you; not working your fingers to the bone on the farm. I'll buy you fancy hats and a new coat you shouldn't wear that old black thing."

"I'm in moaning," she replied to him and at the same time thinking that she really was still grieving for her lost love and no-one else, not even the kind, generous and handsome Mog Morgan could take his place.

Looking quite dejected Mog placed a kiss upon her cheek; "I'll be getting back then."

Thanking him for walking with her she set off down the hill; stopping by the old chapel to wave to him as she knew that he would still be watching.

Passing the village school and wending her way up the rocky path his words kept going over and over in her mind. Had she been wrong to turn him down? He had a good job with good pay in the local pit and this wasn't the first time he had asked her; over the last six months he had on many occasions asked her to marry him and each time she had refused. He had told her he would wait for her that there would be no other woman for him. As she lay in bed at night it was not of Mog's arms around her that she dreamt but of her beloved John; in her dreams she was back with him in the boat house his naked body lying next to hers. How could she, feeling as she did, let another man enter her it would be a violation of all that she held dear.

"Surann wait for me."

Dewi came racing up behind her; "Can I push the pram?" In his excitement forgotten was his stammer. "We'd better get a move on Mother will have tea ready and today it's going to be really special."

In a way the day had been like any other Monday; the same chores having to be done but tea-time was really special as they all gathered around the big oak kitchen table. Grancha at one end nana at the other the two boys on the bench opposite Surann and their mother and baby gurgling away happily in her high chair. A three layered sponge cake took pride and place in the centre of the table with Merryl's name in pink icing and pink flowers decorating the edge and in the centre burned a single pink candle.

"Happy Birthday" sang the happy family.

"God Bless You," muttered grancha and with the help of the boys Merryl blew out her candle. What more could she want than to be with her family?

A silence fell early upon the farmhouse as the family slept; grancha and nana still content to sleep in each other's arms; Mother alone in her big bed still young enough to feel the need for a man to hold her in his arms; but sleep evaded Surann as she opened her bedroom curtains and gazed out across their farm land. The moon shone brightly across the frosty fields, as like day, casting its light upon a fox skulking along the hedgerow how she hoped that the ducks and chickens would be safe. A lamb bleated for its mother; an owl hooted to its mate; a dog barked in the village below and was soon answered by a chorus of others. She was restless; as restless as the night animals; pulling on her dressing gown she quietly crept down stairs avoiding the creaking floor boards. A glass of hot milk and a piece of Merryl's birthday cake might help her to settle.

Removing the fire guard she poked at the glowing embers and soon life returned to the hearth. She placed on the table a rusty old tin box that she had found in the cow shed and now which she kept under her bed and then going to the kitchen she soon returned with a saucepan of milk and the last piece of birthday cake. Placing the saucepan on the fire she watched until the milk began to bubble then pouring it into her mug she sat by the table and unlocking the box she took out her 'diary' an old exercise book in which she kept a record of Merryl's progress from the day she was born in the barn twelve months previously.

"Dear John, Today your daughter had her first birthday.
She is a comely little girl and as each day passes she
grows to look more like you. Her eyes have the same
twinkle as yours – I'll never forget your lovely eyes as
you gazed upon me as I lay beneath you. I knew then
as I know now that you loved me and that one day you
will love me again. She took her first steps today pushing
a trolley that Grancha had made; she has four teeth and
says 'Mamma' and 'Dadda' – it breaks my heart that 'Dadda'
to her is my grand-father."

She went on to write down the presents she had received then closing the book she replaced it in the box.

'One day John you'll be able to read about the years you've missed as your daughter grew – how I hope they wont be too many,' she said these words silently to herself as she finished off the last crumbs of the cake and emptied her mug. Perhaps she should have taken a leaf out of her grand-father's book and added a drop of rum to the hot milk as that really might have helped her to sleep.

For a while she sat deep in thought gazing into the fire that still burned brightly until her mother's voice broke into her thoughts. "Still up dear? Can't you sleep?" Her mother pulled up a chair, "What's bothering you?"

"Morgan has again asked me to marry him. There are so many reasons why I should for instance the farm will have less mouths to feed; Merryl will have a dad and I….." she didn't finish the sentence but just looked at her mother.

"And you dear will have someone to love you," replied her mother.

"I'm fond of him mother but I don't love him."

"A good relationship can grow from deep respect," was her mother's answer.

"Come on let's get to bed or the cock will be crowing waking us all up before we get some shut eye."

Surann fell asleep thinking that the time was not yet right to take such a big step and it wouldn't be just Mog that she was taking on but also his mother.

CHAPTER FIVE

The family were all sitting around the kitchen table when grancha stormed into the room;

"Lost another bloody chicken last night and two ducks; if it goes on like this we'll have no bloody livestock left."

"Is it the fox?" asked Emlyn.

"A two legged one," replied his grandfather.

"Grancha a fox has four legs," chirped in Merryl as she toddled up to her grand-father.

The four year old's words brought a smile to the old man's face. "Aye that he has; didn't anyone hear the dog barking?"

"Not I," said Surann, "I slept like a log."

"I noticed a row of spuds had been dug up; I checked in the barn thinking you had lifted them," said Annie as she poured her father-in-law a mug of tea.

"They're not ready yet; too early for lifting; whoever has been at them will find them like marbles."

"Can you blame them grancha there's folk out there starving," said Surann as she picked up her daughter.

"Are you sticking up for them again girl? I'd give them all I could if they asked but I too have a family to keep and it's been a bad year."

'A bad year', thought Surann as she left the room; it had been more than a bad year for the miners of the valley. It had been strike after strike and now there was talk of a general strike that would put the country at a stand-still.

The summer had been a long hot one and the lack of rain had been bad for the crops and when it did rain there was such a deluge that everywhere was water logged. It was on grancha's shoulders the onus fell to support his family; how often did he tell them he should be retired as the government now stipulated he was past the age of sixty five.

The two boys Dewi and Emlyn worked hard to help their grandfather hardly finding time to play. Dewi never had the opportunity to fulfil his dream to work with the pit ponies as there were not enough jobs for those already employed in the mines. He worked along-side his grandfather and twice a week he would go along to the workman's hall where he sang with the choir. "I'm the youngest there," he would say "and Mr Thomas says I'm one of the best."

As he matured and gained more confidence his stammer had become controlled and only if upset or excited would he revert back.

Young Emlyn was the brainy one and come September he was to go to the Grammar School; luckily grandfather had for sometime been putting money aside for his uniform and books.

A great change had come over Annie no longer was she the loving mother she seemed to have become a stranger to the family. "Put it down to her age," said nana.

Somehow Surann felt there was more to it than that; her mother would disappear for hours on end not telling anyone where she was going or where she had been. If questioned she would say that she had been to visit a cousin in the next village or an old school friend that Surann had never previously heard of. She would start to do the ironing or the cooking and leave off in the middle saying that she had a head ache and would either go to bed or for one of her long walks.

As for herself her life too had changed, drastically; but not for the better as she had hoped. Two years previously Morgan had lost his job and to top it all his mother had been taken ill and within six months had died. No longer able to afford to rent the house that Surann had so admired he had gone into 'digs' with a mate. After his mother's funeral Surann had seen very little of him; he had told her on that sad day that he no longer had anything to offer her and would do his best to try and forget her.

Just before Christmas that year she had taken a train to Pontypridd hoping to make the money that grancha had given her go a little further. Having an hour to spare before her train home she took a walk in the park; it was there that she had come across him sitting on a park bench.

'Morgan', she thought, 'surely it couldn't possibly be Mog.' He was unshaven and shabbily dressed; his dark hair was now more grey than black and as she walked towards him he rose from his seat and with eyes filled with tears he said, "Leave me be Surann I'm finished."

She had persuaded him to come home with her 'just for Christmas', but a week turned into two and by the spring grandfather had offered him work and lodgings and with good looking after and home comforts he soon began to return to his old self.

Merryl adored him and would follow him around begging for stories and asking him to play with her.

That had been a good year when profits were up and now looking back Surann wondered would they ever return.

Gossip ran rife through the two villages and town and soon got back to Surann. Emlyn had come home from school one day with a black eye.

"Have you been fighting?" Surann had questioned.

"Had to 'sis' they were saying bad things about you."

"What sort of bad things?"

"Can't tell you."

"Come on out with it; I can't have you fighting over me."

"They said that Mog was sleeping in your bed and that you were having a baby. I told them that he slept in the barn but 'Titch' Jones said his father had seen you up in the ferns and that's when I hit him."

Surann bathed his eye and told him not to listen to daft stories but at the same time she knew that there had been some truth in what he had heard. Remembering back to the summer when half the village spent time on the mountain slopes harvesting the crop of what the valley folk called 'wimberries'; the lush berries that grew on the mountain slopes amongst the ferns.

"We'll make an early start nna"; had said. So soon after breakfast they rummaged around for all sorts of containers; biscuit tins, basins, anything that would hold the fruit.

"We'll surprise grancha tonight with a lovely fruit tart."

Surann soon got fed up of sitting amongst the ferns picking the tiny berries so leaving Merryl in her mother's capable hands she wandered off; it was idyllic just to have a half an hour on her own to watch the lark soaring high in the sky; and to watch the valley below going about its daily tasks. She could see old Harry with his horse and cart and the postman delivering the mail. Wherever one was life was just the same; one rose in the morning went about one's daily duties; evenings were spent around the kitchen table or like the men folk at the pub; then to bed if one was lucky with your loved one by your side.

'If only', she thought, 'if only he was by my side life would be perfect.' Why could she not get him out of her thoughts? How could she when each day her darling child grew more and more like her father.

She had told her mother she would only take a short walk; in the distance she saw people wandering back down the mountain side so she decided it was time to make for home.

Remembering how she, when a child, had loved to run and jump through the ferns she put all the inhibitions of adulthood behind her and set off at full speed down the slopes. She felt young, she felt free; her freedom was short lived when suddenly she tripped over a hidden rock and fell to the ground twisting her ankle. She tried to get up but each time fell back as the pain shot up her leg; she felt like crying but what good would that do? It seemed like hours that she sat amidst the ferns unable to get up; surely someone would take the same track down the mountainside. She couldn't recall if she had fainted or fallen asleep but she came to when she felt something wet on her face. She opened her eyes to see Jock their sheepdog and then she heard Mog's voice calling to the dog. She had called out to him and he had come hurrying down the slope and had knelt by her in the ferns to take a look at her ankle.

"I don't think there's anything broken;" he had said and then picking her up in his arms he had carried her home. An innocent encounter had been turned into something sordid by 'Tich' Jones father.

Mog too had heard the gossip that was now spreading through the village of their love making in the ferns and that he was on to a good thing.

"Marry me Surann and we'll put a stop to their gossip. I don't want you talked about in the pubs."

"I'm very fond of you Mog but I don't love you," she had said. "Village gossip isn't a good reason for us to be wed; they'll soon find someone else to talk about."

But when Dewi came home from choir practice a few weeks later; his stammer having returned; telling them that he had over-heard a few men talking outside the Workman's saying that they were going to get a job on the farm to get into her knickers she was so upset that she had agreed to marry Morgan feeling that it wasn't fair on her family especially Merryl to have to listen to such gossip.

She had wanted no fuss and wearing a grey suit and a pill box hat, left-overs from her sister that Wendy had sent a few months previously, they were married in the Baptist Chapel with only her mother and Dewi as witnesses and Merryl in a pretty dress holding a small posy.

Nana had prepared a special wedding breakfast for them and that night she had lain in her bed waiting for him, with trepidation. She had retired early knowing that tomorrow would be just another day; no honeymoon for them. Morgan had gone to the Butchers with grancha and they had drunk in the back room with the self-same men who had spread the rumours; on his return he had no sooner got into bed than he had fallen into a deep drunken stupor and was soon snoring

.

Now looking back it was hard to face the truth that theirs was a marriage in name only.

She would go to bed late and rise early; he went to bed early exhausted from the labours of the farm that now fell more and more on his shoulders. They never discussed their lack of sexual contact and at night as she lay beside her snoring husband she would think of John and their love making he would only have to touch her and he would be aroused; yet Mog would lie beside her and feel the warmth of her body and would kiss her 'goodnight' but his manhood would lie flaccid. No words of love passed between them; he would turn over in the night and put his arm across her body and she would lie there waiting, perhaps even hoping for him to caress her breasts and bring her back to life again but now after two years she had resigned herself that this 'brother and sister' relationship was to be her lot.

"No sign of a baby?" Her mother would ask. "He works too hard that man of yours."

The General Strike brought the country to a stand-still and views at home were causing some discord.

"The country has let the miners down again;" said Mog as they sat by the kitchen table.

"Be thankful you are now a farmer," muttered her grandfather from behind the newspaper.

"What's the use of farming when no-one got any bloody money to buy what we produce?"

"It keeps food on the table and a roof over your head; so don't forget that."

"I'm unlikely to forget that whilst you're around."

Surann interrupted what was turning into another argument between her husband and grandfather by asking, "Where's mam?"

"She's gone to visit cousin Florrie."

"I think I'll pop on my coat and go and meet her I could do with a walk. Don't forget to check the chickens there's been no eggs for over a week."

"I've fixed the fence so I don't know how that darned ferret is getting in."

"I expect it's a two legged one."

"You always say that grancha," laughed Merryl. "Can I come to meet grandma with you mummy?"

40

Being a nice evening Surann decided to take the path across the mountain and then across the wood and over the brook to the top village where cousin Florrie lived. She stopped to let Merryl have a swing in the new playground that had recently been put up by the council on waste land at the end of the terrace,

"Hello Surann how is your mother," said a cheery voice, "I haven't seen her in ages."

"Florrie what a surprise I was on my way to see you." As she sat in Florrie's parlour drinking tea she did not mention her mother and luckily the conversation was mostly centred on Merryl.

"She's doing well in school; the headmaster has great hopes for her. She's always has her head in a book."

"No sign of a brother or sister for her?"

Surann ignored the question by saying that it was time they were making tracks.

"May I have one more swing before we go home?"

Surann sat on the bench whilst her daughter played with some of the village children. She gazed across the fields thinking of Florrie's question. Perhaps she should try to talk to Mog would it be wise to ask him to see a doctor. He had lost weight and was always tired; but never too tired to go to the pub; he also ate well.

Suddenly a figure walking across the fields opposite caught her eye; it couldn't possibly be but as the figure drew closer there was no mistake it was her mother. She felt guilty as she watched her walking towards the roadway; then she stopped and turned and it was then that Surann saw him standing on the brow of the hill. There was no mistaking Dai Lewis who owned the farm whose land bordered on to theirs. Lewis had been after their land for years. grancha swore that fences he had put up had been pulled down by Dai Lewis claiming that they were on his land. There was no love lost between the two families.

Dai's first wife had died leaving him to raise their two sons. He had taken in a young girl from the next valley as housekeeper and within a short time she was carrying his child. A daughter was born to them and only when she became pregnant again did he agree to marry her. Then there was a big scandal when she ran off with a travelling man taking her two children with her. Nothing was again heard of her and rumour, at the time, was rife saying that Lewis had 'done them all in' dumping the bodies down the well; a story that died a sudden death.

How could her mother be visiting Dai Lewis? Surann was determined to find out.

Once or twice a week her mother would get dressed in what Surann called 'her Sunday best' and she would say "I'm off to visit Florrie" or "I think I'll take a train and go and visit our Betty."

"Off gallivanting again," her father-in-law would say. "The old woman needs more help it's not fair on her the work she's got on her plate."

"Be back to get supper," was all she would say.

One afternoon a few weeks later when her mother said she was going out visiting and wouldn't be back until supper Surann decided to follow her. Merryl was having tea after school with her teacher and there would be plenty of time for her to find out what was going on and be home before her daughter.

"You off too," said nana as Surann put on her hat and coat. "Leaving all the ironing to me yet again," complained her grandmother. "Annie's been no use for months always complaining she's got a headache or off gallivanting. I don't know what's come over her she was such a loving, caring girl."

Surann had a good view of the village as she took the mountain path; if her mother was going to Dai Lewis' then by taking this route she would be there before her. It never dawned on her, as she made away through the wood and across the brook at the top of the village, perhaps her mother was going to visit a friend. She made her way up the lane towards the back of the farm and just in time she ducked down behind a low wall as her mother walked into the farm yard. It was obvious that she was familiar with her surroundings as she opened the door and disappeared inside. High up on the hill one of Dai's sons was driving a tractor and she had seen the other on horse-back making his way over the mountain to the next valley.

The dogs were already barking so it made no difference as they continued to do so as she made her way along the wall of the house with the idea of knocking on the door but as she passed the window she stopped in her tracks. From the open window she heard voices;

"Annie my love I've been waiting for you; come let me help you off with your clothes."

"You daft bugger," she heard her mother's voice, "I hope you haven't been waiting long you'll catch your death with no clothes on and what would the boys say if they came in?"

"I always make sure they are well out of the way when I know you are coming."

"Oh! Dai bach you are a big boy; come on I'm ready for you."

'What was going on between them', thought Surann not daring to move but when she heard Dai's groans and her mother's sighs she ventured towards the window. She was rooted to the spot as she saw them together against the table. She wanted to turn away in disgust by what she saw but still she stood watching as Dai caressed her mother's voluptuous body; sucking at her breasts like a baby and still she watched as he entered her and she couldn't close her ears to her mother's screams of delight.

She was about to move away when Dai having, satisfied himself, moved; had he seen her spying on them?

She had seen more of him than she had seen of any man; her mother's words rang true 'he was a big boy'.

"Come Annie my girl let's go to bed I haven't finished with you yet."

Surann ducked down just as her mother got to her feet and something made her feel that her mother had seen her spying. She heard the door close and from the room above she heard her mother's laughter.

Surann walked quickly back through the village as it was getting late and Merryl would be home before her.

"Where's nana?" she asked Dewi as she entered the kitchen. The fire had almost gone out and the table wasn't laid for supper.

"Em.'s playing football, Mog came in and then went off in a rush nanna was here then and grancha's in the barn and I don't know where our mam is."

She hurried to get supper ready; there was boiled ham in the larder and she could cook some beans and potatoes and make some parsley sauce; she knew grancha would enjoy that.

Merryl was the first to arrive home soon followed by Emlyn.

"I scored two goals for the school and we beat the High School four nil."

"Will you help me with my sums after supper our Em.?" Asked Merryl

"Hurry up 'sis'," shouted Dewi down the stairs "I've got choir practice at seven thirty."

"Where's nana?" Asked grancha as he hung his hat on the peg, "Is she out with your mother?"

"I don't think so," replied Surann serving the dinner.

"It's not like her not to tell me where she's going."

Supper was soon finished and neither her mother nor nana had returned.

"I'd better go and look for her," her grandfather sounded worried, "she hasn't been herself of late. Caught her sitting with the chickens last week; I didn't say anything but she was still in her nightie and she was talking to them as if they were kids."

"I'll come with you," said Emlyn.

"I'll go down to the village perhaps she's gone to post a letter," Dewi said as he followed the other two through the door.

Surann stayed in the kitchen Merryl's homework forgotten. "Will nana be all right?"

"She said that she was tired perhaps she's sat down somewhere and fallen asleep."

"That's not like nana and where's grandma?"

"I expect she'll be home soon perhaps her train was late."

Surann watched the hands of the clock move slowly around; eight o'clock, eight thirty, nine o'clock and still no sign of anyone. She really was worried. And then she heard the latch of the back door.

"Where's everyone?" Mog's voice echoed through the empty room.

"Where have you been?"

"I had some important things to do."

"Have you seen nana?" asked Merryl.

"Go to your room and get your homework done I want to talk to your mother."

Surann had never heard her husband talk to Merryl so bruskly.

Merryl picked up her books and left the room.

"Well," said Surann;" you've been skiving again. Grancha is getting too old to have to do your job as well."

"He'll soon be doing it permanently," snapped Mog. "I've got a job down Cwm pit. Make better money now I've got a family to support."

"That's the first I've heard of it you've never seemed to worry before about your family."

"Different now I've got a woman and a baby."

"Merryl's far from being a baby or haven't you taken your time to notice?"

"I'm not talking about her you stupid bitch."

Surann just stared at him and was just about to ask 'who then?' when he pushed her to one side.

"Out of my way woman I'm just going to get my stuff I'm moving out; by the way your nan is with my woman I asked her to help she's the only decent one of the lot of you."

"Morgan what the hell are you on about?"

"Hasn't it got into your thick head I've got myself a real woman not a frigid, stuck up bitch like you. I'm moving in with Ivy Roberts she had our baby today a beautiful little girl."

"How could you?" was all she could say.

"Do you really want me to give you the details?" he sneered.

"You never tried to get anything from me," she retorted. "I always thought you couldn't get it up I thought there was something wrong with you."

"Something wrong with me," he laughed. "It's you who should see a doctor, Great putting the blame on me when you made it quite clear from the start that you didn't love me and that was enough to put anyone off. I only married you to keep a roof over my head."

"Pack your bags Mog Morgan and get out of my house."

"You must be joking; your house? The farm will soon be in ruin when I'm gone. I hate the bloody farm Sam's got me a job in the pit. How are you and the old man going to keep it going with your mother off to live with Dai Lewis?"

"Who told you that?"

"Dai's lad; he said that Annie and Dai had been having it off for quite a while and that your mother is a fair bit of stuff as he watches them through a crack in the boards.

Your Merryl must have been a virgin birth as I can't see you letting a man into your knickers. I'll make sure the old woman gets home safely she's only waiting for me to get back." With his last retort he went off laughing and the next time she saw him he was off down the lane carrying a suitcase.

She could not take many more days like this.

A disheartened old man was the first to return; "Can't find your nana anywhere".

"Don't worry grancha she'll be home soon she's gone to help someone who has just had a baby." He'd find the truth out soon enough.

She sat down by the kitchen table gazing into the fire. The dishes were still on the supper table when nana returned. Surann didn't know what she was going to say to her but she had no need to worry because as nnna came in through the kitchen door she said "Get the kettle on Surann there's a love I'm puffed." She sat down by the table and kicked off her shoes.

"It's a funny old world isn't it girl? When Morgan asked me to come to the village with him as Ivy Roberts had had a baby and was all on her own I didn't realise then that he was the dirty old bugger who'd got her in the family way. I just thought poor Ivy whose husband was killed down the mine only last year leaving her pregnant. It is when he got me there and Maggie May, the midwife, was leaving he told me it was his and he was leaving you and that he hadn't known who else to ask to stay whilst he fetched his things. I'm sorry lass if only I'd known. Where's our Annie she should be helping you I know how upset you must be?"

"Mother's not home yet; you know what they say nana it never rains but it pours well Morgan just told me she's having an affair with Dai Lewis and that she's going to live with him."

"In the name of God what next I'll get a gun and fill his arse full of shot that will stop his philandering. I know she's been lonely since your dad was taken from us but to pick someone like Dai Lewis I don't know what to say. He'll give her more than a headache."

It was a very subdued family that said 'Goodnight' as each made their way to bed.

Merryl came down from her studies and in all innocence asked "Why has Mog left us?"

"I'll tell you again said her mother kissing her 'Goodnight'.

The boys trying to be tough said that they hoped he'd get buried alive in the pit.

"Don't say things like that", reprimanded their sister "None of us know what our future holds."

"We'll take good care of you lass," said grancha giving her a hug. "Trust in the Lord my girl he has our life mapped out for us."

She lay sleepless upon the bed that for such a short time she had shared with Mog thinking what had she done to deserve the life that was hers? She thanked God for her lovely daughter but still deep inside, when alone, was the chasm that was growing bigger as the years rolled by; it was the yearning she had for her one and only love. Still she wrote in her diary the happenings in Merryl's life. She unlocked her box and took out her diaries; their number mounting one for each year of Merryl's life.

She turned the pages reading randomly; the first brought a smile to her face as she read of the time when Dewi took her for a walk in her pushchair and how when he had met his friends he went and played football and came home crying that the gypsies had taken her. "I was watching her sis and then she just disappeared." Just as she was going to box his ears Mrs Williams from the big house brought her home saying that she had seen the boys wandering off and called to them saying that she'd take the little one home.

Then she read of Merryl's first day at the village school and how she had cried when she had had to leave her at the school gates. She had kept for John a copy of each of Merryl's school reports showing how well she worked and how she was praised for her achievements.

Reading what she had written comforted her in a way yet didn't clear her head of the thoughts of why Mog had left her. Perhaps she was to blame; she could easily have taken him in her arms and showed him a kind of loving if only she had perhaps he wouldn't have strayed.

CHAPTER SIX

She had at last fallen into a restless sleep and the following morning slept late only to awaken with nana bringing her a cup of tea.

"Take your time girl; there's no rush. After the bad day we had yesterday things can only get better."

"I doubt it; I wonder what mother will have to tell us when she returns?"

"I'll leave her to you I'm going down town but should be back by one o'clock. By the way I'm not going dollally I believe my old man told you that I had been talking to the chickens it is just that I had read somewhere that if you sit and talk to them it will help them to lay better. I'm off now and remember don't let Annie upset you again."

She was standing by the kitchen window when she saw her mother coming across the yard. The look upon her face was enough to warn Surann that there was a 'storm' brewing.

Annie slammed the kitchen door behind her as she entered the kitchen. "Saw Mog in the village he told me that he had left you; how he has stood it this long with you I'll never know you are nothing but a stuck-up bitch; think you're above us all. How you got pregnant in the first place remains a mystery to me. I've come for my things as I suppose you've already guessed I'm going to live with Dai. By the way did you enjoy your 'peep-show' yesterday? Now you know how it's done you'd better find yourself a man before you dry up."

Surann just stood there lost for words not knowing how her mother could speak to her like that; her loving, caring mother who never said an unkind word. Was it the 'change' having a bad effect on her mind or was she ill?

All Surann could say was; "What about the boys?"

"Well, what about them? They're old enough to look after themselves I've waited on you all long enough."

Surann sat in the parlour waiting for her mother to finish packing; surely she would come and apologise; her words had hurt but Surann made the excuse that her mother was hiding her embarrassment at knowing she had seen her with Dai..

She heard her mother's footsteps on the stairs and as she stood in the passage she half turned and glared at her daughter; "Hell will freeze over before I set foot in this house again. My dad was right I should never have got involved with the bloody Lloyds."

Surann heard the door slam and from the window she saw her mother cross the yard and then noticed that Dai Lewis was waiting for her with the horse and trap. Now the whole village would know that Annie Lloyd had left them.

Her grandmother found her sitting at the table with her head in her hands sobbing as if her heart was broken.

"What's the matter lass I see she gone? Well good riddance to bad rubbish. I saw her leaving with Dai Lewis if you grancha had seen him he would have taken a shot gun to him. Our Thomas is up there looking down I don't know what he'd make of it all I told him that she wasn't farming stock; no stamina. How about a nice cup of tea I'll put a drop of your grancha's 'medicine' in it; he always says that it is a pity the doctor doesn't prescribe whisky and brandy instead of the rubbish he doles out." The old lady filled the kettle then turning to her grand-daughter said; "How about a nice piece of Bara Brith I'll put lots of butter on it for you? Where are the boys? They've not gone and left us too?"

"No nana they'll be home soon and our Merryl with them."

Dewi was the first to appear; "I thought I saw our mam coming home where is she?"

"Gone Dewi."

"What you m-m-mean g-g-gone?" He stammered.

"She's left home Dewi she's gone to live with Dai Lewis."

She had never seen Dewi so upset; he went red in the face and thumped on the table. Forgotten was his stammer; "I didn't believe them," he shouted, "I heard them talking in the

Workmen's about Annie having it off with Lewis and they'd go all quiet when I joined them but I didn't think it was our mam. How could she he's a dirty old bugger. I'll kill him."

Hush Dewi don't talk like that mother has been lonely since father got killed she needed someone you'll understand when you are older. By the way there's more to come I may as well tell you Mog's gone too; he's gone to live with Ivy Roberts she's had his baby."

"He's left you for that 'slag' he must be mad. You're the best in all the world sis. Do you want me to tell our Emlyn?"

"If you wish but don't say too much."

As they sat down to supper there was a silence that one could have cut with a knife until Merryl broke it by saying that they should all have a day out at the sea-side. She went on to say that the Sunday school was having their annual outing to Barry Island and that it would be a good idea if they all went.

"So you think a swim in the sea will wash away all our worries and then we can come home and start afresh?" said grancha.

"How are you going to manage now that Morgan has gone? Questioned Surann.

"I've been thinking about that; I was wondering what you'd all think about taking on a few new hands say a shepherd and someone who can do all the odd jobs; fencing, ditching and the like?"

"Can we afford it grancha?" asked Surann.

"If we make a few cut backs and anyhow we've got two less mouths to feed."

"There's Bert Morris he's married with five kids and another on the way. He told me that he's lost his job as a surface worker and that if something didn't come his way soon his family would end up in the Workhouse. I know he can turn his hand to most things," said Dewi. "Only last week he asked me was there anything going."

"Well lad tell him to come and see me that is if you think he can be relied upon."

"There's cousin Florrie's husband he's good with animals; he's been caring for sheep since he was a lad. Florrie told me that he's been out of work for three months. Shall I call round and see if he'd like to work for us," asked Surann.

"Don't know about that Surann he worked for Lewis didn't he?"

"Yes, I know that but Lewis' sons tormented him because he was a chapel deacon and when he complained Lewis sacked him. According to Florrie they really treated him awful."

"Things are falling into shape we'll soon be back on our feet won't we old girl?" said grancha putting an arm around his wife. "Come on old girl let's hit the sack it's way passed our bedtime."

Surann left the boys playing cards and Merryl with her head in a book and putting on her cardigan called Molly the dog; "Come on girl let's go for a walk." Only Molly slept in the house the other farm dogs slept in the barn. As she closed the kitchen door behind her she looked up at the sky; 'what a beautiful sunset', she thought, 'I wonder if John is standing in his garden and seeing the sunset and has a thought about another time and another place that just will not come to light.'

She crossed the yard and closing the gate behind her took the path across the field towards the mountain. From her vantage point she could see across the valley and the pits that now lay silent with the men now on strike; she thought how green and pleasant the land must have been before the mine owners sunk their pits and emptied the bowels of the earth into the looming, menacing slag heaps and coal tips. Yet when there was no work the valley died. From where she stood she could see three of the many pits; the one below her had spewed up its waste to make a black mountain of slag just beyond the village; the one above her high on the mountainside now lay idle and the small terrace of houses built to house the workers were almost derelict just two remaining whose tenants refused to leave the place where their parents had lived and where they had been born. They survived on a meagre living of raising a few hens and pigs and tilling the rocky soil to grow enough vegetables to feed their family. Below in the town was the deepest pit in the valley around which the town had grown with its terraces built on either side of the valley; its steep hills taking the wind out of many a miner. Once so long ago the river ran pure but now it too appeared like a black snake winding its way to the sea. What price man paid for coal death and poverty for the miner and wealth for the mine-owner.

'I should count my blessings,' she thought; 'I just hope that there will be a better world by the time Merryl has to make her own way in life; what of Dewi and Emlyn? There was a good chance that Emlyn would go to University his teachers had said that he was the cleverest lad they had taught for many a year but what of Dewi? All he had going for him was his love of music; where would that get him? Of course there was always the farm.'

She called the dog and began to make her way down the mountainside back to her home taking one last look at the village and thinking of her husband lying next to Ivy Roberts and their baby. She thought back to the days when Mog had wooed her and of the many times that he had declared his undying love for her; why hadn't she showed him that she had cared? Now left alone with no man to lie beside her she realised that she had cared for Morgan more than she dared to admit if only her love of a 'memory' did not posses her.

As the sun set in the west like a red ball of fire Surann made her way home. She saw mister fox skulking along the hedgerow and called to him, "You leave our chickens alone." She smiled to herself at her childishness in talking to the fox. She felt relaxed after her walk and hoped that she would have a restful sleep the first in many a night.

After checking the barn and that the poultry were safely shut up for the night she let herself into the now sleeping household. She made herself a warm drink and sat down with her knitting; another hour and she should finish the bathing costume she was making for Merryl ready for the family's day out at the sea-side. The old grand-father clock struck mid-night as she quietly made her way upstairs. She placed the costume on the foot of Merryl's bed and then stood for a moment watching her sleeping daughter saying quietly to herself, 'You are so much like your father how I wish that he could see you,' and wondering what the morrow would bring.

The two men were only too eager to be taken on and soon the farm once again began to return to its old routine. Grancha appeared to take on a new lease of life and nana once more began to sing as she worked around the house; all be it hymns.

School was off for the summer making extra hands and many a day Emlyn's friends would delight in helping with the haymaking and fruit picking. Nana, Surann and Merryl were kept busy preparing the fruit; nana making the jam and preserves and Surann the bottling. A big earthenware vat of wine stood fermenting in the kitchen and a smell of home-made cakes and pastries constantly wafted through the open door out into the yard an enticement for all who passed by. Keeping constantly busy cast their troubles to the back of their minds and life was harmonious.

The weeks rolled by and soon came around the promised outing to the sea-side. Merryl had been delighted to tell her Sunday school teacher that 'all' the family would be going; mummy, nnna, grancha, Dewi and Emlyn.

Merryl was up bright and early and eager to put on her new bathing costume. "I'll put it on under my dress and then I'll be the first in the sea," she said.

"Don't forget to pack your vest and knickers," said nana, "you'll be in a sorry state if you have to travel home in your wet bathers."

Sandwiches were made and packed along with cake and biscuits and bottles of lemonade. Everyone laughed when grancha joked that he couldn't find his bucket and spade.

Bert brought the horse and cart around to the back door and with grancha up in front and the rest of the family in the cart they set off for the station. Since the family upset Surann had avoided the town and left all the shopping to her grandmother and Merryl and she was now on tenterhooks as she stood on the platform aware of groups of gossiping women and the odd looks she was getting.

"They're talking about us nana."

"Don't worry girl if they're talking about us they are leaving some other poor bugger alone. Mark my words it will all soon be forgotten."

At last the train appeared; slowing down as it came under the town bridge; "I want to go in the front carriage," said Emlyn.

"You'll get all the smuts from the engine there," said grancha. "I see they've put on extra carriages they must have known we'd need one for ourselves," he joked.

"How are you Mrs Morgan," said Merryl's Sunday School teacher, "I'm so glad you could all come; your Merryl is a treasure in Sunday school she is so good with the little ones. Is there room for myself and my sister in your compartment?"

"I'm sure we can squeeze you all in," said grancha. So soon the compartment was full as they were joined by the two sisters and their four little ones.

The whistle blew; the train got up steam and puffed its way out of the station.

"We're going to the sea-side, the sea-side," sung the little ones and then one began to sing; "I'm H.A.P.P.Y.; I'm H.A.P.P.Y.; I know I am I'm sure I am I'm H.A.P.P.Y." Soon they all joined in the singing with nana's lovely voice leading them.

"A good start to the day," said grancha, "Let's hope the sun continues to shine I ordered it especially for us."

That night Surann took out her diary and wrote:

> *My dearest John how you would have loved to have been with us today. Merryl really enjoyed herself; she was, as she had said, the first in the water and was soon joined by the boys (I still think of them as boys but Dewi is nearly 20) How we laughed when she came running up the beach her bathers sagging with water almost down to her knees. She will never forget today it will always remain a happy memory for her. Everything*

*tasted so delicious even the sandwiches that crunched
with sand. Grancha and the boys went out on a boat;
memories again dear John of our boat on the river and
how that day ended. I'll put some photos in the box when
I have them developed. John, dear John will we ever meet
Again and if we do will you then remember me my love?*

CHAPTER SEVEN

More photographs, letters and school reports were added to Surann's 'hoard' that were now locked away in an old suitcase amongst these were photos from Merryl's first day at Grammar School and her first lower school party dress. Yet another Christmas came and went and a new decade loomed ahead with the country still in turmoil but a kind of 'peace' reigned over the farm. It had saddened Surann that she had not heard from her mother at Christmas not even a card for Merryl or the lads. Rumour was always rife in the village; the latest being that they hadn't seen Annie for many a week. 'Perhaps he's thrown her down the well with the others'; grancha had overheard in the 'Butchers'.

"Should I call and see her," Surann had asked her nana.

"That's up to you girl but I don't think it's a good idea at present as the forecast says that we're in for a good fall of snow."

"We need that like a sore thumb," said grancha, "a few of the ewes are ready to 'drop'.

The forecast proved correct and snow fell for almost three days making it almost impossible to leave the house as the high winds had caused the snow to drift. The two farm hands were unable to turn up for work and Surann constantly worried about her grandfather going out to the ewes suggested that she'd keep him company.

"I'm tougher than you think girl I've been doing this since I was knee high to a grasshopper and it'll take more than a few snow drifts to keep me indoors."

By the end of the week the snow had ceased but the icy winds had now caused a big freeze; Merryl unable to go to school had the job of feeding the orphaned lambs and Emlyn in his last year at school worked along-side his brother trekking the mountainside looking for lost sheep.

The month was almost ending before the thaw set in with torrential rain.

"Don't know which is the worse the snow or this bloody rain," moaned grancha as he changed out of his sodden clothes "Where the 'ell do you think you are going," he shouted as Emlyn came running into the kitchen dripping wet and his boots covered in mud.

"Dai Lewis is coming across the mountain; he's on horseback and he seems in a mighty big hurry."

"What the hell does he want? I'll get my shot gun he'll not trespass on my land. If he gets off that horse I'll show the bugger; he wont be able to sit down for the next six months."

Surann was concerned as the unwelcome visitor tethered his horse and strode into the yard.

Surann held up a restraining hand to her grandfather; "You stay put I'll answer the door."

Because of the barking of the dogs Surann did not hear her grandfather's retort; "treating me like one of the kids now."

Before opening the door Surann took a deep breath; then turning the key she came face to face with Lewis. "Mr Lewis may I ask what brings you to, "Gelli Uchaf"?

"Mrs Morgan forgive me but I had to come it's your mother; she's in hospital."

"You'd better step into the hall Mr Lewis and explain when this happened and what ails her."

"She hasn't been herself for months; the last weeks she's been unable to leave her bed crying all the time complaining of pains in her head. I couldn't get her to eat she's nothing but skin and bone. On her better days she's get out of bed but she was like a stranger shouting at me and calling me by your father's name. There were times I had to hold her down as she got so violent."

"Didn't you get the doctor to visit?"

"I couldn't get to him we were snowed in during the weeks when she was at her worse. When I did manage to get Dr Howells he took her straight into hospital. She's been in a coma for the last week but when I visited today she seemed to be a little better and begged me to come and get you saying that she wanted to make her peace with you."

"What did Dr Howells say was wrong with her?"

Lewis sighed, "Oh! Dear God Mrs Morgan I don't know how to tell you," he sighed again and then said, "it's was a growth on the brain and they can't operate as she's too far gone and there's no hope for her she's not long for this world. She was so beautiful and I loved her so much."

He sat down on the settle in the hall his clothes dripping onto the tiled floor and putting his head in his hands he cried like a baby.

"Come Mr Lewis I'll make you a nice strong cup of tea; let me take your coat."

There was little welcome awaiting him as he followed Surann into the kitchen.

"What the bloody 'ell is he doing in my house," shouted her grandfather; "He'll not get my land over my dead body."

"Shut up grandfather; Mr Lewis has brought us bad news. My mother is in hospital and wishes to see me," she paused for a moment and then continued, "She is dying."

Her grandmother and grandfather just looked at each other and then her nana said; "Sit down Dai the kettle will soon be boiling."

"He needs something stronger than bloody tea woman give him a drop of brandy."

"I'll get my hat and coat and Dewi can take me in the trap to the hospital; thank you for letting us know Mr Lewis."

Her heart was racing and over and over in her mind she recalled that harrowing day when her mother had left her family. She had thought then that the vile words her mother had thrown at her were not from her dear mother's mouth but that of a stranger. If only they had known then that she was ill perhaps something could have been done. How long had her mother been suffering? Looking back she recalled that for a good many years there had been a gradual change in her loving mother.

"Mrs Morgan I am so glad that I have caught you," as she entered the ward she was stopped by Dr Howells. He sat with her in an anti-room and tried to explain everything to her.

"Can't you operate?"

"The cancer has gone too far there is nothing more we can do. We are keeping her sedated; if she lingers too long and the drugs have no effect she could become violent and then we would have no option but to institutionalize her."

"No. No not the workhouse for my mother."

"Let's hope that it will not come to that she's already in a very weak state."

"Can I see her?"

She followed him to the end of the ward to a screened off bed and as the doctor pulled back the screen she almost collapsed when she saw how frail her mother had become. She had lost most of her beautiful hair; her face was pallid and her eyes sunk deep into her face.

'God help her', thought Surann as she sat beside the bed taking her mother's bloodless hand in hers; how cold she felt and she looked so lifeless. "Dear God," Surann prayed, "Take her home to You; please Lord stop her suffering."

A nurse 'popped' her head around the screen, "I'll come back," was all she said and Surann was left alone.

"Mother", she whispered, "Mother can you hear me? We all love you and miss you so much." She continued talking aimlessly.

"Sarah, my Sarah Ann," her mother's frail voice sounded like music to Surann's ears.

"Hush mother I'm here."

"Don't leave me."

"I wont I promise."

There was a long silence and all Surann could hear was her mother's erratic breathing. For how long she sat here just holding her mother's hand she knew not. The same nurse came and went without saying a word.

'What is she waiting for?' thought Surann. She must have drifted off to sleep because a sudden noise startled her. It was her mother, who still lay as if in a deep sleep. The noise that came from her throat started Surann and brought her near to tears.

"God help her please," she prayed.

How many times had she heard the old women talk of the 'death rattle', the noise made by the dying.

A sudden cramp in her cold feet caused her to move.

"Don't leave me."

Surann looked down at her mother so pale; so deathly.

"Forgive me Surann; forgive me." Her whole body seemed to tremble.

"There's nothing to forgive dear mother go back to sleep."

A sigh rattled from her mother's throat and Surann felt the last breath leave her mother's body yet she still sat there holding her mother's hand until a nurse put her hand on her shoulder and said, "I'll call Dr Howells; you can go now Mrs. Morgan."

Surann stood and watched as the nurse pulled the sheet over her mother's face; she wanted to cry out 'Don't she's only sleeping' but now words left her mouth.

As she walked slowly back through the ward an old lady called to her, "Has she gone to her Maker?" She didn't answer but walked on through the corridors the smell of disinfectant filling her nostrils hiding the smell of death.

The door ahead of her swung open and the dishevelled figure of Dai Lewis came towards her. "She's gone Dai," was all she could say.

She walked out through the hospital's swing doors and began walking down the road that led to the main entrance. The rain was pouring down and she was soon drenched to the skin.

"Surann," a familiar voice called, "Surann have you forgotten me?" She stopped and looked up into Dewi's face.

"She's gone Dewi; we'll never see her again."

Dewi got down from the trap and putting his arms around his sister they just stood there oblivious of the pouring rain.

Dewi was the first to break away, "Come on sis. we'll catch our death standing here." He wished that he could have undone his when he looked into his sister's forlorn face.

"Someone will have to tell Dai Lewis.

"He knows," was all she said

.

They travelled up the hill from the small village the horse taking them home as the two sat together. The rain had ceased but the day remained as dull as their spirits. The old horse found the going tough as the rocky lane to the farm was awash with water.

"Come on old girl take us home," said Dewi

The welcome light of the farmhouse and the smoking curling up towards heaven brought Surann back to her senses; she had to be strong as they all needed her. Was there never going to be any peace for her and why now at such a time did her thoughts turn to John? 'John my love, how I need you; I need your arms around me to make everything better. I need a man to love me.'

Her mother was laid to rest in the mountain cemetery above the town. A wintry sun shone down upon the villagers as they turned out to show their last respects for a woman who had been born and bred amongst them and until the dreadful curse had changed her had been loved and highly thought of by all. Dai Lewis stood along with her grandfather and her sons by the graveside as they lowered her into the yawning abyss. The men's voices, led by Dewi, echoed in harmony and were carried on the wind to the valley below; "Bread from Heaven feed me now and evermore."

CHAPTER EIGHT

Spring came and with it Merryl's twelfth birthday; she was a constant reminder to her mother of John as she grew more like him; in character as well as looks. She made a special tea for her and her school friends. How easy it was to buy her presents as all she ever asked for were books.

The months and years flew by and Surann's grand-parents now let her handle the finances of the farm and each month she would put a little away for Emlyn and Merryl's further education. Dewi was given a wage like the farm hands; his needs being few as his only pleasure was his singing.

"One day I'm going to sing in the Albert Hall with the hundred voices."

"When you do Dewi I'll be there to cheer you," Surann told him.

"I'll keep you to that sis.."

At Easter time Surann took flowers and laid them on her mother's grave; she sat for a while looking down at the town below and thinking where did the valley folk get their strength? Each day was a fight to survive; the baby fought to come into the world; the man to put food on the table; his wife to keep the family together. It was the mother who had to be the strongest to make ends meet in times of strife; to support her man as he fought for his rights against the mine owner.

Her thoughts turned to her two brothers; hopefully Emlyn would be off to University in the autumn. He had achieved so much and would make a good teacher; he was so patient and so kind. Dewi worked hard alongside his grandfather; he too had dreams as he talked about leaving the valley and the country and journeying to foreign countries. Well into his seventies grancha worked as hard as a man half his age and nana in the eyes' of the family never changed and the two had a relationship that Surann would say was 'true love'; a deep lasting affection for each other.

Time to stop daydreaming and to make her way home; tomorrow she had planned a special dinner for the family and come Monday it would be like any other Monday the family wash to be done how she hoped for a dry, sunny day as there was nothing worse than wet clothes steaming around the boiler. Little was she to know that 'Monday was not to be just like any other Monday'.

Nana was up to her elbows in the wash tub and Surann was pegging clothes on the line when she noticed a man and child walking up the lane; 'visitors to the big house' she thought and went on pegging out the clothes until a familiar voice called her name; "Sarah Ann may I have a word?"

She turned and gazed at the forlorn figure of Mog Morgan, her estranged husband, who was carrying a battered old suitcase and beside him stood a pretty little girl with tight curly hair. She hadn't seen Mog since the day he had left her she had heard that he had left the valley with Ivy and their baby to look for work.

"You'd better come into the parlour." He picked up his suitcase and followed her.

Not knowing what to say to him she motioned to him to take a seat; "I'll ask my grandmother to make some tea; what would you like little girl?"

"My name is Minnie and I go to school; can I have some pop please?"

Surann smiled at the child; "of course you may dear." and made a hasty retreat. She could see the way Mog looked at her it was the same look as all those years ago when he had courted her. She felt nervous in his presence remembering his last words to her.

"Nana", she said, "we have a visitor it's Mog and he has a little girl with him."

"What the devil does he want? Tell him he's not welcome."

"Do you mind making some tea and will you take the little one to see the chickens as he says he wishes to talk to me; about what I have no idea." She was soon to find out after nana left hand in hand with the little girl.

"Well Mog what have you to say for yourself?"

"Ivy's dead; she died last winter of the dreaded T.B. I've tried to care for Minnie but I lost my job a month ago when I had to stay home to look after her.

"She's not caught her mother's illness?"

"No she had the measles and the doctor said that her lungs were fine but fresh air would be good for her. I have no job' no money and I've lost the house and it's the workhouse for us unless," he paused and looked longingly at Surann, "unless you can take my little one. I can sleep rough and go and look for work up north and then I will be able to pay you for her keep. Please; please Surann I know it's a lot to ask but don't let my little one suffer because of my stupidity."

Surann could see that he was near to tears and her heart grieved for him. "When did you have the last good meal?"

"I had food for Minnie two days ago. Please Surann take my child and treat as your own."

He stood up; "her few clothes are in the case I'm going now I cannot bear to say 'Goodbye' to her."

She hadn't said that she would take the child but he knew her well enough to know that she could not turn a child from her door.

"There's no need for you to leave Mog we will need more hands here when Emlyn joins the navy." For a moment her thoughts turned back to the day when Emlyn had broke the news to them that he wasn't going to University as he wanted to realise his ambition of going to sea.

"Sorry," she apologised, "I forgot what I was saying."

"You said that Emlyn was joining the navy."

"Yes. As we will need more help perhaps you would like to stay on and earn a wage. There's room in the house for Minnie and you can bunk down in one of the barns; that is if you agree."

Mog moved towards her and taking her in his arms he hugged her; she could feel his wet face next to hers and she did not pull away from him as he cried, "I'm sorry Surann; so very, very sorry for the way I treated you."

How she hated to see a grown man cry; she moved away from him feeling very near to tears herself; if only she had treated him better perhaps he wouldn't have turned to another woman; deep down she felt as much, if not more, to blame. Why had she turned her back on his love for a memory?

Around the supper table that night Surann had quite a bit of explaining to do. After supper she got out the old camp bed to put in Minnie's room; there wasn't enough room to swing a cat but it was better for Mog than to sleep in the barn as she first suggested.

Mog was true to his word and did more than his share of work taking the burden from her grancha's shoulders. His work load had increased when Dewi had surprised them by packing his bags and telling them that he was off to Spain to fight 'the cause'. He had surprised them all by one morning coming to breakfast dressed in his best suit.

"You're not planning on mucking out the pigs in your bit of best?" Grancha had asked.

"I'm off to Spain; I'm not good enough for this country's army but Spain will have me."

"In the name of God what's got into you lad I never thought my grandson would turn into a bloody red."

"Pity there wasn't more 'bloody reds' in Wales as you put it and then we might not be so down trodden."

"You don't know what you're talking about lad you're talking through your hat." Grancha had pushed his chair to one side and stormed out of the house.

Having said her 'goodbyes' Surann had watched as Dewi crossed the yard to make his peace with his grandfather. She saw the old man taking his grandson in his arms and then handing him an envelope. She knew that grancha wouldn't let him leave without that little extra to see him 'all right'.

Soon the time had come for Emlyn also to leave home. She hugged Emlyn, tears filling her eyes, as he made his departure to join his training ship in Portsmouth. Why hadn't things worked out as she had planned? How she missed Dewi's company and now to see the youngest leave the fold was just too much. Had it been fate that Mog had been sent back to them? She knew that come the following year Merryl too would be leaving home to study law in London. Arrangements had already been made that she would stay with her Aunt Wendy and Uncle; these arrangements had eased Surann's thoughts of her daughter being alone in the big city but why had she decided to follow in her father's footsteps; if only she knew that in the big city lived and worked a man who remained close to her mother's heart. How many times had Surann wanted to tell of his existence but had always found an excuse not to. Had the time now come for her to tell her daughter that her father wasn't killed in the war but he was very much alive and living in the city? 'Why make waves', thought Surann the city was big and they would never meet.

"Happy New Year everyone"; shouted grancha as he returned from an evening in the 'Butchers Arms'. "Here's to 1937. Have you got the elderberry wine ready?"
"I think you've had enough."
"I'm beastly sober me old darling." He turned and hugged his wife.
Surann toasted the New Year in but felt so depressed. She was tired and lonely and dreaded the year that was ahead the year when her darling daughter would leave home. What had she left?

Come July she was sitting in the school hall as she watched her daughter receive her school certificate; many subjects passed with distinction. One thing was certain Merryl brains had not come from her mother.
It was a beautiful young lady who came down stairs dressed in her ball gown ready to be escorted to the school leavers' ball on the arm of the head boy.
She could not imagine how she would face the parting with her daughter; she sat gazing out of the window across the fields and as she wiped a tear from her eyes she heard a little voice.

"I wont ever leave you mother," said little Minnie "I love you too much;" she was such a sweet child. It still felt strange to hear Mog's daughter call her 'mother' but from the beginning the little one had taken to her.

The day came too quickly for Merryl's departure to London. Mog brought the old van that grancha had bought that spring, around to the front door and as Merryl got in beside him Surann could stand and watch no longer. They had said their 'goodbyes' the previous evening and now all Surann could do was blow a kiss and turning fled indoors the tears she had tried to hold back no filling her eyes.

The house felt so empty; grancha had wished Merryl 'good luck' at breakfast and had handed her a 'little something' the same as he had done for the lads. Merryl had been lucky to get a scholarship but things were going to be hard to see her through.

"I'll get a part-time job," she had told her mother.

The same old thoughts ran through her mind; 'Why hadn't she told John Lloyd of the existence of his daughter? Why had she kept the truth of her father from Merryl? Surann threw herself down on her bed and burying her head in her pillow she let the tears flow.

Pulling herself together she decided to take the opportunity of having the house to herself and have a bath. Soon the water was hot and taking the old tin bath off the nail in the yard she closed the kitchen door. Frothing up the water with some soap flakes she lowered herself into the warm water. She closed her eyes hoping to shut out all her worries she must not linger too long as Mog would be back and he would be wondering why the doors were all locked. The water was beginning to cool and getting out she knelt by the bath to wash her hair. Reaching for a jug of clear water she let the towel slip from her body as she saw Mog standing there staring at her.

All she could say was; "I thought I'd locked the doors."

"My God woman you are more beautiful than ever I remembered." He crossed from the doorway and picking her up in his arms he carried her into the parlour. His hungry lips were upon hers and his rough, work worn hands caressed her still damp body. Her hair dripped wet upon the rug by the fireplace where he had laid her. She watched as he undid his bracers and his trouser buttons but she did not move. It was time to put the past behind her; she wanted to be loved. He lay besides her kissing her lips, her breasts; his hands roamed her body bringing to her a sensation that had all too long been forgotten. As he filled her with his manhood she cried out; it was as if she was a virgin and he had broken her in. She clung to him as they reached the height of their passion and together they lay as one.

"Let's go upstairs." She said to him and taking his hand she led him to her bed. The sun streamed in across her bed as she lay waiting for him to undress.

"You look like a Goddess," he teased, "with the sun shining on your body."

She reached out and touched him; "It seems I haven't yet finished with you," he said. "You've been driving me mad all summer long. I've wanted to catch hold of you and take you as I watched you milk the cows; even when you've been bending over the wash tub with your bare arms and your blouse open at the neck showing just a glimpse of your breasts."

There were no inhibitions as he lay beside her; she wanted him as much as he wanted her. "You are a 'big boy' Mog Morgan," she said as she caressed his body.

"Well dear lady I'd better put 'him' to good use."

She felt like a young girl as they teased each other; hard work had kept her body youthful and firm and good feeding had made Mog the man he once was.

Their love making took on a more serious, but pleasurable aspect, as for the second time that morning he entered her.

"I love you," he whispered.

Still she could not say the words; all she did say was; "make it last." She ran her fingers through his tousled hair as his head lay upon her breast.

"Come on sleepy head time to get up."

"I want to stay here forever you've worn me out woman."

"Grancha will be wondering where his lunch is and nana will be back from the shops; back in the kitchen she made a flask of tea and packed two pasties and some Welsh cakes for the two men and she watched at the window as Mog strode off whistling towards the high field.

She emptied the bath and rinsed out the towels then after making some preparations towards the evening meal she took herself off upstairs. Smiling to herself as she looked upon her rumpled bed she muttered to; 'I know what I will do.'

"What the dickens are you up to girl?" Nana's voice called up the stairs. "I thought you were coming through the ceiling. I'm just making a cup of tea would you like one?"

"Lovely," shouted Surann, "be with you in a tick."

"What the devil have you been up to on such a hot day? That walk up the lane nearly killed me had to stop for a breather a couple of times; must be getting old."

"You should have asked Mog to meet your bus." Smiling to herself as she thought to herself what nana would say if she really did know what she had been 'up too'.

"Did Merryl get off all right?"

"Yes; the train was on time for once in a while; she was really excited. I'm glad Wendy and Glyn will be there to meet the train at Paddington. By the way, you asked what I've been doing. I've been moving Millie's things into Emlyn's room."

"Good idea she shouldn't be sharing a room with her father at her age."

Surann said no more nana would find out soon enough that she had moved Mog's things into her room.

"Soon be finished upstairs nana; the meat is in the oven and the vegetables are all ready to put on. Grancha said they'd be in by seven."

"You want to take things a bit easier girl you're looking quite flushed."

It was Minnie on her return from school that let 'the cat out of the bag'. "Mother, mother," she shouted, "I love my new room and the pretty curtains. Daddy will be pleased he hasn't got to sleep on the camp bed any longer he'll like it better in your bed. You wont feel so sad now Merryl's gone to London with daddy to keep you company."

"What did the girl say?" questioned nana. "Mog sleeping in your bed."

"Well he is my husband," was all she said as she went to put the cloth on the table for supper.

CHAPTER NINE

"Happy Christmas everyone," shouted Emlyn as he came through the doorway with his kitbag slung over his shoulder.

"Is he Father Christmas" questioned Minnie as she gazed upon the bearded sailor.

"It suits you," said Surann to her brother; "now if it was grey you could pass as Santa."

"What have you got in your sack?" asked Minnie.

"Presents for everyone but they've all got to go to Santa; I thought you said Merryl was home."

"She's just 'popped' to town to do some last minute shopping."

"You're looking good sis. the extra weight suits you; you were nothing but skin and bone when I left."

Surann just smiled and went on rolling out the pastry for the mince pies.

"Any news of our Dewi?"

"We had a card a few weeks back he said that he is fine but things are bad out there."

"They're bad here too; we could do with him at home helping us," remarked grancha as he sat in the corner smoking his pipe. I just can't do as much as I used to thank God we've got Mog."

"You've got to sleep in the box room Em. I've got your bedroom now," said Minnie.

"I'm home," called Merryl shaking the snow from her coat. "I think we're going to have a white Christmas."

"How are you getting on in London I thought that you'd have been staying there over Christmas?"

"Aunt Wendy and Glyn were going away and I so much rather be home I miss mum's cooking."

"A little bird told me that you've got yourself a boyfriend."

"He's not my boyfriend; we're just good friends. I've got myself a part time job as a filing clerk in a law firm and he's my boss' son. We've been to the theatre a few times and out for a meal once with his mum and dad. His dad is very nice but I'm not fond of his mother."

"I can already hear wedding bells," teased Emlyn.

"Don't go getting serious at your age you've got a lot of hard work in front of you," grancha said as he re-lit his pipe. "I want someone to keep me in luxury when I retire and our Merryl is going to be a famous lawyer one day."

Everyone was in a good mood; everyone except Surann. Emlyn was the only one who had noticed that she had put on weight. She had missed two of her monthly cycles and at first had put it down to her age and perhaps an early start to the menopause but now a third period had been missed and noticing changes to her body and sickness every morning she now realised that she was pregnant with Mog's baby.

She just didn't know how she felt about it and as yet hadn't told her husband. She had so much responsibility from young Minnie to her elderly grandparents. Nana seemed to be failing; she got so exhausted and now left all the shopping and housework to Surann. Grancha took twice as long to do things and Mog often complained that the old man was more of a hindrance than a help.

"Something smells goods," said Mog as he opened the back door and let the cold air and a flurry of snow into the kitchen. "It's snowing quite heavy and I'm sure I heard Santa's bells."

"It's too early daddy; our Em. is home and he's got to sleep in the box room 'cause I've got his bed," laughed Minnie.

"Just in case it was Santa don't you think you should be in bed?"

"Do you like the trimmings daddy?" Minnie said changing the subject, "Mother and I made them this afternoon."

"Don't forget to leave a mince pie for Santa", said grancha, "perhaps he'd like something to warm him up."

"That's a good idea; coming for a pint?" Mog suggested to the old man.

"Not tonight Mog it's too cold for my old bones."

"Do you mind if I join you," said Emlyn as he came down the stairs, "I've missed the taste of a good Welsh bitter."

"Don't be late," shouted Surann as the two men put on their top coats.

"Warm the bed for my love," shouted Mog as he opened the back door.

"Close that door it's like a morgue in here," complained nana. "I'm off to bed."

"I may as well come too can't here the wireless with all this interference," grancha tapped his pipe against the hob and put it in the rack on the mantelpiece.

"Sleep tight," said Surann as the two made their way to bed.

Her mince pies and sausage rolls were made; the turkey stuffed and the fire banked up for the night and everyone's presents ready for the morning Surann decided that she might as well go to bed. The two old folk were fast asleep snoring in unison; she crept into Minnie's room taking the empty stocking from the foot of the bed and replacing it with her Christmas stocking hoping that when the men returned they would not wake the sleeping child. She then tapped on Merryl's door; "I'm off to bed; so nice to have you home."

"Where's my stocking?" asked her sleepy daughter.

"Santa will bring it when he comes," said her mother as she put her daughter's stocking on the floor at the foot of the bed.

"Goodnight mum; Happy Christmas."

"Sweet dreams," replied her mother giving her a kiss.

Quickly Surann undressed; it was really too cold to linger but for a moment she stood naked in front of her mirror and placing her hands on her rounded belly she said to herself, 'by next Christmas I'll be filling your stocking.' She slipped on her nightdress that had been warming on the oven brick that was wrapped in her old cardigan. 'I'll tell Mog tonight if he's sober enough'. She could not complain about Mog's drinking habits as he had changed so much and seldom went to the pub unless it was a special occasion

She looked at the clock; it was almost eleven; 'stop tap was at ten o'clock they should have been home by now,' she thought as she tucked the eiderdown behind her back. She heard a creek on the stairs and Mog's voice, "Quiet you daft bugger you'll wake the baby."

"Ho, ho, ho," was Emlyn's reply, "I'm Santa Claus".

"Happy Christmas Santa Claus," said Mog.

"Is it Christmas daddy?"

"Not yet sweetie pie go back to sleep."

Silence fell once more upon the household as Mog closed their bedroom door.

"Still awake?"

"I've been waiting for you; you're late."

"It's treacherous out there; we had a job to make it up the lane took three steps up and two back. Good thing I brought the ewes down yesterday. Hope you've warmed the bed I'm freezing."

She watched Mog by the candle light as he undressed. "I'm leaving my long johns on tonight it is too bloody cold," he climbed in beside her. "Been waiting for me have you?" He teased and then his mouth sort hers and he kissed her passionately. "Got a present for me have you?" He said as his hands fondled her breasts.

"Not tonight Mog I've got something to tell you."

He lifted her nightdress and began to touch her.

"Mog listen to me I'm having a baby."

"All right my love we'll make one tonight," as he spoke he lay upon her; there was no stopping him. She really didn't wish to as he had aroused her passion'

"Midnight my love; Happy Christmas. That was the best Christmas present I've ever had." He said kissing her.

"Happy Christmas Mog now will you listen to me I've got a better present for you."

"Where is it?" he leaned over the side of the bed as if to look for his present.

"No Mog it's not under the bed it's here,"

"Where?"

"Under my nightie."

"There's nothing under your nightie only you

Mog sat up in bed and once more lifted her nightdress, "You've got me there."

"I tried to tell you before you attacked me; we're having a baby."

"We're having a baby," he yelled.

"Hush love you'll wake everyone."

"How come?"

"Do you really want me to explain?" she laughed. "Well, it's like this, if you can remember back to when we first got back together when you found me having a bath and…..," her words drifted away. "Do you really want me to go into detail about how we made love?"

"You'd better not or I might want to do it again," he gently touched her belly. "No kidding is this really our baby?"

"No kidding come next June we should have a son or daughter. Blow out the candle and lets 'cwtch' up the bed is getting cold."

"Goodnight my love you really have given me the best present. I hope it's a son but there again girls are lovely especially if she looked like you."

She opened her bedroom curtains to see the new day and the land covered in a blanket of snow. Her husband still lay asleep although way passed his usual time of rising. Life on the farm didn't stop just because it was Christmas but she was loath to disturb him as he slept so peacefully.

"Come on sleepy head there's work to be done."

"Did I dream it or is it really true that you're having a baby?"

"Hush, I don't want everyone to know, not just yet. It will be our secret."

"Why not I want the world to know?"

"I don't know what they'll think? Merryl's almost nineteen and I'm sure our Em. will think I'm past it. I'm going on down I want to get the turkey in and I doubt if grancha or nana are up and the fire wont have been opened up and it will take an hour for the oven to warm and I want dinner to be ready by one o'clock."

Mog couldn't keep their secret for long and by the time the new year of 1938 had been celebrated the family all knew of Surann's pregnancy.

"I always wanted a brother or a sister," said Merryl as she kissed her mother 'goodbye' as the train drew into the station. "Take care of yourself mum and don't worry about me I'm happy."

"I think this young man of yours is more special than you are letting on."

"I'll bring him home to meet you at Easter."

Emlyn had returned to his ship a few days previously and would soon be sailing to the Mediterranean. Surann had been upset at his departure concerned about his well-being with all the trouble in the world and constant talk about war.

"Never know sis I may end up in Spain then I can meet this Spanish girl that our Dewi writes about."

"Sometimes I wish that life could have stood still and we were all home together."

"I'm glad you've got Mog and his little one is such a sweetie and come the summer you'll have plenty to occupy your days."

"You cheeky devil," she pretended to hit her brother, "how do you think I now spend my days as a lady of leisure?"

For a few days after Emlyn and Merryl's departure the house seemed very quiet. Minnie was back at school and Mog busy with the farm.

Christmas had been a happy family time but Surann now felt an underlying apprehension that 'things' weren't quite as perfect with her grandparents. Both now seemed locked in their own little world and no longer did everyday life interest them. 'Happy New Year', she thought 'I wonder what the year will bring?'

CHAPTER TEN

It was a beautiful summer's day; and Surann was putting a few things into a suitcase. She took a coat hanger off the hook on the door and carefully folded a pretty lilac crepe dress and jacket; placing on top of the clothes some tissue paper she closed the case. She couldn't believe that she was going to London to spend a week-end with Wendy and Glyn to celebrate Merryl and Richard's engagement. When she had first read Merryl's letter she had been upset and had told Mog that there was no way that she could go.

"I can't possible take David."

"David and I will be fine after all it is only a week-end and I'm still off on the sick I'm not back in work until Tuesday and don't forget we've got Minnie to help us."

Remembering Mog's words she lifted the suitcase off the bed and put it on the landing with her overnight bag.

Mog had visited the doctor with a badly swollen face; the doctor said it was 'blast' but it turned out to be a bad tooth; to put it mildly he had been 'like a bear with a sore head' until Dai 'Tooth' had extracted it.

She knew they'd get on fine but it still bothered her as David was only just turned one year old and so dependent on her. Her mind was racing thinking of the many reasons why she shouldn't go; how would they manage with his nappies; his bottles and at bedtime? She felt so tired; the last year had been so hard. She lay down on the bed and closed her eyes.

'I'll have five minutes before they get back' she thought knowing that Mog would stop at the shop to buy Minnie some sweets after school or stop to show off his son to one of his mates. Rest was to evade her as so many things kept going through her mind. The happy family time at the Christmas of 1937 had soon been forgotten when early in the New Year nana had fallen and broken her leg. She had been hospitalized for a few weeks but on her return home had taken to her bed. From that time on life for Merryl had become hell' to say the least. Grancha had got so upset when she seemed to forget whom he was. How she wished that her brothers had been at home but there was no chance of that Emlyn had written saying that he was married.

"We'll be living in Portsmouth," his last letter had said, "going to be a dad so had to hurry the wedding along before I sail off again."

Letters from Dewi were few and far between; he too was married and his last letter had said that it would be a long time before he would be able to return to his homeland; if ever.

There weren't enough hours in the day to complete her chores and as her baby grew inside her she felt she had no time at all for herself or to prepare for the child's birth.

She recalled, as if it was yesterday, the day nana died. It was just a few weeks before David's birth. Nana had got up from her bed, that had been brought down to the front room, saying that she was going to make tea for her son as he was coming home from the army. Surann had put her arm around her and had suggested that she went back to bed when she suddenly collapsed in her arms and died almost immediately from a massive heart attack. Grancha had been so distressed that he hadn't had time to say 'goodbye' to his darling girl. She could not grieve; she had thanked God when He had taken nnna as she had felt relieved as she couldn't have gone on much longer. How she had hated washing and changing the old lady and daily changing her bed. She seemed to have been washing every day and not once had Wendy come to visit to offer some help.

'Flaming June' lived up to its name and it was with great relief that her baby arrived on time; it had been such a wonderful event when she held her son in her arms. Not born in a barn like Merryl but in a hospital bed. Mog had brought her flowers and Minnie had been delighted with her baby brother. Surann smiled as she recalled Minnie's words; "Daddy said I have a half-brother, I don't understand he looks all there to me." David's birth had been a delight to Mog who worshipped his son from the moment of his arrival and he also doted upon by Minnie.

Merryl had come home that summer for a fortnight's holiday as Richard had gone to America with his parents. She too had been enamoured by the baby. "I'm going to have four children when I get married," she had said.

Surann recalled asking; "When is that going to be?"

"When he's qualified; he's going into the family business."

"I can't wait to meet this young man of yours."

"Perhaps we'll be able to come home at Christmas."

It had been good to watch her daughter enjoying the haymaking and having fun with young Minnie.

The long hot summer had passed; the autumn days brought high winds and torrential rain. "We're in for a bad winter," Mog had said as the month of December brought flurries of snow.

Grancha was lost without his 'help mate' and would spend hours sitting in their bedroom gazing out towards the mountains.

"Come down for tea Grancha I've made your favourite pudding."

"It's going to snow I'd better see to the ewes first."

"Mog will do that," she remembered telling him.

"The ewes are my job." He had put on his old coat and hat and turning to her said, "Keep my tea warm."

The pudding had stood on a saucepan of warm water waiting for his return, six o'clock had come and gone and then seven o'clock. Mog had come in drenched to the skin. "It's snowing heavy and the wind is like ice. I'm not going out again come hell or high water. The ewes are settled down."

"Is grancha with you?"

"No. Haven't seen him about surely he didn't go out in this?"

"He went out about five to see to the ewes."

Her eyes filled with tears as she recalled that night; she remembered how Mog had put on his coat and hat and had ventured out to look for the old man.

It was gone ten o'clock when he returned shaking his head, "It's no good love the weather is getting worse I'm sure there are six foot drifts out there. I've walked up to the top farm and there's no sign of him it's hopeless."

Three days had passed before the snow had ceased and the sun had come out but not for Surann it was one of her darkest of all when her grandfather's body was found.

"Well preserved", she remembered one of the farm hands saying.

The old man was laid to rest besides his beloved Kate. "Never seen such a good turn out," said the landlord of the 'Butchers'. "He was well liked by all. It wont be the same up here now Mrs Morgan what do you intend to do with the farm?"

"Sell up," she had replied. "I've had enough of farming and all the hardships it brings."

Her daughter's planned visit at Christmas was not to be and by the time the daffodils began to bloom Surann had sold the farm and had bought a terraced house in the top village. A house with a front garden and a view of the mountains that she so loved. Across the road beyond the woodland gardens she could see a field where the spring lambs frolicked by their dams; beyond was the wood whose trees sported the green of spring and then the brook and the purple headed mountains. Life here she hoped was going to be free from worry and she could enjoy her family and be content. Luckily Mog had been able to get a job as a surface worker in the town pit and over the last months Surann had made a perfect home for her husband, son and Minnie.

"That's where you are," she heard Mog's voice, "lady of leisure taking an afternoon nap. Sorry I can't join you; all packed I see."

"I'm not going," she said, I'm happy here I don't want to go traipsing off to London."

"You'll regret it if you don't go; might not have a chance for a while there still talk of war."

"I don't think it will come to that we should have learnt our lesson last time."

"What time does your train leave?"

"Eight-thirty; do you really think I should go?"

"I didn't buy you that new outfit for nothing; go and show your sister how glamorous you are; as good as any of those city birds with their fine feathers."

"What's for tea mother? I'm starving."

"Ask your father he's in charge until Monday."

That night they made love with the curtains open and the moon shining in through the window across their bed. "I love you so much Sarah Ann Morgan; don't ever leave me."

"Where do you think I'm going? I've made my nest here and I'm content."

Content she may well be but that night she dreamt of her lost love; they were lying together in a boat drifting down the river.

CHAPTER ELEVEN

She was met at Paddington Station by her sister's husband; "The 'girls' are up to their necks in party preparations."

She was a little disappointed that Merryl had not been there to meet her.

"Taxi," shouted Glyn stepping out in front of a big black car.

"Where's Big Ben?" asked Surann as she settled in the back seat.

"Driver," said Glyn pulling back a little window that divided them from the driver, "Scenic route please."

She was tired from her long train journey and felt too weary to enjoy the famous landmarks of the city as they drove passed Big Ben, The Houses of Parliament and Buckingham Palace. "See the flag flying that means the king is at home. Shall we 'pop' in for tea," Glyn joked. "There's the Albert Hall and when we pass Harrods we'll nearly be home."

"I hope Wendy has the kettle boiling."

She gave out a gasp of amazement when she heard how much their 'site seeing' had cost Glyn. It was half of what Mog earned in a week.

"Here's our humble abode," said Glyn as he helped her from the taxi.

'Humble', she thought, 'there's nothing 'humble' about this three storied Victorian terraced house that loomed above her.

Merryl stood by the open door looking every inch the modern young lady.

"Mother have you had a good journey?" Merryl hugged her mother. "Auntie Wendy said to put your bags in the 'green' room. Here let me take your coat mum it's the maid's day off. I can't wait for you to meet Richard."

Merryl hadn't given her mother chance to get a word in and when she did speak she felt afterwards that it hadn't been herself that had uttered the words. "About time too you've kept him well hidden." Trying to cover it up she said, "Where's Wendy?"

"She's on the phone in the library making the final arrangements. I'm so excited."

"How's your studying going?"

"Oh! Not now mother dear I want to forget about everything until after this week-end. I've got so much to tell you. You'll meet Richard and his parents at dinner tonight. Let's go up and unpack your case and see what you're going to wear. We always dress for dinner."

Surann was flabbergasted and all she could say was; "Well dear, I do hope you do I wouldn't wish to see you come to dinner in the nude."

Merryl laughed, "Oh! Mum you are so funny."

'Funny', thought Surann, 'I was trying to be sarcastic.' Something flashed through her mind she had a feeling of deja vu; the thought made her shiver.

"Are you cold mum? Aunt Wendy has put the heating on in your room."

"No dear I'm not cold just a ghost crossing my path." Why did that ghost feel very close?

"I like your outfit are you going to wear that tonight mum?"

"No dear; Mog bought it for your party tomorrow."

"It would be more suitable for dinner tonight I want you to look your best when you meet Richard. Have you another case with your evening dress in?"

"Evening dress?" Surann questioned.

"Yes mother it is evening dress tomorrow night it was on the invitation."

"Invitation? I had no invitation only your letter."

"Don't worry we'll sort that out tomorrow. Aunt Wendy will get Harrods to send something suitable round."

Surann had had enough how she wished that she was back in her little house in the valley. Had London and Wendy made a snob out of her daughter?

"Sarah Ann darling I'm so glad you've arrived." Wendy 'floated' into Surann's bedroom wearing a Japanese Kimono and her hair tied back in a black satin bow.

"You're looking good having the baby has taken years off you. How is the little darling? Have you any photos to show us?"

"David is fine he had a lovely birthday in June."

"Sorry darling I've been so busy I clean forgot. I really must try and pay a visit you'll have to let us know of a good hotel now that you've moved to your **'little house'",** she stressed the last words. "We are thinking of selling up here and buying a property in Wales now there's so much talk of there being a war."

Wendy and Merryl chattered away over Surann's head about the guest list for the next evening, about who were coming and who wasn't.

"We'll have to sort mum out with an evening dress as she didn't get out invitation."

"There was a time when my clothes fitted her but I can see that's not possible now; how do you manage to keep so slim darling?"

"Hard work," was Surann's reply.

"I must give the caterers a ring I want everything to be just perfect for dinner tonight.

"Caterers?" said Surann to her daughter as Wendy left the room. "Doesn't she cook?"

"As little as possible; Uncle Glyn does quite a lot but for tonight as she wants everything to be perfect. Richard's father was honoured in the King's New Year honours and his grandmother is a Lady."

Surann 'tut'tutted', 'I'm a lady too', she thought but said nothing.

"Mum?" Merryl's tone had changed she sound more like the girl who had once lived in the Welsh valley. "I so want you to like Richard I love him so much; he's bought me a lovely diamond ring and he's taking time off next week we're going house hunting. How I wish you could stay and then we could go together. Auntie Wendy is kind but she's not my mum."

"I wish you all the happiness in the world my darling. Richard must be earning good money to afford to buy you a house."

"His mother's parents left him money and his paternal grandmother is giving us money."

"You're a very lucky young woman. When do you plan to marry?"

"Hopefully next Easter; I always wanted to be an Easter bride and have the church full of daffodils; I'll be Mrs Richard Smythr then; how I wish I had a father to give me a way. I heard of a wedding where the bride's mother gave her a way. That would be nice mum. When

I was growing up and didn't have a dad I always thought that grancha would live forever and he would give me a way. Since I've met Richard I've been thinking about you a lot life has been so hard for you; are you happy mum?"

"I am now."

"When I was a little girl you always seemed so sad. I supposed you missed my father. How I wished that he had lived I always felt left out at school not having a dad. You'll like Richard's dad he's adorable but I'm not so fond of his mother and don't tell Richard but I'm scared stiff of his grandmother she's so Victorian and so severe."

Where will you live if Wendy and Glyn move to Wales before you marry?"

"I expect Richard and I will get a flat. Come on mum there's the gong for tea."

They met Wendy in the hall replacing the telephone; "Richard's mother has just phoned his grandmother can't make it tonight she has a cold coming on."

"Good", whispered Merryl to her mother.

"Perhaps it will be best if you take your mother to Harrods in the morning or to that nice little dress shop in Kensington High Street. I'll book a table for you to have lunch at the Dorchester; all on me as it seems I forgot to post your mother's invitation."

'Accidentally on purpose', thought Surann.

"I'm a late riser," Wendy continued, "especially after a social evening and I've got to look my best for tomorrow evening. By the way, if you'd like a bath before you dress the water is nice and hot. The bathroom is on the third floor Merryl will show you no need to hurry as our bedroom has an en suite."

'En suite', thought Surann, 'what the devil is that. She's forgotten about sharing a tub in front of the kitchen fire.'

'Peace at last', thought Surann as she flopped down on the bed. How she missed her big iron bedstead with the patchwork quilt and she knew that tonight she would miss Mog's muscular arms around her and most of all young David cheeky grin and mop of dark curly hair; he was so much like his dad in appearance but as each day went by he seemed to have more of her character. She took their photos out of her handbag and placed them on the dressing table; Mog, David and Minnie her new family.

"Mum," called Merryl tapping lightly on the door, "Do you wish to use the bathroom or shall I go first?"

"You go dear I had a scrub in the tub last night. I'll just have a wash later."

"Sweet dreams sister dear?"

"Wendy you startled me I must have dozed off. Wouldn't think one would get tired sitting down all that time but the journey was so long and it really tired me."

"Go and have a nice bath I've run the water for you and put in some of my expensive bath salts. We're expecting Richard and his parents about eight o'clock for pre-dinner drinks that will give you a good hour to get ready. First door on the left up the stairs," said Wendy as she 'drifted' out leaving a trail of perfume behind her.

The only perfume Surann had ever had was the Lavender water that Millie had bought her for Christmas. As she passed her daughter's open door Merryl called to her, "We'll go down to dinner together mum."

'Phew', she said as she opened the bathroom door, 'it's like grancha's Turkish bath'. She had to admit as she stepped into the foaming water that this really was luxury. Stepping out she wrapped herself in a huge luxurious bath towel and then using a fluffy powder puff she dusted herself with talc that smelt of roses. 'What would Mog say if he saw her now?' she thought. More than likely it would be what he would do; she smiled to herself as she guessed that he wouldn't wait to get her to the bedroom he would take her there on the bathroom floor. Her breasts tingled as she thought of Mog's love making; it was a wonder she hadn't got pregnant again he was so demanding. Now that he worked shifts he would often take her in the afternoon as David had his nap. He would put his hungry lips upon hers to silence her moans as the little one slept in the next room.

"They'll hear you next door," she would say as the bed squeaked beneath them. "Remember we've got neighbours now."

Not just satisfied with their love making in the afternoon he would be ready for her as she climbed into bed beside him but at night they tried to curtail their sounds of pleasure as Minnie slept across the landing.

"It's nearly seven thirty mum are you all right?"

"Be out now," she called back letting the towel fall to the floor as she took her old wool dressing gown off the hook catching a glimpse of her naked body in the long mirror. Her breasts were firm and well-rounded and her waist hadn't changed much since a girl and as Mog would have said "she had a lovely bum." All in all she didn't look a woman who was nearly forty.

Back in her room she slipped on her silk French knickers that Mog had insisted on her buying when she shopped for a brassiere; something she had never worn, but felt that it would be nice under her new outfit. The silk felt nice against her body and just as she slipped on her matching silk petticoat Wendy's head peeped round the door as she gave it a light tap.

"Well sister I must say you've got a better figure than you had twenty years ago. Mog must be keeping you at 'it'; busy I mean. I feel a little bit guilty so thought I'd better warn you that you're in for a surprise tonight; I'll not say no more.

Feeling rather bewildered Surann slipped on her dress and then put her feet into her new shoes that had just a little Cuban heel; she really felt elegant after always wearing flat shoes; lastly she put on her jacket.

"Ready mum?" said Merryl who had a slight blush of excitement upon her face and was looking radiant in a pale blue chintz dress.

"I believe Richard has arrived so we'll make a grand entrance," laughed Merryl.

'A grand entrance' was not the words Surrran would have used; she almost fainted as a tall, grey haired man turned to greet them

Rchard introduced her; "Father I'd like you to meet Merryl's mum Mrs Sarah Morgan. Mrs Morgan my father John Lloyd-Smythe.

In a daze she took his out-stretched hand. "Mrs Morgan I'm delighted to make your acquaintance Merryl has told me so much about you.

She just stood as if turned to stone; so this was Wendy's surprise; how could she have known all this time and not told her. She looked across at Wendy who had turned a bright red and just shook her head as if to say 'he doesn't know you.' As he let go her hand it just flopped to her side. "Angela", he called "I'd like you to meet Merryl's mum."

A rather tall, horsy looking lady stopped talking to Glyn and ambled across the room.

"Delighted," was all she said as she limply took Surann's hand.

She turned to her husband "John dear Glyndwr was saying that they are thinking of moving to Wales; with all this talk of war perhaps we should think of a place in the country." Ignoring Surann she returned to where Glyn stood by the French doors. "A breath of fresh air darling," she said as she took another cocktail from him, "I need some fresh air."

'So do I', thought Surann, 'why doesn't he know me? Have I changed that much?'

"Your daughter is such a lovely girl and doing so well with her studies I had hoped of keeping her on in 'the firm' when she qualifies but I expect she'll have other ideas now they plan to marry. Do you know Mrs Morgan there seems to be something very familiar about you have we met before?"

"I hardly think so." She wanted to shout out 'yes, yes; we were in love.' She was saved by the bell and Wendy saying "Glyn dear will you escort Sarah into dinner."

He sat opposite her at dinner and on a few occasions she noticed him watching her and although hungry she ate very little nothing could pass the lump in her throat or could it be the pain in her heart? Her daughter was so happy; how was she to tell her that this love could not be as Richard Lloyd-Smythe was her half-brother. Why? Oh why had Merryl always referred to him as Richard Smith or to be correct Smythe as John's mother would always insist? She could remember their first meeting as if it was yesterday and the words he had said; "I'm just plain John Lloyd." What was she to say to Merryl; now everything would have to come out as there was no way possible that she could marry Richard.

"More wine madam?" She placed her fingers on top of her glass and at the same time shook her head; she wanted to keep a clear head what was she to do?

"If there's going to be a war I'll be the first to join up," said Richard who was seated between herself and Merryl.

"No way will I let my son enlist; your father will see to that. You've just turned twenty-two and talking about flying aeroplanes how could you be so cruel?"

'Twenty-two,' thought Surann, she was trembling now with anger remembering John telling her she was the only woman in his life and him having a son by that bitch. No wonder his mother sent her packing; had he been already married when he seduced her in that fisherman's hut all those years ago?

"Merryl has told me that you've given up farming; I always dreamed of being a farmer imagining how idyllic it would have been to be a shepherd."

"It's a hard life there's nothing romantic about it when you have to search six foot snow drifts for a lost ewe and then find her and her baby frozen to death."

"Shall we change the subject," said Wendy with a look of disdain at her sister.

The meal seemed to linger on and on and Angela appeared to have had more than her fair share of drink and over the desert she began to criticize her husband. "Merryl tells us you have a baby," she sneered; "John wouldn't know how to make one." Then turning to Wendy she said, "Is Glyn any good under the sheets Wendy dear?"

Wendy ignored the remark and said, "Shall we have coffee in the drawing room?"

"Do you mind if I smoke?" asked John.

"In the conservatory if you don't mind; there's a decanter there do help yourself. Glyn dear will you escort Mrs Lloyd-Smyth I'll follow with Surann. Richard, Merryl come along."

"I'll be with you now," said Surann as Wendy took her arm. "I'd like to sit here for a moment."

"Don't make trouble," whispered Wendy.

"Why didn't you tell me?"

"Are you two coming?" said Merryl, "The coffee smells good."

"Don't be long Merryl will wonder where you are."

"Tell her I've gone to the bathroom."

She sat by the table sipping the wine, no longer chilled, that she still had left in her glass; she needed some Dutch courage. What was she to do?

"Mrs Morgan don't sit there why don't you join me if you don't mind the old pipe."

She slowly crossed the room to where he stood by the open doors. "Do you think there'll be another war?"

"I hope not," he puffed away at his pipe the smell of the smoke instantly bringing back memories.

"Did you serve in the last war?" she asked.

"Yes. I was in the Norfolk Regiment and was invalided out just at the end but I don't wish to spoil the evening by burdening you with that tale."

"Please continue," she looked into his eyes; those same eyes that had once looked down on her naked body.

"I was wounded and suffered amnesia; there is still a period in my life I cannot recall. Sometimes I seem to have flashes of memory but nothing makes sense."

She looked at his hands, so unlike Mog's work worn ones John's were lean, his fingers long and his nails clean and she also noticed that he wore no wedding ring.

"Your son and Merryl seem so very happy."

"I hope they make a go of it she's so good for him and I think the world of her."

"You married during the last war?" Surely he must think it strange that she was asking so many questions; stupid questions at that as she recalled the article she had read in the paper after Merryl's birth.

"No. Let me see it must have been about 1919 Angela was a young widow with a son and somehow or other my mother pushed us together."

Surann sighed; a sigh of relief to know that Richard wasn't his son. How she longed to tell him about Merryl but what had Wendy said, "don't make trouble."

"Are you all right Mrs Morgan?" he put his hand on her shoulder.

"Just a little tired it has been a very long day."

"Shall we go in? They'll think we've run off."

'I wish I could,' she thought and shivered as he took her arm.

"Cold?" he said.

He was as handsome as she remembered and still the perfect gentleman and out of her reach.

"Merryl often talks about your home cooking and especially your Welsh cakes. I seem to remember tasting them once but don't know where or when."

She wanted to tell him but now wasn't the right time; when would be the right time? Seeing him had stirred up the old memories and the love she had felt for him; the love she still felt for him.

CHAPTER TWELVE

Not only were the 'storm clouds' gathering over Europe they were gathering in her very being; she was drowning in a sea of despair would she ever find a safe harbour where she would find peace?

She was going home; home to Wales and the valley she loved the big city wasn't for her. It had saddened her to have to say 'goodbye' to her daughter but yet she felt deep down that city life was fast changing her daughter's views on life. It had been a tearful departure as Merryl had kissed her mother; "I promise mum I'll be home for Christmas. The papers' say that if there is a war it will all be over by then."

Surann said nothing thinking of past promises that had never borne fruition.

"I'm so glad you got on so well with Richard's father", her voice was silenced as the train's whistle blew, "Give my love to Mog and Minnie and a big hug for David". The train got up steam and carriage doors were slammed shut, "Love you mum," she shouted. The corridor was packed with men in uniform and hopefully Surann looked for a seat; "There's a seat here ma-am," said a young man and as she went to lift her case onto the luggage rack he offered to assist her and then sat next to her. "I've got a week's leave so taking the opportunity to visit my parents; goodness knows when I'll see them again if there's a war."

'War', thought Surann the word that was on everyone's lips. 'What would happen to Merryl and Richard's relationship if as he had said he joined up? Was it strong enough to survive long separations?' She closed her eyes as her thoughts turned over and over in her mind; 'if Merryl did come home for Christmas perhaps it would be a good time to tell her about her father'; she thought but then dismissed it as being unwise as it would ease her conscience but how would it affect Merryl?'

"John, John, John," the train seemed to say as she drifted into oblivion. The train stopping at Reading brought her back to reality and it stressed her that her thoughts were not of her husband but of John and the feelings she knew that had lain dormant for a time but were now uttermost in her mind. She shivered as she remembered the closeness they shared as they danced at the engagement party on Saturday evening. His very closeness making her wish to hold him even closer; to kiss him; to love him. 'Why? Why?' she now asked herself, 'after all those years had the love she had felt for him not died?'

He had told her how lovely she looked in the blue evening gown that Merryl had chosen for her, "Blue is my favourite colour," he had said. They had sat together and talked; talked about everything; the young couple, the war, his business, farming and even his wife; his wife who had kept her distance most of the evening as she flirted with all the male guests; age being no obstacle.

"We live separate lives," he had said, "always have done. It was a marriage of convenience we just stayed together for Richard's sake and now I suppose it is the business and as Angela puts it, 'my good name'". When the time came to say 'goodnight' he had held her hand and lightly kissed her on the cheek. "Do you know I still have that feeling that we've met before and the longer we're together the stronger it grows; silly isn't it as you say we haven't met."

She had looked into his eyes; how blue they were just like Merryl's. 'The mirror of the soul', she thought and what they revealed was a kind, loving man; the man she knew that she still loved.

Yesterday he had taken them to lunch; Wendy and Glyn declining the invitation saying that they had a prior engagement. He had driven them in his luxurious car to a hotel on the banks of the Thames at Windsor and whilst Merryl and Richard had taken a stroll, hand in hand, along the river bank they had sat for a while in silence; she not knowing what to say and he appearing to be deep in thought and then taking his pipe from his pocket he asked, "Do you mind if I smoke?"

"No." she almost whispered, "I rather like seeing a man smoking a pipe; a sign of contentment."

He laughed, "I'm far from contented, well perhaps I am at this moment in time," he said giving her a curious look and for a moment he 'puffed' away at his pipe before continuing, "I seem to have a memory of a time when I used to take a boat down the river near my home in Norfolk it is a pleasing memory as at the back of my mind I think I must have had a pretty young lady with me; blast!" he said "how I wish I could remember if only I could have I'm sure my life would have been different."

How she wanted to say to him "I was that girl; I sat by you in the boat and lay with you in the boat-house," but common-sense prevailed as she recalled that she had read it was unwise to tell someone suffering from amnesia about their past life; if it was to return it had to be a natural occurrence. 'If' was the operative word she thought, 'why after all these years hadn't it happened? Perhaps it never would.'

"All change; all change."

'Cardiff,' she thought 'I'll soon be home; home to Mog and the children. It had been a dream this was reality she must forget him and make the most of her life with her husband and the children.'

A fortnight later on 3rd September war was declared between Britain and Germany and Mog was all for 'joining up' but was told he was 'too old.'

"Too old be buggered I'm not yet forty five."

"They need young men," she had said "anyhow, you are doing a worth-while job the country would come to a stand-still without coal."

A letter from Merryl had arrived at the beginning of December sending her apologises that she wouldn't be able to make it home as Richard and her would have very little time together as he only had a two day leave and after Christmas she was off to start her training with the W.R.A.F..

'Someone else to worry about' thought Surann as she read the Christmas card and letter from Emlyn's wife saying that she was worried about her husband on his ship in the North Atlantic with all those German 'U-boats' about; "our second is due any day and all I can think about is me being left a widow with two kids."

By the time Christmas arrived the war that they had said 'would be all over' had escalated bringing with it the rationing of petrol and the thought of more rationing to follow in the New Year. The promised rationing started on 8th January with bacon, butter and sugar being rationed and everyone was issued with ration books.

"Perhaps we should have stuck to farming then at least we might have had more food on the table; 'dig for victory', we'll not be able to grow much to feed Britain in our little garden."

"We can grow our own vegetables."

"Can't live on veggies alone; it makes my mouth water to think of all those sides of bacon that used to hang in your nana's kitchen I could do with a few slices now what the devil does the government think we can do with four ounces of bacon each it's not enough to make a sandwich; I heard a rumour that old George is going to kill one of his pigs on the 'q.t'"

"Don't you go getting involved in the Black Market".

The New Year not only brought more trials for the country but also for Surann. "Are you all right," she had called to Minnie whom she could hear coughing in the scullery. Having no reply she had left off her dusting and went to see what was wrong and seeing Minnie with her head in her hands she asked "Have you taken your medicine?"

Minnie just shook her head and then held out a blood stained piece of rag, "Look Mother it happened when I coughed I knew it couldn't be my medicine as I haven't taken it."

Surann put her arm around the girl's shoulders, "Don't worry love you must have strained yourself coughing let me give you a teaspoonful of your medicine and then go and have a lie down. Fear filled her heart as she watched the girl slowly climb the stairs. She put the kettle on the make tea for herself and a hot drink for Minnie and was just pouring the hot water on the blackcurrant cordial when her husband returned with David.

"Are you O.K. love? You look as if you've been crying."

"I'll just take this up to Minnie and David can have his afternoon nap."

"I'll carry him up for you; why don't you have a nap as well."

"We need to talk I'm worried about Minnie."

Back in the kitchen she poured two cups of tea and cut a large slice from her newly baked cake for Mog. "Aren't you having some?" he asked.

"I'd choke on it," she said and sighed, "Mog our Minnie is coughing up blood we'll have to get the doctor out to her she was too weak to walk up the stairs and her face is like a sheet."

"God no," he said "That's how it started with her mother. I noticed on Sunday when she put on her coat to go to chapel that it was hanging on her I thought then that she must have lost weight but assumed it was just a woman's thing. I knew she shouldn't have gone to chapel it was freezing cold but she insisted telling me her cold was better."

"Don't blame yourself I've been too tied up in my own thoughts I should have noticed before. I did tell you before Christmas that I didn't like the cough she had but put it down to the 'flu that was going around."

"I'll 'pop' down the town to the surgery and have a word with the doctor; hope I'll be able to get and see him Ianto said there was a queue right down the hill last night and they closed the doors at 6 o'clock turning dozens away."

Everything seemed to happen so quickly the doctor had called that evening at 9 o'clock and within days he had found her a bed in Talgarth the hospital for those with the dreaded disease of T.B.. It broke their hearts that they weren't able to visit; not just because she needed complete rest but also because of the heavy snows that blocked the roads and made everywhere impassable.

"We're almost down to our last lump of coal the ton I ordered couldn't make it up the hill passed the pub it's early to bed for us tonight old girl we'll keep each other warm under the clothes mind you I got a job to find you with all you put on to go to bed."

"It's the only way to keep warm; I've put my old coat on David's bed I'm really worried about him he's not his usual playful self I do hope he hasn't caught Minnie's illness."

 "You worry too much about everyone. God girl I've been worrying about you since you went to London. Talk about not 'being himself' it is you who haven't been yourself. You've been in a world of your own. If you are really worried about David I'll try and get through tomorrow and get the doctor out to him."

That night she lay in his arms his words going over and over in her mind had she really been neglecting him, putting herself and her lost love before those who really loved her? When Mog turned over and lay upon her she did not push him away instead she closed her mind to the world outside and hungrily her lips closed upon his.

"What's got into you tonight old girl it hasn't been as good as this for a long time. I was beginning to think you didn't love me any more."

"Of course I do and watch whom you are calling 'old girl' I expect it's the change of life that has made me feel so down."

"We'll have a holiday this summer when our Minnie is better and this war is over."

"Do you really think it will be over by the summer? Our Merryl said in her letter that Richard is being posted abroad she hasn't been told where; everything is 'hush, hush'; obviously they now will not be able to get married at Easter. I hate to think of her living in a hut on an airfield; mind you she does look smart in her uniform."

"There you go again worrying about everyone else how about making me a happy man I hope you can remember what we used to get up to." His kisses that started on her lips warmed her passion and by the time his mouth reached her secret places all thoughts had left her mind."

Having drifted off to sleep she stirred in his arms hearing a sudden noise then hearing the wind howling outside she turned over and pulled the eiderdown over her ears.

"You've got all the clothes," said her husband tugging at the eiderdown.

"Didn't know you were awake too," she said.

"I thought I heard a noise."

"Go back to sleep it's only the wind; I hate to think what it will be like in the morning there's already a couple of inches on the sill in the bedroom. Did you bring the spade in?" There was no answer her husband was already snoring.

By now she was wide awake and lighting the candle by the side of the bed slipped her feet into her slippers and taking her dressing gown off the bed made her way to their son's room. Deep down inside she had a feeling that the noise she had heard was not the wind but her baby crying yet now there was silence. Just as she crossed the landing the candle flame flickering in the draft she again heard the noise; it wasn't the happy gurgling sound her infant made but a rasping, wheezing noise.

"Mog, Mog come quickly I think our David is ill; I'm sure he's caught Minnie's illness." She bent over the little one as he lay in his cot and picking him up she held him close. "Mog, Mog," she yelled "David is choking," She held him against her shoulder and patted his back as she did to bring up his wind; she thought this had helped but then panic stricken as she realised that he wasn't breathing putting her lips to his she tried to breath air into his lungs.

"What's a matter," asked Mog as he appeared in the door way dressed only in his shirt.

"He's not breathing help me Mog, do something."

"Perhaps he choked on something put your finger down his throat."

She continued to try to breathe life back into her little one but now he lay limp and cold in her arms. Mog put his arms around her shoulders and held the two of them close. "It's no good my love he's gone."

"He's gone to sleep Mog I'll sit here and nurse him for a while."

She sat in the basket chair by the side of the window that was now completely covered with snow and sung softly to her baby; "*Hush a bye baby on the tree top when the wind blows the cradle will rock;*" and outside the wind still raged and the valley lay asleep swathed in a blanket of snow.

"Come back to bed my love you'll catch your death sitting there," no sooner than the words had left his lips he regretted what he had said but his wife didn't appear to notice what he had said and continued rocking her baby. He got a blanket off the bed and put it around her shoulders.

"Thank you," she said and by the flickering light of the candle he saw her smile; "I didn't think of the blanket I'll wrap him Welsh fashion and then I'll go down and make a warm bottle for him and we can have a cup of tea." She put the baby in one end of the blanket and rolled it tightly around him and then tucked the other end in underneath leaving her arm free and the baby nestled close to her bosom.

"Shall I take him?" asked Mog.

"No you get dressed and go and get the doctor just in case he's caught Minnie's illness he might wake up and start coughing again."

"Come back to bed my love and put David in his cot he'll sleep until morning and we'll get the doctor then."

"No I don't want to disturb him he's cosy here I'll go and open up the fire and it will be nice and warm when you get back."

"It is still snowing and I doubt if I'll get through."

She turned and stared at him her eyes glassy and lifeless, "You did hear me I said get the doctor."

What was he to do? He put on his long johns and his working trousers tucking his flannel shirt in and tightening his belt he slipped on his waistcoat and over his top coat he pulled on an old mackintosh that hung on a nail behind the back door then pulling his socks up over his trouser bottoms he pulled on his working boots. He left her sitting by the glowing embers of the fire still rocking and humming to her baby. "Be as quick as I can," he said as he opened the front door letting in not just a flurry of snow but the soft snow that drifted up against the door. She did not reply; taking the spade he began to dig himself out the biting wind already stinging his face and the snow settling like ice upon his whiskers. "God help us," he prayed. "Dear Lord what shall I do?"

Their doctor lived a mile down three hills in the town below there was no way that man or beast could get through. He straightened his back and in doing so his eyes caught the flicker of a candle in the bedroom of the house three doors down; had his prayers been answered? Old mother Williams lived there and in a peculiar way she was the answer to his prayers as she was the one that all the village called upon when there was a death in the family but how was he going to get her attention if he could make his way to her house as he knew she was as deaf as a doorpost. 'Funny saying,' he thought as he made his way down the garden path using the spade to make a way through as the snow in some places being up to his waist. He slipped down the four steps that led to the road landing in the soft snow that had drifted against the wall. In patches the road was clear but then he came face to face with another huge drift and almost found it impossible to get up the steps of number twenty-three. Stupid thoughts were going through his mind, he felt as if he had one to many to drink as he cleared a path way to Mrs Williams' door, 'She'll thank me in the morning for clearing her path.' He picked up a handful of snow and making it into a ball he threw it up towards the window where the candle still flickered. The first and second time he missed; his fingers by now felt as if they were dropping off he put his hands in his pockets for warmth and there found some small change this gave him an idea; in the dark of the night he could not find any small stones to throw at the window to draw the old lady's attention so placing in the snow ball a few farthings he took aim and this time he hit his target.

'How stupid I am', he thought 'she'll never hear that' but to his amazement the curtains were drawn back and her head appeared at the window bedecked in her mob cap to hide her metal curlers. On seeing him she waved her hand and disappeared behind the curtains that she had again drawn. He waited a few moments almost frozen to the spot before the front door was opened and Mrs Williams called out "Is that you Morgan? What's wrong to get you out of your bed on a night like this? Come on in lad and I'll make you a hot toddy you need a drop of something strong to thaw you out."

"It's my little one Mrs Williams he's dead," he almost choked on the words suddenly realising what the words meant. She wont put him down my Surann thinks he's asleep yet she wanted me to go and get the doctor."

"It'll be the fourth little one I've laid out this week; Mrs Jones lost her two youngest and our Maggie May her little baby only born before Christmas and Reverend Davies' four year old; with all his praying it didn't save his little one from the diphtheria."

"Is that what's taken our David?"

"I can't say until I see him but I should think I'm right it's running rife through the valley; one doctor over in the Rhondda saved one little one's life by operating on the kitchen table cut a hole in his throat and put something in to help him breath; mind you lad I don't know if it is true you know only too well how rumours start. I'll go and get some warm clothes on and see if I we can make our way back to your place; mind you might have to carry me all sixteen stone of me."

"I will if I have to Mrs Williams I don't know what else I can do I've never seen my Surann like this before she's always been so brave."

"Losing a little one can sometimes do strange things to a mother."

Mog sipped his hot drink and felt the warm liquid reach the 'cockles of his heart' and then turning to the dresser he poured his self another stiff whisky he would need it if he was going to get Mrs Williams safely back to his house.

"Pour me one lad whilst you're at it I'll need something to keep out the cold and give me the strength to face what lies ahead."

The wind and snow had eased a little and a watery moon had made its way from behind the snow clouds and the snow lay crisp and deep beneath their feet and sparkled like diamonds by the light from the moon. It seemed an eternity since he had left the warmth of their bed when Surann had called to him until the time when he re-entered his cold, dark house. The candle that had been burning on the mantelshelf had long since burned away but in the faint glow from the dying embers Mog could see that his wife still sat there nursing their baby.

"Hello Mrs Morgan just 'popped' in to see if there was anything I could do to help. It's a devil of a night out there and when I saw Mog and he said that he was going for the doctor I thought I'd come and see what was wrong I was a nurse in my younger days."

"It's all right Mrs Williams he's sleeping peacefully now we'll get the doctor in the morning." Surann's voice sounded distant. "I don't really want you in my house I know what you do when you go to people's houses my baby is asleep you can go home."

Mrs Williams just ignored her words and said, "Shall I ask Mog to put some more coal on the fire you'll catch cold sitting here?"

"We've only got one big lump of coal so there's no need to waste that as it has to last until the coalman gets through."

"I've got plenty in my cwtch you can have a bucket of through and through tomorrow so if I was you Mog I'd go and get some in and make the fire up enough to last us until morning. Then we can get the kettle on and have a nice hot cup of tea would you like that?"

"I need the milk for David's bottle."

"Shall I nurse him whilst you go and make one?"

Surann just looked at the old lady and then burst out crying, "I know why you're here it's because of my poor little baby."

The old lady put her arm around Surann and held her close and with her free hand she gently took the baby away from her; turning to Mog she said, "Take her back to bed and stay with her I'll see to the wee one."

It was two days before the doctor followed by the undertaker were able to get through and a week to the day since Surann and Mog's little one had died he was laid to rest in the new cemetery. His little coffin had been carried from the house, where it had lain in the front room for all the neighbours to call to offer their sympathy, and by friends Mog worked with underground. The hearse bedecked with numerous wreaths was followed by the one family car. Family and friends had tried to persuade Surann that it wasn't 'the done thing' for women to attend the burial but she had insisted and accompanied by her husband and daughter she sat in the back of the big black car with Mog on one side and Merryl on the other all holding hands afraid to look at each other unless the tears would yet again start to flow. Each side of the road that led from the village the inhabitants of the tiny cottages and terraced houses lined the way; the men doffing their hats and the women wiping a tear from their eyes with the corner of their apron but unaware of the sadness of the day the girls continued to play their game of hop scotch and the boys kicked their ball aimlessly between each other.

It was the saddest day of her life as she stood beside the small, yet deep abyss and listened but did not hear the words the minister spoke; neither did she sing the well-loved words of the children's hymn; *'There's a friend for little children above the bright blue sky…'* She stood still, as if frozen to the spot, as the coffin was gently lowered into the grave. Then taking from her bag her child's favourite teddy she let it drop upon the coffin before the first grains of soil were scattered with the minister's words "Ashes to ashes….." She heard no more as she turned and taking Mog's arm she led him back to the waiting car. Her heart was breaking no longer would she see his bonny face or see his curly head; never again would she hear him call her 'Mamma'. What had she done to deserve such punishment? Was God punishing her for turning her back on her family and for not being content with the life he had decreed for her; she had sinned by lusting after a man that was not hers to have. Yet now in her hour of grief she still could not get him away from her thoughts as she turned and looked at his daughter; their beautiful daughter.

They had kept David's death from Minnie as she herself lay, so near to death, upon her hospital bed. "Come spring when the weather gets warmer," the doctor had said, "we'll be able to take her out into the garden and the clean fresh air will help her lungs. Where there is life there's hope."

CHAPTER THIRTEEN

"Where the hell have you been woman? I've been sitting here like a bloody lemon can't even get to the lav."

Surann slammed the front door behind her she had had just about enough. She had been queuing most of the morning just to get some tea and then again at the butcher to get a bit of meat for Mog's dinner.

"Suppose you've been gossiping about what a hard life you've got; well you're better off than those poor buggers in London I heard on the news that the Luftwaffe launched a massive raid on London they flew 350 bombers from airfields in France and dropped 300 tonnes of bombs on the docks and the streets of London."

Mog had been a little more content since Glyn had given him a wireless that he no longer needed. "More money than sense," he had said at that time but had soon placed it on the window sill near to his chair where he sat turning the knobs tuning into the home service.

"Dinner wont be long I managed to get two chops from Fred and Ianto just dropped off a rabbit he caught last night so I'll keep that for Sunday I'll make a stew with a few veggies from the garden."

"Why didn't Ianto call in haven't seen him in over a week?"

"He's doing double shifts." Saying no more she closed the door not to disturb him further and went to the scullery to prepare dinner.

In the eight months since David's death she had aged ten years no longer did she tend to her appearance; her hair that had grown quite long and was now streaked with grey and she wore it in a knob on top of her head. She had had no new clothes since her visit to London; 'London,' she thought 'that now seemed a life time ago,' yet each night as she lay in bed she would think of him; her John. Since the accident Mog no longer slept by her side now having his bed in the front room. What a day that had been when they brought her blood stained husband home not knowing at that time the extent of his injuries. His face and head had been dressed at the hospital and they had said that the cuts would soon heal but they didn't know how badly his eye sight had been affected. A further examination a week later had shown that he had totally lost his sight and that the hearing in his right ear was also impaired. The comments from the superintendent of the mine was that he had been negligent; Ianto confirmed this to her later saying that since the death of their little one Mog hadn't seemed to concentrate on his job.

From that time her loving husband had changed refusing even to try to do anything for himself. She would get him up in the morning, wash and dress him and then feed him his breakfast. His mates had brought Minnie's bed down from the spare room when he had refused to climb the stairs to bed saying that if he fell down the stairs it would be the end of him and that would let her off lightly. Just as he had today he would leave the fire go out not trying to pick up the tongs to put some coal on the fire.

On a few occasions when things hadn't pleased him he would strike out at her but instead of hitting her he would hit himself against the dresser and when that happened the air would be blue.

If he couldn't sleep at night he would ring the bell that she had left by the side of his bed and nine out of ten times he wouldn't need anything. "Come in bed with me wench and make me happy I suppose you think 'cause I'm blind I wont be able to find my way there I've found my way there in the dark many a time," he would taunt her.

She had done all her crying after David's death and even when she had learned that Mog would never regain his sight she could not weep; there were no tears left. The excuse she made for his bitterness and what now appeared to be his hatred of her was because of the loss of his son. She arose each morning and went to bed each night as just a matter of course there was no spirit left in her.

She lay in bed at night thinking of her sister and the good life she had; after their visit home for David's funeral they had gone house hunting and had bought the big house at the top of the village. After a little persuasion from Glyn she had agreed to give a home to two evacuees; two little girls that Wendy delighted in dressing in pretty dresses and having them to accompany her to church on Sunday. One good thing had come from her sister returning home was that she had agreed to give Minnie a home. "The clean, fresh mountain air will do her lungs the world of good", the doctor had said "so I'd advise you to take her up on her offer."

Wendy had taken her on with a few conditions one being that she would help about the house; but by the time Minnie had been there two months she was doing nearly all the house work. Surann did not worry about Minnie as the fresh mountain air was doing her the world of good and for the first time in many a month she was looking much improved. She called once a week to see her father bringing produce grown by Glyn in his large garden. "I suppose his lordship thinks he's digging for Victory," had been Mog's snide remark when Surann told him what Minnie had brought.

She had heard him telling his daughter only the previous day that it was because of her that he had had the accident "It's her bloody fault I'm an invalid if only she had looked after our baby properly I wouldn't have been thinking of him and I would have seen the tram coming."

"You can't blame mother," Minnie had said.

"She's not your bloody mother remember that girl and isn't it about time you came home to look after your dad living up there in that big house will turn you into a snob like them." She; he nodded his head towards the living room, "she doesn't do a thing for me. See this black eye she did that pushed me into the dresser."

"Hush dad Surann will hear you. You should be glad Wendy gave me a home I've got a lot better since living up there. You should use your stick more then you wouldn't bump into things."

"It comes to something when my own daughter calls me a liar; I can tell by your voice that you don't believe she did this to me," he pointed to a large bruise on his forehead.

"I'll see you before I go just going to get Wendy's basket back from Surann."

"Don't forget I'll be listening I can hear more than she thinks."

Back in the kitchen Minnie asked Surann why her dad was so nasty.

"It's all been too much for him David's death and then the accident in the pit was the last straw that finally broke the camel's back."

"But why does he blame you for David's death?"

"I don't really know; I suppose in one way he felt so helpless on that terrible night but believe me Minnie even if the doctor had been called earlier nothing would have saved our darling boy."

"Will dad get better?"

"I hope so; let's get this winter over. I think perhaps not just here at home but all over Britain things are going to get worse before they get better."

"I'll stay with dad if you want to go out for an hour."

"Thank you Minnie you're a good girl but there's nowhere for me to go."

"Why don't you take a walk up to see Wendy; I know she'd love to see you. She told me yesterday that she might take in another evacuee if things don't get better in London. She's changed a lot since she had the little girls."

"Another time perhaps I've already been to town and had to queue ages for just our four ounces of tea and these two chops for your dad's dinner."

"Don't give him the two have one yourself; he's not a working man now."

"I bloody heard that," shouted her father from the front room. "I'll have you know I slogged my guts out for you two."

"I'll be off then," said Minnie.

A knock at the front door stopped any further reiteration from Mog; "Anyone home?" shouted Ted Morris, "me and the lads have brought up a few bottles to cheer our old mate up."

'Not again' thought Surann as she waved to Minnie as she turned the corner of the road, remembering the previous week when his mates had called round leaving him in a drunken

108

state. He had called to her to help him undress but as she went to help him he had put his arms around her and pushing on his bed had almost raped her it was just luck, if she could call it that, that saved the day. As he had gone to lie on her he had fallen giving her time to get away from him.

"Surann," he had shouted "help me up you bitch."

"Get up yourself you're quite capable," and she had left him to it only when returning to find him still sitting on the floor in his own vomit in a drunken stupor.

"He's not to have more than two doctor's orders," she said as she showed the six men into Mog's room.

"The misses' orders not the doctors; come on in lads I hope you got some good gossip to cheer me up the old woman does nothing but nag."

"Why don't you come down the pub with us? You've got your white stick and anyhow we'll see you get home all right."

"That's the best idea I've heard yet I think I feel up to it now boys; I've had enough of being house bound she wont let me go out anywhere afraid I'll fall."

'Liar,' she thought as she watched them helping Mog down the steps, 'it's you who has been afraid to go out.' To a degree she felt sorry for him but the last months had driven any love that she might have had for him from her heart and now all she felt was hatred and many a night she had prayed for a quick release from her burden. She closed the door and turning the key in the lock made her way upstairs knowing that they wouldn't bring him back until stop tap she decided to have a lie down hopefully to sleep and to dream of happier days. Her last thoughts, before falling into a deep, well deserved sleep, were of the two, still uncooked, chops sitting on a plate in the scullery.

When she awoke the room was in darkness; 'how long had she slept?' she wondered and where was Mog? She slipped her feet into her shoes and lit the candle she kept at the side of her bed and saw that the time was just gone eleven o'clock. Stop tap was at ten o'clock surely the boys would have brought Mog home by now; they wouldn't be daft enough to leave him sitting on the doorstep? Or would they?

She quickly went downstairs not bothering to switch on the light because as yet she hadn't drawn the curtains and she didn't wish for anyone to shout to her to "put out that light", and just as she made her way through the passage there came a knock on the front door. She blew out her candle just in case someone had seen the candle light.

"Mrs Morgan are you there?" Sergeant George's voice boomed through the empty passage. "Has your husband come home?"

She turned the key in the lock and on opening the door came face to face with the burly figure of the local bobby. "No George; isn't he still with the boys in the pub?" As she spoke she could just see by the light of the moon a group of men standing in the road.

"According to Ted they all were kicked out just after ten and he and Fred were going to bring Mog home but after saying 'goodnight' to the others they couldn't find him."

"What do you mean 'couldn't find him'; it is hard to miss a blind man with a light top coat and a white stick."

"He didn't have his coat Ted found he'd left it in the pub. When they couldn't find him they knocked up old Pete to check if he'd fallen asleep somewhere in the pub."

"You just said he came out with them."

"I've got to be honest with you Mrs Morgan they all were too drunk to know anything."

"Are you trying to tell me my sick, blind husband has gone walk about without his coat? He'll catch his death and I expect he's as drunk as a lord."

"No Mrs Morgan Mog only had one pint he just sat there reminiscing about the past and the good times you had when you were farming. He was saying he wished he'd never gone back down the mine."

"You said you would see him safely home Ted so where the hell is he?"

"We've all got together and we're going to look for him," as Ted spoke the moon went behind a cloud and suddenly there was a deathly darkness and a fear crept into Surann's heart a feeling of dismay that perhaps her prayers had been answered. "If the moon doesn't come back out you'll not be able to go looking."

"We'll get some torches," said Fred.

"I think Sergeant George will have something to say about that," said one of the younger lads, "we don't want Hitler dropping bombs on us."

"We're all local lads and we'll soon get used to the darkness we'll find him for you Mrs Morgan."

She closed the door and returned to her cold living room; the fire had long since gone out or as her dear grandfather would have said 'gone next door'. She was just about to draw the curtains when Mrs Davies her next door neighbour tapped on the window. "Your back gate was open so I just called round to see what George wanted I hope everything is all right."

At any other time she might have thought of her neighbour as being a busy body but on this occasion she was glad to see the friendly face.

"It's Mog he's gone missing; the boys took him down the pub and somehow or other he left them."

"Oh dammo girl you've got no fire; come on in our house cariad the fire is half way up the chimney and the kettle will soon be boiling what you want is a nice cup of tea and a little drop of something."

Taking her old coat off the peg on the back door she followed Mrs Davies through the yard and up the back steps to the back lane almost stumbling in the now pitch blackness of the night. "They'll never find him unless the moon comes out again," she said to Mrs Davies as the two hooked arms as they made their way over the uneven surface of the lane.

After two hours the men gave up their search promising to continue at first light. "Stay with us tonight cariad; you can have our John's bed."

"I'll be all right Mrs Davies thank you so much for your kindness."

"What are neighbours for? I know you've gone through a lot this last weeks can't keep much from ones neighbours the walls are so thin I've heard the way he's shouts at you."

"He hasn't been himself since the accident; I suppose I should say since David's death."

"It is us women who carry their bairns for nine months and then to lose them after is a terrible loss that's hard for us to get over. I lost two of mine one to the scarlet fever and one like yours when she caught diphtheria and she was only two and such a bonny little one but there let us not talk about such things it happened so many years ago and I raised four healthy sons after that and my darling daughter. She made me a granny last week I went down to Swansea to be with her as her husband is serving God knows where with the army; it is awful that these children are being born without a dad being there for them and not knowing when or if he'll ever see them." Mrs Davies went on talking and at the same time pouring Surann another cup of tea, Surann not making any effort to leave the warm kitchen for her cold home or Mrs Davies suggesting that they made their way to bed.

It was almost day break and many cups of tea later and if one looked closely one would have observed that a bottle of whisky on the table was now half empty or as her grandfather would have said "half full".

"How about trying to get forty winks?" asked Mrs Davies as she saw that Surann had suddenly gone quiet and was resting her head upon her hand.

"I'll go home now it is light enough to see my way."

"No, no dear you just 'pop' upstairs here I'll call you if anyone needs you. Don't you fret now they'll find him safe and sound before you'll know turn around."

Sergeant George called round just after nine saying that once again they had to give up the search; some of the men hadn't slept all night and others having to be in work. "We've searched the wood down as far as the river, been up the golf course and as far as the reservoir even looked round the old workings at top pit but there's no sign of him anywhere."

"Have you checked with his daughter up in the big house?"

"Yes Ted and a few lads went up there and Glyn joined them in a search of the forestry."

"You can't just give up," said Surann as she appeared by the front door.

"We'll keep up a look out Mrs Morgan but there doesn't seem any more we can do now."

Suddenly as if struck by lightning a thought entered her head, "Sergeant George didn't you say the boys said he'd been talking about farming and the 'good old days'?"

"Yes. Ted said that was all he talked about all evening."

"I know where he is; he's gone to Gelli Uchaf."

"How could he possibly find his way there in the dark?"

"He is permanently in the dark sergeant; I suppose one could say he could 'see' better than us in the dark. Mind you there were times of late that I thought he could see more than he let on. It's his headaches that worried me."

"I'll call back at the station and get a few lads."

"Let's not waste time I'll come with you."

"But Mrs Morgan what if….," he had no time to finish the sentence as Surann had already began to make her way down her neighbours path.

"I'll get my coat," said Gladys Davies "she might have need of me."

She got very little pleasure from her ride in the police car as the young policeman drove them through the village to the lower village passed the school and up the rocky road to her old home.

She quickly alighted from the car and was dismayed to find that the old farmhouse looked quite derelict. Seeing the look on her face the sergeant said, "Been for sale since last summer all the boys joined up and Mr and Mrs. Jenkins went down west somewhere to stay with their daughter."

"Morgan," she called "Mog where are you?"

As she turned to cross the yard she found his white stick lying in a pool of water; "He is here," she called, "I've found his stick."

The police sergeant and the young constable hurried to her side; "You stay with Mrs Davies we'll have a look in the barn.

She stood in the centre of the yard with neighbour's arm around her and neither moved or spoke as they waited for the policemen to return.

It was a rather sombre looking Sergeant George that crossed the yard towards them; "Stay put Mrs Morgan we've found your husband."

"Is he all right?"

"I'm sorry….," but he had no chance to say no more as she broke away from Mrs Davies and ran towards the barn.

She could see a pool of blood and an old sack covering the head and shoulders of a man's body.

"Stop where you are Mrs Morgan I'm afraid it's not a pretty sight."

She did as she was told and stood dead in her tracks the body beneath the sacking could not possibly be Mog.

"What happened?" she managed to ask.

"I'm afraid your husband has shot himself."

"But how? Where would he have got a gun?"

"It seems there are a few old shotguns hanging up in the barn."

"But how was he to know they were there and who would leave a loaded gun?"

"Ted told me that he had been saying that he had been up to the old farm last winter because he was thinking of buying the place. He must have seen the guns then and remembered where they were and old Jenkins got in the end that half the time he didn't know what he was doing I expect he left them loaded ready to use; he was always shooting at something or other.

"I still can't imagine how he could possibly shoot himself."

"I hate to go into detail Mrs Morgan but I think it took more than one shot to kill him and remember he was known for being a good marksman."

How she got over the following weeks she could never recall. There had been an inquest and the verdict had been accidental death. Why hadn't they just said that he had committed suicide? Because in her mind she knew that is what he had done the once strong, handsome Mog Morgan could not face life as a blind man beholden to his family and friends. She also learned, at the time of the inquest, that the accident had not only caused the loss of sight but it had damaged his brain. "He knew the extent of the damage caused by the accident," the doctor had told her. Why had he kept it from her? The headlines of the local paper were not quite so diplomatic; "Local miner suffering from depression blew his brains out."

Because of the verdict she was able to lay her husband's body to rest besides his beloved son; poor Minnie wasn't well enough to attend the shock of her father's death had brought on a bout of coughing and with it bleeding and once again she was hospitalised with now little hope of her recovery.

'What a year', thought Surann as she closed her front door to the world. She just wanted to be on her own. Merryl hadn't been able to have leave as a step-father's funeral wasn't classed as 'a necessary journey'. The posters that now adorned every railway station asking – 'Is your journey really necessary?' What was happening to the world? Her world had really fallen to pieces before her eyes.

She drew the curtains and put on the light; taking a few logs that Mrs Davies' husband had been so kind as to chop for her she made up the fire and putting on the kettle to boil went out again to the passage. She soon returned carrying a large suitcase and as she placed it on the kitchen table she noticed an envelope sticking out under the lid; surely she couldn't have been so careless it had been before she went to London that she had last looked at the contents. Taking the envelope she noticed that her name was written upon it in Mog's scrawl. She looked puzzled how could Mog possibly have put a letter in the case that she always kept locked and hidden away in the cwtch under the stairs.

She tore it open and read the letter that it contained:

My dear Surann you will never know how much I loved you. I expect by the time you find this I will be dead. I told Ianto to shove this letter in the lid of the case knowing that as soon as I was six foot under you would find it. I have always known that your heart belonged to someone else but until you went to London I hadn't realised how much you had kept from me. I have always known about your diaries but have never before pried into your personal thoughts until it got the better of me when you went away. I have read some of the contents of the suitcase and feel hurt that you could never bring yourself to tell me about Merryl's father or worse still that you've never told her. I also saw your diary that you left unlocked when you went to change David's nappy the day after you returned from London. Can't quite recall the exact words that you wrote but I remember quite well these words 'I still love him'. What a mess you've got yourself into with your lies and deceit. Was all our loving just a game? Well my darling Surann you are free now to go to him but I don't think he'll fancy you any more; no longer are you in the first flush of youth you've grown old. Excuse my scribble but as you are aware I have lost my eye sight; that's not quite true as over the last few weeks I have seen faint images; images of your face and I've 'seen' enough since my accident to know that you now hate me even if once you did love me a little – well I hope you did because I've always loved you. Be happy if you can Mog.

Surann just buried her head in her hands and wept. Now she was really alone for the first time in her life with no-one to care for and no-one to love her. Wiping her eyes with the kitchen towel she opened the case and took from it her latest diary and read what Mog had seen now over twelve months ago: '*at last after all these years I have met him and as I looked into his clear blue eyes all the memories of our time together came flooding back. How I wished, as we danced together at Merryl and Richard's engagement party, that he would pick me up in his arms and carry me to his bed where we would make love all night long; I ache for him; I long for him; I love him still and always shall. Will the time ever come when he will remember me and our lost love and will it ever be possible for us to rekindle that love?*' She closed the diary and replaced it in the suitcase and not bothering to lock it placed it back in the cwtch under the stairs. It had been so foolish of her to write down her innermost thoughts all these years. What if it had been she who had died and left the unexplained contents of the case to be found by her daughter? She must try to explain to her daughter but in her mind at that moment it seemed an impossible task.

So many thoughts turned over and over in her troubled mind; had she ever loved Mog? Sitting there now thinking over the last year she realised that after David's death she had felt no closeness what so ever towards her husband there had been times even before his accident when the sight of his body reviled her. Looking back she realised that he had never been that loving or gentle with her it had been his needs that she had succumbed to; had he ever tried to please her? She had done her best to make him happy; he had been a good father to Minnie and to David and would have gone on being a doting father to his son if he had been given the chance. Why had God taken David from them? Had it been her fault that she hadn't noticed that he was ill; could the doctor, if called earlier, have been able to save him? So many questions but no answers; she realised she now had all the time in the world to find an answer to the questions that at that moment in time she could not answer and the heartache was intense; would it ever leave her?

The evening was getting cold and the fire was getting low no longer could she afford to waste the coal as in future it would be hard to come by Mrs Davies had said that she could always have some through and through off them and that she was never to be afraid to ask. Mr Davies now brought her logs for the fire on a regular basis but the heat had not just gone from the hearth but from her heart. She turned on the wireless and listened to the latest news and was dismayed at what she heard; now not just London was the target for bombing raids but also Bristol, Cardiff and Swansea; the war was getting too close to home.

Remembering that she hadn't eaten anything since her porridge for breakfast she took some stale bread and putting the poker in between the bars of the grate to bring some life back to the dying fire she put the bread on the old toasting fork and sat there waiting for it to toast. She then warmed some milk and water in a saucepan and poured it over the toasted bread with just a tiny sprinkle of sugar. 'Sop', grancha would have called it; how he loved his bowl of 'sop' on a cold night before going to bed.

How long would the government leave her in peace? Soon she expected they would be informing her that she must do her part for the war effort. What were her options either to take in an evacuee or go and work in a factory? She began to wonder was she too old to join the land army surely her knowledge of farming would give her good chance. She rinsed her bowl with a drop of warm water; checked that the doors were locked; put the guard by the fire, switched off the radio that was now making a buzzing sound, as obviously she had lost the station, then lighting her candle she switched off the lights and opening the stairs door made her way to bed. In the silence of the night she could hear the Davies shouting about something or other and as she made her way upstairs she could hear the new baby crying in number twenty seven; life went on.

CHAPTER FOURTEEN

Her bags and suitcases were already in the passage all that was left to do was to put a strap around the old tattered suitcase that held all her diaries. 'Ironic,' she thought as she tightened the strap that was an old belt of Mog's.

It had been a long, hard winter; a winter of discontent, as she tried to find a solution to her problems. Wendy had suggested that she take in an evacuee; "Two boys would be nice," she had said "You are so good with boys; you always handled our brothers well."

'How would you know,' thought Surann 'you were never there.'

Then Glyn had suggested that she take in two Bevin Boys; "These lads need a good home and good food the ones I've seen are nothing but skin and bone. They're not cut out to be miners."

It was on a visit to the doctor at the end of January that her problems were solved. She had sat in the waiting room listening to the gossip; "How are you Mrs Jenkins?"

"Feeling a bit better; it's a wonder we're not all ill trying to survive on such a meagre ration. What brings you here?"

"I'm here with my leg it swells up like a balloon every evening. Doctor told me to rest it and gave me some medicine now I'm spending half my time in the lav.."

Surann smiled to herself as she imagined the lady that had the trouble with her leg arriving at the surgery without it; how many times had she heard the same words; 'I'm going to see the doctor with my leg or arm or whatever;' it was a typical valley saying. It was almost six o'clock and it seemed as if she would be the last patient to see the doctor so picking up a magazine she began to flick through the pages until she noticed the heading 'Situations Vacant'; she read on down the page until her eyes alighted upon the words 'Companion Wanted'. *Mature lady required for semi-disabled lady; live in; no housework or nursing. Situation will suit lady with no family ties. Duties will be to accompany Lady to social functions, theatre etc.. Apply in writing to: Mrs B. Johnson "The Lindens", Penarth.*

"You'll be next Mrs Morgan."

"It is gone six so I wont waste the doctor's time; do you mind if I take this magazine with me?"

The nurse nodded and then said "But if you're feeling poorly Mrs Morgan you should see the doctor."

"As a matter of fact I'm feeling a lot better." She picked up her bag placing in it the magazine noticing the strange look the nurse had given her she left the surgery.

Once home she hung up her hat and coat and before slipping off her shoes went and got a few pieces of kindling and a couple of lumps of coal she 'opened' up the fire. Filling the kettle with water she placed it on the fire. 'A nice cup of tea and then I'll settle down to write that letter,' she said to herself as she went to the drawer to get out her note-paper. There were only two sheets and one envelope left from the pretty paper that Merryl had bought her before the war; how glad she was that she still had some left it would make a good impression.

She lay in bed that night thinking about what she had written; she had told Mrs Johnson that she was a widow lady who had years of experience in catering to the needs of others. She had no family ties as her daughter was serving with the W.R.A.F. and was engaged to be married; one thing puzzled her though and that was why she had signed her name 'Lloyd.' She slept that night more peacefully than she had for some time.

The next morning she was up bright and early and after breakfast she slipped on her hat and coat and picking up her basket walked to the village shop to post her letter.

"Hello sis. you are out bright and early you must have heard Charlie has had some cheese in I've had our half a pound; there's a queue half way down the terrace."

"I don't think I'll bother to queue for two ounces of cheese you're lucky you've got the girls. I'll just post this letter and I might walk on down the town."

She had already decided to take advice from a solicitor into what would be the best thing to do with regards to her house if she got the position; 'putting the horse before the cart'; grancha would have said.

120

Each morning she waited for the post to arrive; letters came from Dewi and Emlyn. Emlyn couldn't say where he was but told her that he was safe but worried about his wife and children with news of all the bombs that were being dropped on Britain. Dewi's letter hadn't really told her much; he had said he was doing 'hush, hush' war work and was just looking forward to the day when it would be all over and they could once again meet up. "I still have dreams about singing in the Albert Hall remember sis. you promised you would be there when that time arrives."

Merryl too had written saying that Auntie Wendy had written to her saying that she was worried about her sister as Sarah Anne was acting strange and was up to something. 'No stranger than usual', she thought as she opened up an old envelope and scribbled a few lines to her daughter telling her not to worry that she was 'up to something', and would let her know if it bore fruition.

She had almost given up hope of receiving a reply making excuses that perhaps she should have put a stamped addressed envelope in with her correspondence or that she wasn't 'posh' enough for this lady until one morning almost three weeks later she picked up an envelope from off the doormat her heart missed a beat as she noticed the neat hand writing. She quickly tore open the envelope and read:

Dear Mrs. Lloyd I am pleased to advise you that I would like you to attend for an interview on Friday 14th February. To make travelling easier for you I would like us to meet at noon in the restaurant at David Morgan's in Mary Street, Cardiff. Just ask for Mrs Johnson. Yours sincerely B. Johnson (Mrs)

Surann heart missed a beat she just couldn't believe her eyes she had got an interview but then when she had had time to think she realised that perhaps there were others to who would be interviewed but there again why ask to join her for lunch? The next problem was what should she wear? The only decent coat she had was the black one she had had for David's funeral and the little black pill box hat; perhaps she could brighten it up with a pretty scarf or add a flower to her hat but then what would the neighbours say her being a widow lady. 'To hell with the neighbours' she thought as she delved into the back of her drawer and at last found what she was looking for a pretty silvery grey chiffon scarf and a pink fabric gardenia. She neatly stitched the flower onto her hat and then when trying it on was disappointed as since the last time she had worn it her hair had grown long and no longer did the hat suit her. Then smiling to herself she replaced the hat in the hat box and putting the guard in front of the fire, locked the back door and then putting on her old hat and coat set off for town and then she caught a bus that took her to the next town five miles away.

She stopped for a cup of tea and a Welsh cake in the church hall; "Fund raising for the forces," said the vicar who looked as ancient as Methuselah. She sat with a few other ladies all deep in conversation about the bombs that had been dropped on Welsh cities. "Coming too close to home for my liking; you'll not get me going to Cardiff."

"They got these things called barrage balloons flying over the city supposed to deter low flights by enemy aircraft."

"My two daughters are working down in Treforest they've got to get up before daylight to get to work on time; but there they're doing their bit for King and country."

"Have you got anyone serving in the forces misses sorry I didn't get your name?" The vicar asked as he joined the ladies.

"Morgan," she replied. "Yes my daughter she's with the W.R.A.F.. Excuse me but I really must go or I'll miss my bus home. Can anyone tell me if there's still a hairdresser in town?"

"There's one on the square but she only opens once or twice in the week you can try there."

"Thank you," she said and leaving the hall placed a sixpence in the box by the door for a special flag day; there were so many special flag days for one cause or another. She made her way around the corner and soon found the shop she was looking for and on trying the door found it to be open. A little bell tinkled in the back of the shop and an elderly lady appeared from behind a curtain.

"Can you fit me in for a cut? I'm sorry I haven't made an appointment."

"No need for appointments these days I'm lucky to get two customers in a week. Do take a seat and I'll see what I can do for you. Your hair has a natural curl perhaps it would look nice in a bob; if you would like it washed I'll have to light the old geyser; the boiler I mean not my old man." She went back to the back room laughing at her own joke.

An hour later Surann left the hairdressers feeling like a 'new woman' she walked up the street to the chemist shop where she treated herself to some Ponds cold cream a 4711 lipstick, powder and rouge. She had to make the best of herself if she was going to get the job as a Lady's Companion.

As she alighted from the bus by the town bridge she bumped into her sister Wendy; "My you are looking glamorous have you got a new man in your life? Sorry Sarah Anne I shouldn't have said that I was only joking. I can tell by the look on your face though that you are up to something."

"You will know all about it as soon as I do," was all she said and crossed the road to the butchers shop to see if he could spare her a nice chop for her tea.

"You're in luck today Mrs Morgan you've got the choice of pork or lamb."

"I'll have a pork chop please Fred."

"That'll be 1s 2d go or a 'bob' will do being it's you."

"She took a shilling from her purse and handed it to the butcher.

"Come to think of it Mrs Morgan but there seems to be something different about you; I know what it is you've had your hair cut taken ten years off you if you don't mind me saying."

She certainly didn't and now all that was left was for her to make a good impression of Mrs Johnson.

The day for her journey to Cardiff soon came round; was it a good omen that the sun was shining? It had rained continually for over a week and she had begun to wonder what hat she should wear if the rain continued.

Luckily her lilac two piece still fitted her; she had washed her hair the previous evening putting in a few metal clips so that her waves would stay nicely in place. She was at last ready; the bus had gone up the road and that would give her enough time to put on her hat and coat. She locked her front door and slipping the key into her bag made her way to the bus stop. The service was only twice a day but it was a Godsend when one didn't wish to walk to town. Her train left at ten thirty and if on time she should arrive at the General Station by eleven thirty that would give her thirty minutes to get to David Morgan's'.

The usual signs greeted her as she bought her day return ticket; *'Is Your Journey Really Necessary?' Keep Mum You Don't Know Who's Listening'*.

Sitting back in her compartment she looked at the pictures of sea-side resorts that adorned the carriage; *'Come to sunny Western-Super-Mare; Rest Bay Porthcawl; Llandudno and Aberystwyth.'* 'One day perhaps I will,' she thought.

"All change for Bristol Templemead……" She had arrived at her destination. The station was a hive of activity; men and women in uniform; women with children kissing their husbands 'goodbye' with tear filled eyes and there were those that were welcoming home their men folk also with tears in their eyes as they led them away from the crowds; the men who would not return to the front; the war was over for them; men with crutches to aid the loss of an amputated limb or bandaged heads to cover their eyes that had been blinded; what suffering was all around her. She recalled being in the same place at the end of another war; seeing the same thing. Wasn't that supposed to have been 'a war to end all wars?' A war that had taken her one and only love; 'Come on Sarah Anne Lloyd pull yourself together and think positive; think of the future not the past.'

She had made up her mind that no longer did she wish to be Surann Morgan if she got the position she would be sure that her old family 'pet' name would be brushed under the carpet and she would only answer to Sarah Anne.

Considering the shortage of food it surprised her that the restaurant was so busy; she was just about to ask a young waitress to direct her to Mrs Johnson's table when she noticed sitting at a table by the window overlooking The Hayes a woman of about her own age smartly dressed with a fur shoulder cape and matching fur hat. Her hair dark hair was neatly groomed and her make-up immaculate. How glad she was that she had made the effort to smarten herself up. "Mrs Johnson," she said as she joined the lady "I'm Sarah Anne Lloyd I do hope you haven't been waiting long."

"Just arrived," she smiled at Sarah Anne "Please take a seat I love to sit here then I can watch the comings and goings in the square."

Sarah Anne removed her coat and sat opposite and for a moment just gazed out of the window not quite knowing what to say.

"Do order what you fancy but I'm afraid you'll have to be prepared for the waitress to say 'It's off'; I remember before the war my husband and I would dine here and the food was simply delicious I can't say the same now but old habits die hard I still come if it's only for a cup of tea and that now tastes like dish water I think they use the tea leaves over and over one is a lucky if one get the first cup."

Lunch consisted of a bowl of vegetable soup and a dry bread roll; even if there had been a delicious desert Sarah Anne couldn't have eaten any more as her stomach was churning over with nerves.

"Relax Mrs Lloyd I shouldn't really keep you on tenterhooks; I just wanted to meet you but I liked what you wrote in your letter and now from meeting you I can tell that we will get on. Just one condition to your employment and that is please do not refer to me as 'Mrs Johnson' I want us to be friends and friends use only Christian names so please do call me Betty."

Suddenly Sarah Anne felt guilty of having not being completely honest with this lady; "I really must apologise for not being quite honest with you I wrote to you using my maiden-name it is just that I wish to put the past behind me and look to a brighter future."

"Sarah Anne will do for me; well perhaps that is a bit of a mouthful if it is all right with you I'd like to call you Sarah. How soon can you start your duties?" Before she had time to reply Betty Johnson had suggested the second week in March. "I hope that will give you time to make all the necessary arrangements. My chauffer will be here in five minutes so we'll say our 'goodbyes' now and I will write to you with all necessary details.

On the train journey home Sarah Anne's mind was in a whirl; in the short time together she had learned that her employer's husband was a Major in the British Army and was now stationed in India. Betty's long-time companion had left to take care of her ailing parents; "It's this old heart of mine that stops me from doing what I wish I had rheumatic fever as a child and it has left me with this weakness I just get tired very quickly and cannot walk long distances but I still like to continue with my charity work and fund raising and that's why I like to have a companion. The evenings are also long when one has no company; my housekeeper come cook is ancient; don't let on I said that I think the world of her and her husband is my chauffer, butler and general dog's body. By the way Sarah can you play cards?"

Sarah had been puzzled by the question until Betty informed her that every Saturday evening she held a whist drive. When Sarah had said that the only card games she could play were the ones that her grandfather had taught her that he played in the pub Betty had laughed and said she would soon learn.

There was so much to do and now what appeared to Sarah, so little time to do it in; Wendy was the first to tell her that she was mad to give up her home and go and live with a strange woman; 'strange' thought Sarah Anne there was nothing strange about Betty Johnson she already felt from the one meeting that she had always 'known' the lady.

She wrote letters to her daughter and brothers telling them of her new address and what she would be doing; she had been pleased with the response from her daughter who had sent her a pretty card saying 'good for you mum'. She had then visited her solicitor and on his advice had agreed to rent out her home. Once her neighbour heard that the house was to rent an agreement was set up between them that Mrs Davies' daughter would rent the house as it would be good to be near her mother to get away from Swansea with her three children. She decided to sell her furniture as she no longer had need of anything. Mrs Davies bought the bed and the bedroom suite and the chest of drawers and the rest old Mr Jones bought for his shop in the market. She also sold some of her old clothes and also her husband's clothes and tools; she felt quite rich as she banked the money 'for a rainy day,' she would have enough to live on from her employer's generous wage and also a roof over her head.

She had said 'goodbye' to Wendy and Glyn the previous evening; Wendy promising her that should Minnie improve there was always a home with her. She took one last look around as she heard the 'toot' of a car's horn; she was going off in style. At first she had planned to travel by train but Betty had written saying that her chauffer would pick her up with her baggage; "don't worry about the petrol as the journey is really necessary."

Word had soon got round that Surann Morgan had got too big for her boots and was leaving the valley to go and live in the city. The children had gathered around the vehicle and had gazed with amazement at the uniformed old man who sat behind the wheel; "Got a penny mister?" asked one scruffy child. As she was driven through the village she felt that all eyes were upon her; the women stood on their doorsteps with their sleeves rolled up having left their wash tub to see her departure and faces peered from behind lace curtains.

"You'll be back," Wendy had said but somehow Sarah felt that she would not see the valley again for many a year to come.

CHAPTER FIFTEEN

Betty Johnson was waiting eagerly for her arrival; with afternoon tea was ready in the dining room.

"Have you had a good journey?" she enquired.

"It really amazed me how quickly we got here; it nearly always took well over an hour to travel to Cardiff by bus." The ice was broken as Betty, after taking her coat and hat, ushered her into the dining room. "I'm sure you are ready for a nice cup of tea and I will tell you now it is far better than what we had in town. Thanks to my husband we got well stocked up before war broke out. I didn't believe him when he said that there might be a shortage of food but how right he was."

As they sat together dining on salmon sandwiches; home-made cake and a delicious cup of tea Sarah mentioned how upset she was about the damage caused to Cardiff during the air raid of January.

"I will never forget that night it was so terrible; the colour of the sky was horrendous. I had been fast asleep when the sirens alerted us; Mary had tried to persuade me to go down to the cellar but I just stood there by my bedroom window that gives a view across the bay. I learned the next day that a land mine had fallen on our beautiful cathedral at Llandaff and another on St. Michael's College by the Black Lion; I don't know if it is true but the report was that tombstones were found half a mile away. Mr White the verger was taken to hospital and the Dean had been blown out of the cathedral but luckily no-one had been killed." Betty stopped talking and poured Sarah another cup of tea.

"What lovely china you have," she said as she picked up the delicate bone china cup.

"I have lots of lovely things my dear; but sadly no-one to leave them too. How I wished we had had children but it wasn't to be. Kenneth has been an army man all his life and we have spent so much time apart. I did go to India with him back in the 30's but the heat was too much for me so returned home and it was then we bought this house for our retirement. That is a joke in itself as Kenneth had decided to retire when he reached fifty and take up market gardening as this property gave us green-houses; orchards and the paddock for the horses.

Kenneth had decided he would breed race horses; dreams, dreams; none now that I doubt will bear fruition."

"Has the war hit Penarth badly?"

"The night of that terrible air raid Grangetown had it the worse there were hundreds killed there; I believe about 30 land mines were dropped on Cardiff. We had our share here too All Saints Church was gutted by fire only the walls remained standing. As it overlooks the docks the town has become one big anti-aircraft battery with search lights; barrage balloons and everyone ready for action. Once summer comes I would so love to take you out to Lavernock Point but I'm afraid that too has become a kind of fortress with a large AA battery. I am sure you will at first find it strange from the silence of the valley to hear the 'whoop, whoop' of the destroyers as they sail in and out of the docks. The Luftwaffe pilots follow the Bristol Channel and then the Severn as they fly their planes towards the Midlands. God help us all; it is so distressing to hear the news and read the headlines. Shall we reach an agreement that unless it is absolutely necessary we will not discuss the war."

"You have never quite explained what my job entails."

"I don't wish for you to think of it as a 'job' I want a companion; or rather a friend who will keep me company and help with my charity work. Whilst you are with me, which I hope will be for quite a while, I want you to treat 'Lindens' as your home; feel free to give my telephone number to your daughter and when she has leave she is welcome to visit. I will get Mary to show you around but I am sure you have already guessed this is a very large property. I had thought about opening up my home to the evacuees but on my own I couldn't possibly have coped. Mary suggested, only yesterday, that we take in some of these American G.I.'s they would be the worse, more boisterous than children."

Betty pulled on the bell pull; "It will take her five minutes before she arrives she is complaining about her arthritis."

"Shall I clear the table?"

"No, no you take it easy; Mary has all the time in the world to clear the table. I just wanted her to show you around the house for you to get your bearings. I have given you the front bedroom to the right of the landing I have converted the back sitting room into my bedroom the stairs have got too much for me; if you can't sleep you can creep back down I don't sleep very well and we can have a midnight snack; it will remind me of my days in boarding school."

"Isn't life strange," said Sarah; "here I am feeling free for the first time in over twenty years and you, I feel, have been without a family most of your life I can hardly envisage what life would have been like in a boarding school only what I've read in children's books."

"You rang Mrs Johnson?"

"Yes Mary; do you mind giving Mrs Lloyd," she paused and looked at Sarah and when Sarah nodded she continued; "a tour of the house and Reg can show her round the gardens tomorrow."

The rooms were absolutely splendid; she smiled to herself when she noticed her bedroom had en suite facilities; 'that's something I can write and tell Wendy', she thought as she gazed from the window across the bay where she could see the search lights criss-crossing the water. This was going to be a totally new life she couldn't wait for the following morning and that night she slept like ' a top'; no 'whoop, whooping' of the destroyers disturbed her rest.

"The misses doesn't get up before 11 o'clock she forgot to tell you last night," said Mary as she cleared the breakfast table. "My old man is ready when you are and he'll show you the gardens."

"I'll just get my coat," said Sarah "shall I meet him in the garden?"

"No lass he's in the kitchen I expect he's having his second cup of tea. We've just taken on two of those poor men injured at Dunkirk they're no good for military service but will able to do some gardening; the place is going to rack and ruin since the gardeners joined up; my old man has tried his best but it's too much for him with his rheumatics."

"Chauffer, gardener, general dog's body that's me," said Reg as he got up from his chair by the kitchen range. It's nice and warm here and now I got to go out in the cold and my poor old bones will start to complain again."

"Stay there Reg I'll find my own way around it will be fun exploring alone." Sarah said as she buttoned up her coat.

"Take my scarf off the hook by the back door it is freezing cold out there the wind is blowing up for a gale."

True enough the wind was quite keen; from the top garden she had a view across the channel and as the day was clear she could just make out the English coast line; two islands sat in the channel looking just like two pikelets or drop scones as her grandmother would have said. 'Flat Holm and Steep Holm,' Reg had told her as he had driven her along the front the previous day. She saw the two men working in the green house and stopped to have a chat. They told her they were planting cucumber and tomato plants and they had been doing some pruning of the fruit trees; some work that should have been done the previous autumn.

"But there misses," said the one named Joe you wouldn't be interested in our work."

"You'd be surprised," said Sarah, "I once ran a farm; sheep, cows, goats and chickens and we had a lovely vegetable garden my grandfather grew enough to feed the village during the strike." She felt that she might have exaggerated a little but went off smiling knowing that she had impressed the two men.

"If you have time to spare misses you can always come and give us a hand," shouted Mike as she made her way towards the orchard and the paddock.

"I might do that," she shouted back.

A very rosy cheeked, windswept Sarah made her way back to the warmth of the kitchen where she found Betty writing by the table.

"Just writing out plans for our afternoon with the 14th Penarth Boy Scouts they are a great group of lads; I've just suggested to Mary that it might be a good idea to make some biscuits we can sell them four a penny and help raise funds for the lads."

She pulled up a chair and sat down, "Do you know Betty you've just brought back memories I remember how my sister and I spent a whole week making preserves and bottling fruit and on the day we made batches of Welsh cakes and sponge cakes all for sale at the church fete that's where I met….." She said no more but just sighed.

"You were saying?" questioned Betty

"Perhaps I'll tell you about it one evening when you have nothing better to do."

"As you wish my dear; I shall always be ready to listen what friends are for? We are going to be friends aren't we?"

"Of course we are," smiled Sarah taking Betty's hand. "It is a long story and really I don't know quite where to start."

"The beginning is usually the best place."

"Do you mind if sometimes I help Joe and Mike in the garden I so love gardening?"

"I've already told you to make yourself at home and when we're not entertaining or going anywhere special the time is your own to do as you wish as long as we can sit together in the evenings; they seem so long with the black-out. How I used to love to sit with the lights on and the curtains open and look out across the garden. Now our windows are all taped up and heavy blackout curtains on the windows make the evenings so dreary. How are you off for clothing coupons?"

"I haven't used any since January; why do you need some?"

"No my dear it's just well, I suppose the best way is not to beat about the bush. I couldn't but help to notice when you unpacked last evening that you have only one evening dress and one best suit and as you will be attending a great many functions with me I would like you to go shopping, on me, for a new wardrobe."

"But I couldn't do that I have some money of my own."

"It is because of me that you have to buy new clothes so we will go shopping tomorrow; we'll get Reg to take us into Cardiff and we'll go to a nice little restaurant I know and I hope that they might find some cream cakes to go with our refreshment."

Sarah was surprised to find Betty up bright and early and looking forward to their visit to the Cardiff shops. "Do hope they have something other than 'utility clothes' for you to choose from; they can be quite smart but I do miss not being able to buy a fully pleated skirt most on sale today have just the one kick pleat and some even look like divided shorts."

"The fashion shops have really cut back on the use of material but there I suppose the forces have more need for clothes than we have. I have a friend who made her new Sunday coat from a blanket and she trimmed it with an old fox fur and I really must say it did look smart."

Betty smiled; "I can go one better than you there's a lady in town who is busy making boiler suits like Churchill wears for all the young lads from their father's left over coats and blouses for the girls from parachute silk."

"I hope you will help me choose Betty because I have no idea of what is worn to these grand functions that you attend."

By lunchtime the two were feeling in need of refreshment after having a very fruitful morning. Sarah had ended up with two long dresses; suitable for evening wear; a little black dress that Betty had said 'would take her anywhere'; a fashionable suit, although utility and a very smart pill box hat, gloves and some underwear. How Betty had laughed when Sarah told her that only when she had visited London for her daughter's engagement party had she ever worn a brassiere.

"Well I think you should perhaps buy two and some slips and matching..." she whispered in Sarah's ear "knickers."

Reg had been waiting to take the purchases back to the car and Betty told him to go to his favourite pub for lunch and return to pick them up outside David Morgan's' at three o'clock.

"Do you know Betty I would love to take a ride on one of the trams?"

"We'll have to do that one day as yet I haven't been on one either it does look like fun."

That evening as they sat each side of the fireplace listening to 'I.T.M.A' on the wireless Sarah asked; "Are you tired it has been a long day for you?"

"Do you know my dear I think you are a better tonic than all the medicine? Shall I turn the wireless off then perhaps you can tell me a little more about yourself?"

So, that evening as they sat by the glowing fire Sarah told her all about her lost love and her daughter's birth and now, after all these years he had come back into her life and would be Merryl's future father-in-law.

"I cannot find a way to tell her; she has asked many a time about who will give her away on her wedding day. She had suggested Mog and even myself after Mog's death."

"You have told me that you have kept cuttings from the press and diaries since her birth why not tell her on her next visit that you have something to show her and gradually unfold her life to her?"

"I don't want to cause her any stress; I know it is a coward's way out but I shall wait until they fix a date for the wedding and I cannot see that happening until this war is ended."

"Surely they will want to get married if the war continues much longer and at the moment I cannot see an end. I would so like to meet your daughter why don't you invite her to stay next time she has a few days' leave?"

Summer came early that year and the lighter evenings gave her the opportunity to spend more time in the garden; it was lovely to have fresh fruit and vegetables from the garden and she also took it upon herself to make up baskets of fruit to distribute to the local hospitals. Sarah's days were really full; she accompanied Betty to flag days; W.I. meetings; concerts and charity events. Then there were Betty's cocktail parties and bridge evenings and whist drives.

When Betty would take an afternoon rest Sarah would walk through the Alexander Gardens down to the esplanade where she would sit on a bench and gaze out across the channel and day dream; life was good but still she could not rid herself of her dreams; her dreams of John.

On a few occasions when she had gone to town on her own to queue for some rations she had been roped in to rolling bandages in the hall in Albert Road and had also helped at the

British Restaurant at the end of the arcade in the town centre to serve a cheap meal to the homeless or a traveller; all in all she felt that she was doing her bit to help the war effort.

She also enjoyed an evening stroll down to the pier where she would watch dozens of anglers fishing either from the pier or the beach; she never ventured down to the sea shore as Betty had told her she wouldn't find it like the beach at Barry as it was rather pebbly.

As yet she hadn't got used to answering the telephone and found it extremely peculiar that she could speak to her daughter as if she was in the room when she was hundreds of miles away.

One morning as she sat having breakfast Betty came into the morning room; "You're up early this morning Betty are you all right?"

"Never felt better; well I'll rephrase that I was feeling good until Mary brought me my breakfast she took the opportunity to tell me that they were handing in their notice as they were getting too old to cope with a big house and wanted to go and set up home in Pembrokeshire, to be near her sister, before the winter set in. I just don't know who I will be able to get to drive the car and how will we manage without a housekeeper."

"Don't stress yourself Betty; I'll let you into a little secret I've driven an old bone shaker of a van; mind you I don't know if I can manage the car but I'll give it a go and as for housekeeping, well if you don't mind me suggesting, we can close up many of the rooms in the house."

The winter that followed was a long, cold, hard one and Betty's enthusiasm for fund raising and cocktail parties had ebbed a little. "Is there anything worrying you?" Sarah had asked her friend.

"You are getting to know my every mood," Betty smiled "I can't keep anything from you; it is just I haven't heard from Kenneth and he always makes sure my parcel arrives before Christmas and I know letters get held up but I haven't had one for two months."

Sarah had no answer for Betty knowing that if she said 'that no news was good news' it wouldn't help matters. So many of the country's women were in the same situation; many had received that fateful telegram telling them that their loved ones had been killed in action or missing believed dead.

"Perhaps I have some news that will cheer you up Merryl has said that she will be able to visit us over Christmas; just two days leave and as Richard is stationed abroad she would like to spend it with us."

"We'll kill the fatted calf," jested Betty. "I know a man who knows a man who will be able to get us a turkey but here is the crunch; who will do the cooking?"

"Well we could find the best chef in the country or there again perhaps I too know someone who knows someone who will do the cooking; I understand she is a very good pastry cook and makes the most delicious mince pies."

"Are you teasing me?"

"What do you think?"

"Are you telling me that you are prepared to do the cooking? I'm going to ask a farmer friend of mine if we can have a tree from him and hopefully some holly. We're going to close our doors and shut out the war for the two days that your daughter is home with us."

Sarah cried when she met her daughter at the station; Merryl looked so grown up in her uniform; 'silly me', thought Sarah, 'still thinking of her as my little girl when she is now a young woman doing her bit for King and Country.'

"Hello mum," Merryl hugged her mother. "Why the tears?"

"It is just I am so proud of you and you look so smart in your uniform."

"I can say the same about you mum you are look fantastic."

"Any news from Richard?"

"Had a letter yesterday; censored of course but we've devised a code where we can tell each other secrets. As far as I can gather he is somewhere in the Far East."

"Betty's husband is in Singapore. Places we've never before known about are now on our lips every day of the year the world is getting smaller. We've closed up most of the house but have aired the bed and what Betty says 'spring cleaned' the room next to mine for you. She is quite excited about meeting you."

"No more talk of war until after Christmas; just one thing I have to tell you Richard's grandmother died two days ago his mother was quite nasty when I told her I was going home to you for Christmas she said that I should be there as Richard's fiancée but his dad was lovely and told me to go and enjoy myself and I was to give you his best wishes. I'm so fond of him mum how I wish I had a dad like him."

Sarah shivered; "Cold mum," asked her daughter.

'If only she knew,' thought Sarah 'that the very mention of his name stirs something within me.'

Betty and Merryl got on like a house on fire and whilst Sarah prepared the Christmas 'feast' Betty gave Merryl her suggestions as to where the decorations were to be placed in the hall and lounge and dining room and that evening a tired trio went eagerly to bed.

Religious services had never played a big part in Sarah's life that was until she came to live with Betty now most Sundays she accompanied Betty to Church and it surprised how she was really looking forward to the Christmas morning service.

"We always leave our presents until after we've been to Church," Betty told them as Sarah eyed the parcels under the tree.

Merryl was quite amused when she saw her mother reversing the car out of the garage; "Before you say anything," Sarah said to her daughter, "our journey is necessary as Betty couldn't make it to church without the car."

"To Richard's mother's annoyance his dad has put the family car on blocks and walks to the office each day."

Sarah was surprised to see such a large congregation and as she knelt besides her friend and daughter she prayed for a safe return of their loved ones and "God Bless my beloved too."

"We shall break with tradition this year," said the vicar "and shall sing as our final hymn; 'O *God our help in ages past.*' God bless you all and keep you safe."

CHAPTER SIXTEEN

Sarah was late rising that cold January morning; Betty had given a fund raising New Year's Eve party and had raised quite a lot of money for the war effort. As she opened her eyes her first thoughts were of what the New Year was going to bring. Peace seemed far away as the war had escalated with the bombing of Pearl Harbour by the Japanese bringing the United States into the war.

"If I was handing out medals," Betty had said the previous evening "You would be the first on my list; copying with all the cooking over Christmas and now organising my party."

It had been so good having Merryl to visit over Christmas but all too short. Sarah felt a little 'lost' after she had watched her daughter; immaculate in her uniform, her gas mask slung over her shoulder with her bag and her overnight case in her hand board the train that would take her back to London. Sarah had to admit that her daughter's bobbed hair suited her; "Just had to have all my locks cut off mum my hair wouldn't fit under my hat." Yet again the time hadn't been right to tell her about her father and what now was on Sarah's mind was; 'when would the time be right?' She would have to know as all that her daughter had talked about over Christmas was that hopefully the next time Richard got leave they would be married. "I will try and let you know mum but if it just has to be 'a quickie' we'll have to have a real wedding after the war."

'What was the world coming too?' thought Sarah as she had watched the train disappear out of sight. Suddenly she had felt like getting away from it all; from the every-day scars of the bombing raids; the queuing for food; the shortage of everything in general and she smiled to herself as she thought; 'and quickie weddings.' Betty and Sarah weren't as bad off as so many other people but the 'stockpile' of food and wine was slowly diminishing and when word went round that certain items were available in the shops Sarah would go off and queue especially if it was for fruit.

One morning in early February Sarah came down to breakfast to find a very distraught Betty sitting by the kitchen table a newspaper in her hand.

"You are up early this morning dear," Sarah had said to her friend.

Betty looked up from the paper her eyes filled with tears; "I thought I heard something on the news but couldn't quite catch it all as the radio lost its signal;" she handed Sarah the paper.

Sarah read the headlines about the fall of Singapore to the Japanese on 15th February. The surrender demonstrated to the world that the Japanese was a force to be reckoned with. It was a great humiliation to the British Government as the Japanese had been portrayed as useless soldiers.

"I only hope my Kenneth is safe they say that some 100.000 men have been taken prisoner I just cannot envisage such a number. In his last letter Kenneth had been quite jovial saying what a good time him and his fellow officers were having frequently dining and socializing in the Raffles Hotel and the Singapore Club and how much better it would have been if I had been there with him; Sarah do you think he is one of those taken prisoner?"

"Perhaps he has left Singapore you say you haven't heard from him for quite a while."

"Trouble comes in threes so they say I had this letter this morning the Government want to commandeer my home saying that they have need of it as a hospital. They have written at the end that they are willing for me to keep rooms for my own use. What am I to do Sarah? You will not want to stay with me now as I will have no need for a companion; there will be no more entertaining or fund raising for me."

"Of course I will stay with you we'll see this through together; I've already got an idea I was only thinking when I watched Merryl go off after Christmas that I would like to get away from all the trials and tribulations and the scars of war."

Betty smiled; "Come on then out with it what is this idea of yours?"

"Well the first question I must ask and I am loath to do so but are you financially secure? I myself have a little put by and I thought that….." Sarah's voice trailed away as she hesitated.

"I trust you Sarah and of course you can ask me anything and please put your suggestion to me I am really interested."

"Well, I was thinking that after the war was over I would like to rent a small holding in Pembrokeshire with some chickens, a few sheep and a garden where I could grow my own vegetables and have enough room to put up my family should they wish to come and visit."

"It is a lovely idea so what are you trying to tell me?"

"Well, if you are up to it, why don't we do it now; you can be the homemaker and I can be the farmer." Sarah laughed to hide her embarrassment.

"I think it is a wonderful idea and then after the war when Kenneth comes home we can all return here unless;" Betty looked at Sarah with a twinkle in her eye; "as I was saying; unless John comes back into your life."

"I will have to resign myself to the fact that we will never be together."

"Never is a long time. I just have a premonition. You've really cheered me up so how do we go about looking for somewhere; way down in the west where we can let the rest of the world go by?"

Sarah laughed, "I've heard those words somewhere before. I thought I saw somewhere advertised in one of your 'posh' magazines."

The two were soon delving through a pile of paper that had been put ready to 'help the war effort'. "Eureka," said Sarah found it; blast it is out of date it is last November's issue."

"What does it say?" questioned Betty.

Sarah sat on the bottom step of the stairs and turning to the appropriate page read; "Small holding to rent in quite village in Pembrokeshire; two miles from nearest town Haverfordwest; sheep; goats and chickens and two milking cows are being cared for by local farmer; all mod. cons. You know what that means? There's water and an outside loo."

"Is there an address or better still a phone number?"

"Yes' it says here if interested phone the farmer and the number is here."

"Shall we phone?"

"But Betty you really haven't had time to think about my suggestion you cannot jump in like that."

"My husband always said that I jump in with both feet before thinking; I only know that it will be better than being stuck here in two rooms with God only knows charging about my home."

"I will ring the number but you must promise not to be too disappointed as I expect someone has already grabbed the opportunity as I am sure there are many like us who wish to get away from it all."

"But surely there are not that many who have the knowledge of farming as you have. So many men have joined up and left the land."

"I know that only too well if it is only my two brothers. Hush, it is ringing."

"James Brown; Estate Manager how may I help?"

Sarah took a deep breath; "I'm ringing concerning an advertisement for a small holding to rent in Pemrokeshire I've only just seen the advertisement and I know it is out of date but I was wondering if it is still available."

"That will be the Williams' place; he joined up last summer and his wife and family have gone to live with her mother; I've been keeping an eye on the place. The place is partially furnished; obviously your husband will be able to work the land and is knowledgeable with animal husbandry?"

"Yes;" was all she said as she tried to hide a giggle as Betty kept asking; "Can we have it?"

"Will you wish to view the place?"

"Well, as things are with petrol rationing I will have to take your word that the place is in a habitable condition."

"You can take my word for that madam the house is spick and span just as Mrs Williams left it; I gather that you are interested so if you will let me have your address I will send you the relevant details."

After giving their details Sarah replaced the receiver; "Well?" said Betty "what's happening?"

"He's sending us the details and we have to send two references one preferably from a bank manager,"

"That will be no problem although he might think I've gone mad. Then what happens?"

"We could be setting up home in Pemrokeshire by the beginning of March just before the government wish to take over your home."

"This is going to be fun," said Betty as she hugged Sarah.

'I don't know about that,' thought Sarah thinking that it might also be hard work but as her dear old grandfather would have said 'hard work never killed anyone.'

References were easily obtained and Betty had explained to her bank manager that the country air would do her the world of good and that it would only be for a short while until the war was over.

"What am I going to do with all my possessions?" Betty had questioned.

"We can pack up your china and antiques and store them either in the attic or the cellar; the clothes you don't need can be packed into the big trunks you have in the attic and the furniture that will not be needed I am sure the Government will arrange to put it into storage until after the war; I really don't know how this commandeering business really works. We can arrange with the removal firm to transport the beds and other items we will need and the large packing cases then it will be 'Goodbye' to 'The Lindens' and 'Hello' to 'Thimble's End'."

"I hate having to leave all the hard work to you;" grumbled Betty as Sarah dragged a large packing case into the sitting room. "I feel so useless."

"Don't be daft; I like having plenty to do then there's no time to worry."

"What are you worrying about?"

"This, that and the other."

"Please don't add me to your list I'm going to be fine; in fact, I've never felt better do you know what Sarah? You are a tonic and I feel like one of these children I used to read about in my story books going off on a big adventure."

"I'm just worrying that it is not going to be awful; big holes in the roof that let the rain drip in on one as one lies sleeping; broken window panes and...."

"You are teasing me; I'm sure our 'friend' James Brown has made sure that the place is perfect. He seems very nice when I spoke to him yesterday confirming that we hope to arrive a week before Easter."

"Voices can be deceptive," was all Sarah said as she locked the last packing case.

"It is good sometimes to know people in high places I had a letter this morning wishing us well and enclosing enough extra petrol coupons to get us to Pembrokeshire."

"Dealing with the Black Market now," jested Sarah.

"I feel a little sad at leaving this place but whilst Kenneth is a way it doesn't seem like the home that we planned together. I've written to him telling him everything I just hope that he will get my letter I just told him that I love him and…." Betty said no more as tears filled her eyes. "It is the not knowing if he is alive or dead and how I pray that he is still alive and not suffering too much. I hate to read the papers and the articles of how bad the prisoners are being treated."

Sarah held her friend close and whispered; "He'll be fine God will take care of him and bring him back safely to you. Listen Vera is singing just for us."

Sarah turned the volume up and the words filled the room; "Wish me luck as you wave me 'goodbye'."

"We'll need it," said Sarah; "as you said this is going to be an adventure into the unknown. I suppose sometimes it is a good thing that we don't know what lies ahead. If you don't mind Betty you can turn that song off because I'm not as optimistic as you and I don't think we'll ever meet again.

CHAPTER SEVENTEEN

With the road map open on her knee Betty navigated their route; leaving behind the town of Carmarthen where they had stopped for lunch; the menu of the day being soup and a roll. They had laughed when the young lady had said; "off, off, off," to all their requests; and when Sarah had asked, "What is 'on'?" and was told "just the soup;" Betty had said; "we've heard those words somewhere before."

The trees were clothed in their spring foliage and everywhere one looked the pasture was green where the sheep and cows grazed and the soil had already been tilled and planted with early potatoes. This was a totally different world; far from the horrors of war and the grime and squalor of the coalfields; the countryside through which they now travelled appeared to the two travels as a little bit of heaven.

Once they had driven through the market town of Haverfordwest they knew that the journey was almost at an end and neither wished to linger knowing that the setting sun would soon disappear leaving them with very little light to find their new home.

"How much further?" asked Sarah as she manoeuvred the twists and turns of the country lanes.

"About two miles; are you getting tired? It is a bit late to say this but perhaps it would have been better to have travelled by train."

"I'm fine but I just hope I don't meet a tractor or a herd of cows as I'm afraid if I do we will end up in the hedge; I'm afraid I am not very good at reversing."

"Sorry," said Betty as she grabbed Sarah's arm "but I am sure we are meant to turn off here; look there's a sign pointing to something Manor I can't read the welsh name and the estate manager told me to look out for the sign and our house is just behind his."

Whilst Betty had been talking Sarah took the right turn off the lane to what now appeared to be just a dirt track. "The first thing I am going to do is buy a horse and trap cars don't seem to have any use in what is beginning to look like some God forsaken place."

"Look there it is there's the manor house so that lovely house behind must be ours."

Sarah slowed to an almost crawling speed and observed the name on the high wall that surrounded the huge residence; "I can't quite make it out the name in this light but this place belongs to some 'bigwig'; so I can only assume the house behind must be the manor house and I am now beginning to wonder where our place can be if we don't find it soon we might end up in a field for the night."

"We can always stop at the manor and ask the way," suggested Betty.

"I'm not stopping anywhere because if I do I will not be able to get the car going again as we are nearly out of petrol and the engine is overheating."

Sarah drove on passed the gates to the manor and a hundred yards further she just managed to see a wooden board with the name 'Thimble's End' painted in white paint. "We'd better take that down," Betty jested "you never know the German's might find us."

"I'll give a bloody medal to anyone who can find us down here."

"Sarah I have never heard you swear before."

"That's my grandfather coming out in me," laughed Sarah as she took a sharp right turn into an even muddy lane from which they could now see a sweet little cottage. Sarah drove the car into the yard and was surprised to find a tall distinguished looking gentleman waiting for them.

No sooner had Sarah turned off the engine than her very eager companion opened the door and stepped out; not exactly onto terra firma but into a muddy puddle that covered her black patent leather shoes and splashed the hem of her coat.

Sarah could not help but laugh; "That's the countryside for you dear friend I am sorry to have to say but this is the life you will now have to get used to and there's one more thing that I forgot to mention and that is the lovely country smells."

"Ladies so glad you've arrived safely; I assume your husbands will be arriving with the furniture."

"I'm sorry," said Sarah smiling sweetly, "I forgot to mention there are no husbands; Mrs Johnson's husband is an officer serving in Singapore and I'm a widow." Before he had time to say anything Sarah continued; "You have no need to concern yourself I have farmed a much larger spread than this and I am also a very good gardener." 'Self-praise is no recommendation,' she thought as she followed Betty into the cottage.

"I've lit the stove so the kitchen is nice and warm and the animals have been fed and watered; I hope that you will find everything satisfactory I'll be around in the morning about seven so I can show you the ropes."

He bid them 'good evening' and calling to his dogs strode across the yard and was soon out of sight.

"Handsome fellow," said Betty as she sat down and took off her shoes. "I'll get my own back on you just you wait and see you could have warned me."

"You were out of the car before I even put the hand break on I thought you were going to fall into his arms. I think we'll leave the unloading of the car until the morning there's not much we can do in this light; anyhow all I want is a nice cup of tea I made sure I put that in my overnight bag and a tin of condensed milk."

"You and your cup of tea all I want to do is roll into bed."

Sarah drew the curtains and lit the oil lamp; "You will be thinking we are in the dark ages there doesn't appear to be electricity here and as for our beds you know they will not arrive until the morning so wonder where we are going to sleep?"

Sarah lit a candle and followed closely behind by Betty wandered from room to room. The kitchen led into a passage from which the door opposite led into the dining room or what Sarah would have 'the parlour'; further along the passage were two more doors opposite each other one leading into a downstairs bedroom which they found to be still furnished with a long mirrored wardrobe, wash stand and chest of drawers and a large brass bedstead on which were two straw mattresses. "Well we've got a bed but as far as I can see no bed linen."

"I just want to fall on to it just as I am but by the height of it I might need a ladder."

"Let's go and see what is behind the other door."

From the light of the moon and their flickering candle they could see that the large room was void of any furniture; no curtains hung on the French windows and there were no carpets or rugs upon the floor boards; to the far side of the room was what appeared to be a pretty Victorian fireplace.

"I think this will make a lovely room for you Betty; you can have all your bits and pieces in here and as far as I can see in this light you will have a lovely view across the garden."

"You are a darling you think of everything nice that will please me and never think of yourself."

"I am just glad to be with you and I have told you many times I love the countryside and all that goes with it."

At the end of the passage they found another room that one might have called a bathroom; an old Victorian bath stood in one corner but didn't appear to be connected to any water supply; the wash basin had one tap so they assumed it was connected to the water main and in the other corner was the kind of boiler that had been in Sarah's grandparents farm and which was lit only on wash days and on the outside wall was a lavatory also connected to the main water supply; "Goodness me," said Betty "I wonder where the waste goes?"

"A cesspit I expect," replied Sarah.

Back in the kitchen they sat each side of the big oak table and drank their nightcap. Sarah couldn't find the tea that she was so certain that she had put in her bag so they both were content to sit and drink a cup of condensed milk and hot water and eating a few dried up sandwiches and the last of Sarah's welsh cakes.

"I hope you don't snore," said Betty as she slipped off her skirt and clambered up onto the bed.

"Sleep tight," replied Sarah "and I hope the bugs don't bite."

"Bugs?" questioned Betty "surely there are no bugs here?"

The following morning Sarah awoke at just after six and throwing her coat over her sleeping friend she quietly left the room. How glad she was that she knew all about these old fashioned stoves and it wasn't long before the kettle was boiling. She opened the curtains to a misty morning; 'sign of a fine day' she thought as she gazed across the yard to the outbuildings and beyond she could just make out the distant hills. Now in the light of day she could see that the kitchen was well equipped and opening a side door she found a walk in larder the shelves of which were laden with home preserves and bottled fruit; 'had their land lord recently stocked the shelves or had they been left by the previous tenant?' she wondered and then seeing a boiled ham in the meat safe and a side of bacon hanging from a hook on the far side of the larder she guessed that it must be their landlord. Sarah smiled; 'perhaps Betty is right he is not only a very handsome gentleman but a kind one at that.'

"That smells good," yawned Betty "What's cooking?"

"Bacon and egg."

"Where did you get the bacon from?"

"I was up early and I just killed one of the pigs. Would you like some?"

"You're doing it again; you are such a tease."

"Behind that door," said Sarah "is the larder and it is full of goodies."

"Kenneth used to have bacon and egg for breakfast but I was never up early enough; I can't remember when I last had bacon and egg. Do you know I'm so hungry I could eat a horse but I'll settle for bacon and egg if it is not too much bother?"

"Do you know what time it is? It is not yet seven o'clock I thought you would have a lie in."

"You know the bible story of Ruth and Naomi? Well I'm Ruth and you are Naomi and to put it in today's words what-ever you do I will try also to do."

"Shall we have an agreement then; if you feel up to it you can take over the household and I the garden and the animals and on market day I can also do the shopping and if you're not too busy you can come to market with me but I'm going to warn you now I'm going to get a horse and trap."

"Just one thing is bothering me."

"What is that?"

"After our journey last evening I have been wondering how the removal van is going to bring our furniture down that terrible lane."

"I've been looking out of the window across the fields and I am sure I could see another road I thought I saw an early morning rider."

"Perhaps it is Mr Brown on his way to see us. I'd better go and brush my hair and powder my nose."

"Well I'm going to see if I can find a pair of wellies that fit me and an old coat and I'm going to see what is what before he arrives."

"Where did you find the tea?"

"On the larder shelf I don't know where I packed ours."

"I'll make a pot by the time you come back."

"Or is morning tea for the estate Manager?"

In the porch Sarah found an old pair of Wellington boots that must have belonged to Mrs Williams and taking an old raincoat off the hook she wandered out into the yard. To her delight she found that they would not have to put money out on buying a horse because as soon as he opened the barn door she was greeted with the friendly neigh of a large brown horse; "And a good morning to you," said Sarah as she patted the horses nose. "Now if you can you tell me if there is a trap also that too will save us money."

"Yes," came a reply that made Sarah jump.

"You startled me. I thought it was the horse." As the last word left her lips she realised how stupid she must have sounded.

"I heard someone talking and thought that you were both up bright and early."

"Mrs Johnson is making a pot of tea shall we go and join her?" said Sarah trying to cover up having been found talking to the horse. She bent and patted the black and white sheep dog that had come sniffing at her feet,

"I can tell you like animals, old Jock doesn't make friends that easily."

"Shall I show you around first and then we can have a well-deserved cup of tea."

"Thank you for stocking the larder."

150

"Mostly farm produce," was all he said and as he strode off across the yard towards the fields she noticed that he walked with a limp.

"The cattle are all down at my place but there are six cows in the field behind the barn I'm sure there is no need for me to tell you that to produce good milk they need good pasture. I'm not sure about the number of goats they just roam freely around the yard and the rough land to the east. I've already got in the early potatoes and the seed has been sewn for hopefully a good harvest. We all pull together at harvest time and what-ever your capabilities all will be a great help. The gardens to the front of the house are yours to grow what-ever you wish and whatever you sell the profit is yours. There are two dogs down at my place that lived here so if you would like them back I am sure they would like to come home. Shall we go and have that cup of tea now? I am still rather amazed that you have chosen to take on such a task."

"What about the land army girls? We women are stronger than what you men give us credit for," quickly changing the subject she said;"the countryside is so beautiful one must be able to see for miles on a clear day."

Back at the cottage she found that Betty had powdered her nose and put on some of her pretty red lipstick; her dark hair was shining as too were her eyes; from somewhere she had found a frilly apron and as they entered the kitchen she said; "tea is brewing I saw you coming across the yard; sorry we've haven't any cake but next time you visit I will be sure to have one baked."

Sarah smiled as she slipped off her muddy wellies and hung up the old coat; Betty had been without a male companion for so long that it was good to see her looking bright eyed and bushy tailed. A little harmless flirting didn't hurt anyone.

CHAPTER EIGHTEEN

It had been a beautiful spring; a delightful time to be in the country or as Betty so aptly put it "away from the maddening crowd". On their arrival Betty had remarked that she had never seen so many snowdrops; masses and masses of the dainty white blooms heralding the spring and the golden daffodils nodding their heads in the March winds. Their place had been filled with the delicate primroses and the golden gorse and as they had stood in their garden they could see the golden hedgerows for miles around; Betty had also been delighted to find hidden away in the corner of the garden a bed of shy little violets. Sarah had remarked to her friend that the country air was really doing her good as no longer did she lie in bed until noon but was up with the 'lark' with Sarah.

"Do you know Sarah I am sure my mother and then my husband made a mountain out of a mole hill about my weak heart I've never felt so good now that there is no-one around to tell me that I shouldn't do this and I shouldn't do that."

"It is mart day today so I'm making an early start are you coming with me?"

"Not today I want to do some baking; you enjoy yourself better without me I noticed how the farmers treat you as one of them I could never go drinking in the Farmer's Arms; anyhow I would cramp your style," she joked.

"I like the way you put that; I don't go 'drinking' as you put it I just have a larger and listen to them discussing prices. Is Mr Brown going today?"

"How should I know and how many times has he told you to call him James?"

Was it the heat from the stove or had her friend suddenly turned a bright red with embarrassment at the mention of James Brown. A day didn't go by without him 'popping' in with some excuse or other and she was certain that it wasn't to see her. The relationship, if that is what one could call it, was doing Betty the world of good.

By the time summer arrived there was less and less for Sarah to do around the farm as James had taken on some local men that had been invalided out of the army; she did the gardening in their quite ample piece of land and the produce she grew she sold in the farmer's market. It had pleased Betty that amongst the fruit and vegetables she found space to grow some flowers that were no sooner in bloom than Betty had them filling the vases in the home.

Sarah would rise early and after breakfast would take the two dogs, come rain or shine, for long walks along the country lanes that twisted and turned as they made their way to the sea four miles away. She had tried to persuade Betty that they would take a journey with the horse and trap and visit the coast. "We'll take a picnic; it will be great fun." Sarah had suggested.

"I'd love to go but not in that contraption I'll wait until I can go buy car."

So Sarah had promised that she would find someone who would service the car and put it in working order.

"I'm off," Sarah called as she opened the kitchen door, "If I see the 'postie' I'll save him a journey; we haven't had any mail for weeks."

Sarah called to one of the dogs who jumped up into the back of the trap; "Sandy is coming with me he likes to see the sheep."

As she turned the corner she looked back towards the house and noticed Betty walking down the lane; pulling the horse to a stop she waited a moment thinking that Betty had forgotten to remind her about something or other but her friend hadn't seen her and Sarah noticed she was making her way to the manor house and as Sarah jerked on the reins she could but not help seeing James Brown coming to meet Betty; 'Morning tea together', smiled Sarah as she journeyed on.

"Good morning Mrs Morgan have a pile of letters here for you and Mrs Johnson they seem to have all arrived at the same time."

Sarah noticed that there were three letters from Merryl and two for Betty with the official 'censured' stamped across the envelope. She was eager to read Merryl's letters but she couldn't really sit there in the middle of the lane and catch up on her daughter's news; so slipping the letters into her bag she journeyed on.

Her produce sold she walked around the Mart ground stopping to talk to the farmers and their wives whose acquaintance she had formed over the last months since their arrival.

"Your friend not with you today?"

"No; she's having a day at home baking."

"I met her the other morning when my husband and I called on James to discuss the price of a tractor he has for sale; they seemed very much at ease with each other. Did you say she was a widow?"

Observing Sarah's embarrassment Fred Barnes jested that his wife was always 'match making'.

The letter's in her handbag were burning a hole in her curiosity so deciding to forego going with the others to the Farmer's Arms she made her way into the narrow street and finding a tea shop she sat in a quiet corner and ordered tea and a cake. She glanced at the three envelopes and noticing the post marks opened the one that she knew Merryl had sent first.

Dear Mum just a very short note as Richard and I are supposed to be on our honeymoon – if you can call it that as we only have the week-end together and are spending time in his grand-mother's old place in Norfolk which as I have told you now belongs to Richard. I know this will not come as too much of a surprise as I have already told you that should the opportunity arise we would get married. We were married on Friday in the registry office and Richard's dad gave me away the only other witness was Richard's friend. I felt a little sad that you weren't there but I promise that after the war we'll have a wedding in a church and you will be there by my side. Richard's dad made it special for us and we had a meal afterwards at the Savoy. I am so fond of him mum and feel a lot closer to him now that he is my father-in-law. Just a word in your ear; I cannot stand Angela, Richard's mother; she declined the invitation to our wedding making the excuse that she didn't agree with our marriage. Got to sign off the sirens are off again have to make our way to a shelter or hide under the bed that'll be fun. Love to you from Richard and Merryl xxx

As the waitress put the tea on the table Sarah turned her head towards the window she did not wish for her to see the tears that now filled her eyes. Why was life so cruel? Yet, there was no-one to blame but herself she should have taken Betty's advice and told Merryl about her father. She had a job to drink her cup of tea as her throat was constricted as she choked back her tears. Replacing the first letter in its envelope she opened the second and on reading this she trembled with shock.

My dearest mum; don't quite know how to write this letter to you as Richard and I are so up-set. His mother was killed in an air-raid on London two days ago; what is more distressing to me is that his father, although appearing uninjured, is in hospital and has been in a coma since that awful night. Richard has been given compassionate leave but obviously we cannot enjoy (to find a better word) our extra time together as we are so worried about father. Don't know how long this will take to get to you but cannot wait to hear from you – miss you so much. All our love Richard and Merryl xx

Sarah again noted the date stamp on the letter and realised it had been almost a week since the letter had been mailed to her. For the first time since leaving Penarth she wished that she was still there and could pick up the phone and speak to her daughter. Her heart was in her mouth as she thought of John lieing in a hospital bed and she wondered what harm had come to him; she wanted to sit by his side; to talk to him, to tell him that she still loved him. How ironic was life that now after all these years Merryl was now calling John 'father' the man that was her natural father. It was time she returned to Thimble's End she could not think sitting there surrounded by people. Leaving her cake uneaten she paid at the desk and unleashing the dog from the drainpipe outside the shop she made her way back to the mart ground. Someone called to her from the Farmer's Arms asking 'if she was going to join them' but she just waved as couldn't bring herself to speak.

As the old horse plodded its way home Sarah thought back to the time when she had returned home in disgrace carrying beneath her coat the result of that all engulfing love that John and she had shared. Why had she kept the lie going so long that her husband, Merryl's father, had been killed in the war? Why, when Merryl was old enough, hadn't she explained to her about her father? There were so many questions and she had no answers.

"Watch where you're going you silly old bat," shouted a young lad on a bicycle.

She had let the horse make his own way down the familiar lane and deep in thought she hadn't noticed the lad on the bicycle. Turning around she apologised and it was then that she noticed it was the telegram boy.

'Oh God!' she thought I do hope it is not bad news. Her first thought being that John had died. She jerked on the reins and the horse increased its pace as they made for home.

How could she possibly breathe a sigh of relief when on entering the kitchen she found Betty with her head on the kitchen table and the discarded telegram lying on the floor.

"Betty; are you all right?" At the same time she realised how stupid her question had been; how could anyone possibly be 'all right' having just received a telegram knowing what they usually contained when one had a husband serving with the armed forces.

Betty lifted her head and at the same time handed Sarah the telegram; "My husband is dead," she almost whispered, "I've been waiting for this for so long and I am more upset because I cannot cry."

"That's understandable," Sarah put her arms around Betty and held her close. "Shock has that effect on some people."

"It is not that; you will not believe what I have to say." Betty motioned to Sarah to sit beside her.

"We've been a part for so long; not just since war broke out in 1939 but for years before. I have only seen him twice since I returned home from India. I have never said anything to you knowing you had enough worries of your own but for years until you came to live with me I have been so lonely. I involved myself in my charity work and worrying about my health. Coming here has done me the world of good giving me a new life and a new love; don't look so surprised I am sure you have noticed how James and I are with each other. It is only in romantic novels that one reads of 'love at first sight' but that is how it was with James and myself from the moment we met. At first he would just call for a cup of tea and a piece of my home baked cake but one morning when you had gone for an early morning walk with the dogs' in the pouring rain; James had turned up at the door drenched to the skin after helping a cow to give premature birth of all places in the high field. He was going to bring her down to the barn but thought he had plenty of time. I really am waffling on because I don't quite know how to tell you."

"You don't have to explain anything to me."

"But I do; I've tried to tell you on a few occasions but something or other has prevented me. Well I suppose the best thing I can do is tell you straight out James and I ended up in bed and since that morning every opportunity we've had we've been together. He's makes me feel like a princess; he is so gentle and so kind and a wonderful lover. I know I've never had much experience in that field but all I can tell you is that I never felt like that with Kenneth; now I realize that I was just there for Kenneth when the need took him and that I am now aware wasn't that often."

"I know it must have been distressing to receive that telegram but if you are not sad because of that was is now making you so unhappy when everything should be just perfect."

Betty sighed; "Obviously what went on between James and myself is private but I just want you to know it wasn't a spur of the moment thing; we had walked hand in hand together and talked; he had taken tea with me and had on a few occasions kissed me lightly on the cheek; yet I know now that both of us were aware of the chemistry between us but we kept it hidden."

"Were you worried about what I would say," questioned Sarah.

"In a way; you had been there for me and helped me so much and we had come to 'Thimble's End' together and I felt that I was deserting you to be with the man I loved and I also felt guilty that I was a married woman if only in name. That morning when he came in looking so forlorn my heart missed many a beat I just wanted to take him in my arms and comfort him. He went to my bedroom to slip out of his wet clothes and I had told him to take the blanket off my bed to wrap himself in whilst I dried his clothes. After he closed the door behind him I stood in the hall feeling like a young girl I wanted to 'peep' through the key hole and watch him undress I wanted to touch him and most of all I wanted him; my whole body ached for him. Then he called to me from the room asking where the blanket was and it was then that I remembered the previous evening you had thrown it over me as I lay on the sofa listening to the wireless. "I'll fetch it now," I called back suddenly aware that he must have known I was outside the door. When I returned the door was open and he was standing by the fireplace his back towards me. Never before had I such feelings on seeing a man's body but when I saw his naked, muscular body all my inhibitions left me and my passion rose to bursting point; "Here's the blanket," I almost whispered and as he turned I knew at that moment that he wanted me as much as I him. As he picked me up in his arms and lay me upon the bed he said the three words I had been longing to hear 'I love you.' The rest dear Sarah I will leave to your imagination because what happened there is James and mine; ours alone. "

Suddenly Betty started to cry; tears running down her cheeks she sobbed, "I love him so Sarah but now I've spoilt it all."

"How; is it because of the telegram? I know you have lost your husband and it might sound a bit callous but now you are free to love James."

"It is nothing to do with this," Betty threw the telegram across the table; "I didn't think it was possible and now I've spoilt everything."

"What wasn't possible? What have you spoilt?""

"I remember you telling me the same thing happened to you and I thought it couldn't be possible but I am; I know I am."

"For goodness sake stop talking in riddles what has this got to do with whatever happened to me?"

"Just like you I thought I was starting the menopause early but it's not that; I'm pregnant."

Sarah could not control her built up emotions and just stood with her arm around Betty and laughed. "I thought you were going to tell me that you were ill; how come you are pregnant I thought you said that you couldn't have children?"

"That's why I never worried about taking precautions I always believed it was my fault that we never had children and my mother always rubbed it in saying that it was a good thing I never got pregnant with my heart condition."

"So why are you now crying?"

"I don't know how to tell James he might think I'm stupid letting myself get pregnant."

"It takes two," jested Sarah bringing a smile to her friend's face.

"He might not want a baby at his age and I'm not a young mother."

"Why, will he be ninety next birthday?"

"Don't tease you know he is almost fifty and has two married sons by his first marriage. How will he tell them about me and the baby?"

"I was your age when I had David."

"I know but David wasn't your first," Betty bit her lip, "sorry I didn't mean to bring that up."

"There's no need to apologise friends can speak their minds to each other. I'll go and see to the chickens but I'll call on James first and tell him that you would like to see him; if he loves you like I believe he does then everything will be fine. Mind you I'm not stopping with the chickens all night for you to have your wicked way with him." Sarah kissed the top of her friend's head and reaching for her coat called back to her, "I've got something to tell you later."

"Keep me in suspense as usual," retorted Betty as she filled the kettle ready for the cup of tea that James always liked.

Sarah fed the chickens and then calling to the two dogs took them for a walk down the lane to the small hamlet that nestled in a hollow surrounded by fields where the cattle grazed to their heart's delight. The evening sun setting in the west was like a ball of red fire and Sarah stopped for a while and lingered on the old bridge that crossed the stream; "Come on walkies," she called to them deciding to journey on a little further to give Betty and James plenty of time together and not just because of them it would also give her time to think; of which she had a lot to do having not yet opened the last letter from Merryl she wondered what it would contain.

Not thinking of the distance that she would have to walk back home her walk took her to the next village; 'at least it would be down-hill all the way back,' she thought as she stood beside the old church.

"Good evening, beautiful evening for a walk," the minister's voice startled her. "The door is open if you would like to go in just tie the dogs by the old horse trough."

For the first time in her life Sarah felt the need for help from God to solve her problems. Tying up the dogs she entered the small church closely followed by the minister.

"Have you lost a loved one?" He asked.

"No; yes, sorry I don't know. I've made so many mistakes and I don't know how to put things right. It is all so complicated and I really must get back I have come too far and my friend will be worried."

"Aren't you one of the two ladies that live at 'Thimble's End'?

"I am going that way to visit a sick friend so if you wish I can take you home."

"I've got the dogs."

"Don't worry about that my wife and I have three and three kids. It is bedlam in the vicarage. Would you just like to sit quietly for a while or would you like to talk?"

"I don't go to church," then as if to make an excuse for what she had said she continued, "I used to go to Chapel and my daughter went to Sunday school in the village church."

"Where was that?"

"Back in the valley in a time that now seems so long ago; how can I put things right?"

"Is it your daughter that you are concerned about?"

"Yes. I've made so many mistakes."

"We all make mistakes none of us are perfect but if we can right the wrongs we've done then the battle is half fought."

"Back in 1919 I gave birth to a beautiful daughter; to save having the name of 'bastard' put upon her I raised her to believe that her father had been killed in the war; I am not trying to make excuse but in a way he had died. We had loved each other deeply and he had promised to marry me at the end of the war placing this ring upon my finger; I have always worn it and have kept his love forever in my heart. I am wasting your time with my memories."

"No my dear I have all the time in the world."

"You said you were going to visit a sick friend."

"Perhaps you need my help; that is if I can give it, more than my sick friend."

"John; that is his name, was invalided out of the war and returned home; to my dismay he did not come to see me and I later found out he was suffering from amnesia. I was 'paid off' by his mother as not being suitable for an up and coming barrister. Giving up I returned home to the valley and to my family. I later found that he had married and yet I still didn't give up the thought that one day we would meet again. I married a local man but without going into further details the marriage failed but later he returned to the farm with his daughter from another relationship his partner having died. We took him in and later he returned to my bed and a child was conceived;" Sarah paused "I really shouldn't be wasting your time. Although I try to shut that time from my mind the loss of my baby has left a deep wound; David was such a beautiful child." She sighed.

"Please continue; I feel that you have led a very troublesome life."

"My mother died followed by my grand-parents and my two brothers left home one to join the navy and the other to Spain to fight for 'the cause'. Luckily as far as I know they are both alive. I sold the farm and with my husband out son and his daughter bought a house in the village; for a while things were good until Merryl told me of the young man who had come into her life. It is hard now to believe that such a thing could happen but Richard, who is now her husband, is her real father's stepson. When I first learned of this association I was concerned for their relationship until all was made clear. I came face to face again with the man that I had never stopped loving; for our short time together he seemed, at times, to have a kind of recognition in his eyes; how I longed to tell him.

The winter after this meeting everything went wrong, I felt that God was punishing me for my sins, our son David died from diphtheria, Minnie my husband's daughter was hospitalized with T.B and then came Morgan's pit accident that led finally to his suicide." Sarah sobbed. "Sorry I can't go on; I just want to tell you that Merryl has found happiness and has a deep affection for her father-in-law; quite ironically he gave her a way on her wedding day. Shall I just let sleeping dogs lie or shall I tell her that he is her real father? I have kept diaries from her birth and all the press cuttings of John's rise in his career but how or when can I do this?"

"What has brought this all to a head at this moment in time?"

"I received three letters today; one telling me that Richard and Merryl were married and that Richard's father had given her away. The second was to say that during an air raid on London Richard's mother had been killed and his father although appearing not to be injured was in a coma; the third letter is here in my pocket and I am afraid to open it just in case it says that John has died."

"Would you like me to open and read it first?"

"If you would."

The minister took the letter and opening it carefully took out the folded paper.
He glanced through it and then read it to her;

"Dear mum; is there any chance that you can come to London? Richard and I are in a quandary his dad has regained conscientious and there appears to be nothing physically wrong with him but he seems to be living in the past; he doesn't recognise Richard and myself and keeps asking for Sarah. We believe this must be you as he tells us to go to 'Oak Manor' and ask Wendy and Glyn where you are and why you don't come to visit. He talks about the horrors of war but we now understand that it is about the First World War that he is speaking. Did you ever meet him? We've enclosed a P.O for your fare just in case. Our love as always R and M xxx."

Sarah just sat in the pew and stared at the minister; at last she spoke, "What am I to do?"

"I know it is going to be hard for you but you must go to London; I suggest that you take with you some of your diaries and before you go to visit John you must tell your daughter and her husband the truth. You say she is happy and has always been; have you always had a close relationship with your daughter?"

"Always; she has always known how proud I have been of her achievements and a day hasn't gone by without tell her how much she is loved."

"If she is as loving as you say she will forgive you easily and in the tragic world in which we live today it will give her a new hope for the future. As for John you will have to tread carefully and I am sure you will be advised by the doctors treating him what and how much you can tell him. Be brave Miss Lloyd.!

"Mrs Morgan," she smiled for the first time as she corrected him. "I changed to my maiden-name when I became a companion to Mrs Johnson; and talking of Mrs Johnson she will be wondering where I've got too; thank you so much for listening you have helped me a lot."

"I do hope I have; perhaps one day you will call at the vicarage and tell me what happened on your visit to London. I hope you find happiness Mrs Morgan you deserve it."

"Where the devil have you been?" called Betty as she entered through the kitchen door we've been waiting for you."

"Talking to a friend," was all she said as she took off her coat.

"James and I have something to tell you; haven't we James?" Betty looked lovingly into the eyes of the man who stood by her side with his arm around her waist. "We're going to get married."

"Good, can I be bridesmaid?"

"This friend of mine can never be serious; of course you can but I think it will have to be matron-of-honour don't you? James has been waiting to open the champagne."

"Champagne," said Sarah, "Where did you find that?"

"Under a bush in the garden," said Betty "I kind farmer left it for us; didn't he James?"

"I've got a few more where that came from but they've got to be kept for our wedding day."

"To James and Betty," said Sarah as she lifted the bubbly drink to her lips, "To a long and happy life together. God Bless you both."

That night she took the two letters addressed to Betty from her hand bag and placing them on a shelf high up in her room she said to herself; 'to be opened at a later date.' No way was she going to spoil her friend's happiness.

All that was now left to do was to put her own house in order and this she knew was going to be a difficult task.

CHAPTER NINETEEN

Sarah wanted to close her eyes to the aftermath of the ravages of the war as she journeyed by train to London. So many villages and towns had been hit by the onslaught of German air raids. What was happening to the world? Her world too appeared to be crumbling around her as the short time of a peaceful existence was lost; her very being was in turmoil as she tried to find a way to tell her daughter about John; how would she go about it? Would it be better to tell Richard first? That would only be possible if he picked her up from the station. 'No', she almost said out loud that was a stupid idea especially if they were travelling by public transport; perhaps it would be better to tell them together but when would be the right time? Sarah felt there was no 'right time' as she wished the train would turn around and take her back to the peace and quiet of Thimble's End.

Paddington Station was a hive of activity and as she stepped from the train her eyes searched the crowds of men and women in uniform; mothers and children and the old and infirm; people of all walks of life, en masse, with one thought on their minds to save their country from tyranny yet at that moment in time all she could think about was 'how was she going to tell her daughter'?

"Mum," a familiar voice called from a group standing by the exit. She first saw her daughter's hand waving to her and then as she pushed her way from within the group she Merryl; gone was the young girl and before her now stood a beautiful young woman; her 'bobbed' hair suited her and the pretty floral dress that she was wearing complimented her figure. Sarah put her suitcase down and mother and daughter embraced

"Let's go and have something to drink and then we'll have to get the tube I'm afraid Richard couldn't bring me as he has been called back to duty; I've got so much to tell you."

"You're very quiet," Merryl remarked as they sat in Lyons Corner House.

Sarah smiled; "Just admiring my beautiful daughter."

"I can't wait until we get home I've just got to tell you I'm pregnant; we're going to have a baby. It is early days but I think baby should arrive around about my birthday. We're going to move to Richard's grand-mother's place in Norfolk. I didn't want to worry you but I was quite poorly so I have been released from the W.R.A.F."

"That sounds as if you've been let out of jail."

"It began to feel a bit like that as I really wasn't suited to the life but had to do my bit for King and Country."

"Have we got to go by tube? Sarah questioned.

"I doubt if we can get a cab."

The journey by tube was something that Sarah did not wish to repeat; she hated the idea of being in the bowels of the earth with the knowledge of all those massive buildings sitting on top of her. Merryl appeared to take it all in her stride as they were jostled from side to side by passengers coming and going and when they did manage to get a seat the rocking to and fro almost sent Sarah to sleep.

"The next stop is ours; be careful stepping down sometimes there is quite a gap."

As she stepped gingerly from the train Sarah had visions of falling between the platform and the railway track; something more ominous was awaiting her as she watched the passengers stepping onto the escalator.

"I'm not going up on that."

"Come on mum it is easy just step on and it will take you to the top; I'll take your case."

Before Sarah had time to retort 'that it was too heavy' her daughter had taken the case and was already reached half way. There was nothing else for Sarah but to step on to the 'contraption' and was immediately pushed to the side as three young men, appearing to be in a hurry, barged passed her as they strode up the moving stairway. Seeing a light ahead of her and her daughter standing at the top smiling down at her Sarah gave a sigh of relief.

"That was fun," remarked Merryl.

"Fun? Don't take me down there again," Sarah moaned.

"It's the easiest way to travel mum and I hate to have to tell you but if there's an air raid it is the safest place to be. We've spent the night there on a few occasions; one meets all kinds of people and while the bombs drop above us it is marvellous to see the courage of the people that you meet. We have a sing song and social classes are completely forgotten; it is a totally different society I've helped old people by listening to their tales and mothers who are worried about their children who have been sent out of London to escape the bombing. We had planned to wait until the war was over before planning to have a baby but life doesn't stand still." Merryl pointed across the road to a park; "our flat is just the other side of the park."

"No escalators," Merryl joked as they entered an elegant Victorian building, "we have a ground floor flat."

The flat was larger than what Sarah had anticipated and as her daughter ushered her into the sitting room she was surprised to see that the French windows gave a splendid view of a tree lined long back garden.

"Richard's parents lived here in the thirties when they were in London but moved to the other house just before the war. Not having use for this place they let out the top two floors and Richard and I had this one. By the way are you up to going to see Richard's dad tonight?"

"Can it wait until tomorrow I have something I need to tell you."

"I know mum."

"What do you mean 'you know'?"

"I'll put the kettle on nana used to say it was best to sit and talk over a nice cup of tea." As she spoke her daughter opened the French door. "Go and sit in the garden mum we must make the most of the nice weather."

Sarah strolled to the end of the garden taking in the perfume of the flowers as she walked by; one could hardly believe in the tranquillity of the English country garden that the world was at war.

"Tea is ready," called her daughter placing a tray on the garden table.

"I should have asked you did you need to 'freshen up' as Aunt Wendy would have said."

"This is lovely," said Sarah as she sipped her tea "did you bake the cake?"

"I'm learning slowly to be the perfect housewife but I don't think I'll ever be as good as you."

"What did you mean by saying you know what I had to tell you?"

Merryl smiled; "Richard and I didn't know what to do or how to tell you as we felt we had been prying into the past. When Angela was killed in the air raid we found in the rubble of the house a box of letters and a letter from John's mother addressed to Angela that she must have hidden away. We read his grandmother's letter in which she had said to Angela to burn the box of letters as if John got his hands on them it would be the end of their marriage. Mystified we opened the box and when I looked at one of the letters I realised that the signature at the bottom was yours. We only read the one mum as we realised they were 'love letters' but the one we read happened to be the one where you had written about your time together and that you would always wear the ring he had placed upon your finger."

A silence fell between them Sarah not knowing what to say and Merryl waiting for an acknowledgement from her mother that she hadn't done wrong in reading the personal letter.

After a moment Merryl broke the silence; "Are you cross with me mum? If you loved John so much how could you go and marry someone else so soon and have me?"

Sarah got up and crossing to where her daughter sat put her arm around her and said; "of course I'm not cross; in fact, I wish you had read more then you would have had the answer to your question."

"What do you mean mum?"

Sarah sat back down; "firstly let me tell you that it is I who should apologise it is you that should be angry with me. It is so hard for me to try and explain; you were right in saying that John and I loved each other deeply and it was the war that separated us; I was living with Wendy and Glyn and we met when he was home on leave and fell in love almost immediately. The war was nearing its end at the time of the letter that you read and John promised that as soon as it was all over we would be married. He told his parents of our engagement and his mother indicated that I wasn't good enough for an up and coming barrister." Sarah paused and pored herself another cup of tea.

"Why didn't you marry when he came home?"

"He was invalided out as he was suffering from amnesia after almost being killed in battle."

"You mean he had lost his memory and forgotten all about you? Why didn't you go to him and tell him who you were?"

"I was told it was far too dangerous as his memory of that time had to come back naturally."

"Why didn't he remember you at our engagement party?"

"He seemed to have a distant memory that we had met before but I was still afraid to tell him and afraid to tell you…." Sarah's voice drifted away and tears filled her eyes.

"Mum why are you crying?"

"Don't you know? Can't you guess what I am trying to tell you?"

Merryl looked puzzled; "I have read that one must not bring back the memories of amnesia patients too suddenly but surely after all these years it wouldn't have hurt to tell him; John would have been glad to know that you were once in love as his marriage to Angela was a big mistake; he always said Richard was the only reason he stayed. Why did you go back to Wales? Surely if you had visited him he would have remembered you."

"There is only one way I can say this to you my darling daughter; John's mother sent me a cheque and told me he was going to be married. I had no alternative I was young and in those days women did not fight for their rights. I went home to Wales and to my family because I had nowhere else to go; I went home in disgrace."

"What do you mean 'in disgrace'?"

"I was having a baby."

"Did you have a miscarriage?"

Sarah sighed surely her daughter being an intelligent young woman could understand or was she pushing her to reveal the truth; "Merryl don't you understand what I am trying to say? I didn't have a miscarriage you are that baby and John is your father."

Merryl stared at her mother and then started to cry. "Mother," she sobbed "I wondered why my father had the same name as Richard's dad but I just assumed..." She stopped talking and wiped her eyes. "I don't know what I thought many times I wished that he was my dad he was just how I imagined him to be if he hadn't been killed in the war. Why did you raise me to believe he had been killed?"

"What else was I to do? Let you grow up in the valley with the stigma of being a bastard? As the years went by it got harder and harder for me to tell you and then out of the blue he comes back into my life as Richard's father. Now how was I to tell you that you couldn't marry your half-brother and that you romance could not be."

"But he isn't my half-brother."

"I found that out by talking to John at your engagement party and believe me I gave a big sigh of relief."

"What about Mog did he ever know?"

"I thought not but after he died I found a letter he wrote saying that he had read my diaries whilst |I had been in London."

"Did you ever love Mog?"

"It was a kind of loving; but always at the back of my mind was the love that John and I had shared. Day by day as you grew up I could see him in you more and more; your eyes, your loving nature everything about you was my beloved John. When you wrote and said he had represented your father on your wedding day I wept and how I wished that I could have said 'he is your dad'."

"I'm so glad I know mum but I do so wish you had told me sooner; did you think I wouldn't forgive you? I love you mum; you've been my best friend, my teacher and most of all the best mum in the world and now I've got a father. How I wish we could all go and celebrate but John doesn't know who I am and Richard is away goodness knows where and the world is all upside down again. It is like history repeating itself the only thing that is different is that Richard and I are married."

"How ill is John?"

"The doctor says he is well enough to come home except for his amnesia and the fact that he is now living in 1918; he just thinks of us as a nice young couple who spends time with him and brings him gifts."

"Is it far to the hospital? Can we go this evening?"

"I'll just make a phone call and see if a colleague of his can drive us."

Whilst Merryl made the phone call Sarah gathered her thoughts; how was she going to handle this meeting with John? Surely now he wouldn't recognise her if he was living in the past.

"Sorry mum Clive is busy this evening but he'll drive us out tomorrow afternoon. Perhaps it is a good thing as you look exhausted. Clive is running the firm single handed with John hospitalised and Richard away. He is a real dear and came out of retirement to help us out."

That evening after dinner as they sat together Sarah took from her case a few of her old diaries and photos of Merryl that had been taken at different ages of her childhood."

"I remember that dress it was my first grown up party dress when I went to the Grammar School and I always loved that one taken at the sea-side with Dewi and Emlyn. Do you think we'll all meet up again after the war?"

"I really hope so; I have a photo here somewhere that Emlyn sent me last Christmas." Sarah delved in her bag and handed the photo to Merryl.

Merryl laughed, "He looks a cross between Father Christmas and Sailor Sam in Rupert Bear. I must admit he looks the very image of a sailor. How many children has he got?"

"Three at the last count; his wife seems to fall pregnant after every leave. By the way I'm sure she wont mind me telling you Betty is pregnant and it will not surprise me that you are both due about the same time."

Merryl looked surprised, "How come? I thought her husband was in Singapore."

"It seems we've got a lot of catching up to do; Betty had a telegram saying that her husband had died in a prisoner of war camp."

"You didn't tell me when you wrote; come to think of it I haven't had a letter for ages."

"Letters seems to take ages these days or perhaps it got lost in the post."

"Has Betty been having an affair?"

"I don't really like to call it that as they have a lovely relationship; in fact, she's a 'new woman' since we've gone to live in Pembrokeshire."

"Come on then mum spill the beans who is he?"

"Our land-lord; James Brown a very charming gentleman who worships the ground Betty walks on in fact just before I left to visit you they got engaged and plan to marry as soon as things can be arranged and I'm going to be bridesmaid and wear a frilly dress; only joking about that as the role will have to be matron-of-honour."

"I hope I'll be invited to the wedding. Will you need anything more tonight mum? I do hope you will sleep well I've put you in the back bedroom it over-looks the garden and the doors open like these so if you fancy breakfast in the garden just tell me; it used to be the dining room." Merryl opened a side door that led off from the sitting room.

"This is a lovely room I'm sure I shall be quite comfortable here." She kissed her daughter and said; "sleep well my dear and dream of happy days ahead. I do hope my revelations haven't upset you."

"Of course they haven't now I know that as well as you and Richard I've got another important person in my life, my father. With his loss of memory and being married there is no way that he could have been in my life before I only hope that he will recover his memory and then we can be one happy family; our baby will have a grandmother and a grandfather and it will be even better if you end up together."

Sarah went to sleep that night with but one thought on her mind and that was to dream that Merryl's words would come true.

CHAPTER TWENTY

She awoke to find the morning sun streaming in through the windows; she felt quite refreshed and when she glanced at the clock saw that it was almost mid-day surely she couldn't have slept that long. She slipped her feet into her slippers and picking up her robe she went in search of her daughter.

"Good morning sleepy head; I brought you a cup of tea at nine o'clock but as you were snoring your head off I let you be."

"I'll have you know that I don't snore."

"I'm just preparing lunch I thought we'd have it now as Clive will be here about one. I just made a pot of tea I thought you might like one."

"Just what I came looking for and then I'll go and get dressed."

She took from her case a blue chintz dress; the memory of so long ago still fresh in her mind of how much he liked her wearing blue. She quickly washed, did her make-up and then slipping the dress over her head she looked at the final result and said to herself; 'well Mog Morgan you said I was old and decrepit you'd have a shock if you saw me now'.

"You look gorgeous mum," said her daughter as she joined her at the dining table "I've got just the hat to go with that dress."

By one o'clock both were eagerly awaiting the arrival of Clive; "I don't know what I am going to say to John."

"Just be yourself and try and answer any question as truthfully as possible but avoid anything that will upset him that's what we've been told."

"But will he know who I am? Remember it is almost twenty five years ago since we were young and in love."

"Perhaps in his mind's eye you will look just the same; we will just have to wait and see."

Clive was late arriving; a jolly man in his late sixties. Sarah wondered if it was safe to let him drive the car but her inhibitions soon left as they left behind the city and he soon made up the lost time as he sped along the country lanes. Sarah had been glad to leave London behind as the sight of the damage caused by the continual air raids really upset her; all around her life went on and as she saw the farmers busy haymaking she felt quite nostalgic; she would really have liked to have stopped the car and gone and joined them.

"Soon be there mum are you all right you are very quiet?"

"Just taking in the beautiful countryside and dreaming dreams. What is this hospital like?"

"It is not what you might call a hospital as such; obviously there are nurses and doctors but it is more like a rest home for officers who need that extra bit of care to recuperate. Some of the patients have lost their sight, others have had limbs amputated and then there are those who have had a nervous breakdown."

Sarah was surprised to see them turn into the drive of a beautiful Georgian Mansion and the first thing that she noticed were the smartly dressed nurses wheeling their patients across the rolling lawns to a lake where wild fowl swam freely.

"They all appear to be enjoying themselves."

"Many of them are happy enough during the day time but they hate to be on their own at night," said Clive as he parked the car. "I'll pick you about five if that's all right I'll go and visit my sister for an hour or two."

They watched Clive drive off and then Merryl turned to her mother; "He always says that shall we go and see what dad is doing with himself today."

"Why dear what does he usually do?"

"Most of the time he spends reading I think he has read every book in the library."

"Well if he reads that much surely he would have read about the war that is going on now."

"I never thought about that unless he refuses to take it in."

"Good afternoon Mrs Lloyd your husband not with you today? Your father-in-law is in the library."

"I'm going to leave you now mum I just think it might be better if you visit him alone I'll go and visit with Richard's friend who likes me to read to him; I'll meet you for tea in the restaurant at four."

How could she spend two hours with someone who might not even know her quietly she turned the handle of the library door and as she closed it behind her she turned and saw him sitting in the window seat with his feet up, just as she would have pictured him as a child, reading a book.

He lifted his head and looked towards her, "Hello Sarah I wondered when you were coming to visit me."

She almost fainted when she heard his words; was he seeing her as she was today or was she the young girl of their youth.

He rose to his feet and putting his arms around her he kissed her passionately. The kiss answered her question she was once more his eighteen year old fiancée.

"I hope they'll let me come home soon I've lost all sense of time in here. I remember you writing to say you were having our baby. I hate this I just can't remember if we got married but we must have seeing the ring on your finger and the fact that you are no longer pregnant you must have had the baby what did we have?

"A beautiful little girl," she replied almost choking on the words. She twisted the ring, the very engagement ring he had given her all those years ago. Would he notice that it wasn't a wedding ring.

"What did you name her?"

"Merryl and she looks just like you."

"Merryl," he said the name as if half to himself. "Merryl I've heard that name somewhere before."

"You once told me that if we had a little girl you would like her to have that name and I remembered how you said you would like it spelt." 'What a stupid thing to say' she thought. The conversation seemed to be getting them nowhere.

"You are so beautiful I love you in blue. I do hope you've brought a photo of our little one."

She opened the bag and took out the photo she had taken on Merryl's first birthday. "You can keep it if you like I have another."

He gazed at the photo for a moment and then he said; "I don't quite understand how long have I been like this? This must be her first birthday and this wasn't taken at mothers or Wendy's home so where do we live?"

"I went home to visit my family," was all she could say. Why couldn't he see her as she was a woman in her forties; surely he must realise that he was almost fifty. He only had to look in a mirror to see his grey hair and moustache.

"Tell me Sarah, tell me about the years I've lost," he was almost pleading with her. "Come sit with me and tell me everything I feel bewildered and lost seeing you has somehow brought memories flooding back and I don't like what I see." He put his arm around her and led to the window seat and just as they were going to sit down the air raid siren let out its piercing noise.

"Blast; we'd better get to the shelter this is most unusual it must be one that's lost his way and just wants to drop his load anywhere; why can't they leave us alone."

They were just about to make their way across the room when Sarah heard the most terrific blast followed by another; the panes of glass in the bookcases shattered and the next thing she saw was a massive hole appear in the ceiling.

"Quickly Sarah under the table," John pulled her towards the table and the last thing she saw was one of the huge beams falling towards them.

She opened her eyes but could see anything; the room was in darkness; remembering the last thing she had seen she tried to move but realised John was lying across her body. 'Dear God', she thought 'let him not be dead'. She couldn't move her arms as the weight of his body pinned her down she tried to move her legs but the pain was so severe that she just cried out.

"John are you all right?" If she could only feel his heart beating or just here one word then she would know; she couldn't lose him now after they had just found each other. As her eyes got use to the darkness she realised that it wasn't as dark as she first thought. John must have managed to get her under the large oak table before the ceiling collapsed in upon them. Her nostrils were filled with the smell of burning timber surely they would be rescued and not be burnt to death. Panic stricken she again tried to move and as the agony of the pain in her legs gripped her she lost all her senses; she felt hot as if she was burning up and as her eyes became blurred she fainted.

"Get me out of here," she screamed "Help me I'm on fire; Merryl where are you?"

"It is all right mother I'm here lie still you are safe."

She opened her eyes but the brilliance of the light was too strong so she closed them again. She couldn't move; her legs were numb and her head hurt. Then she remembered John and once again the same panic gripped her. "John," she called "John don't leave me."

"I'm here my love," she felt someone take her hand. This time when she opened her eyes their eyes met.

"John you are all right I thought you were dead."

"I haven't felt this good in quite some-time; this last bump on the head has done me the world of good." He pointed to his bandaged head. "Just a nasty cut that will soon heal but it has brought me to my senses at long last hasn't it Merryl?"

"Where am I?" she asked as she tried to raise her head.

"You are in hospital mum; it took a while to rescue you and dad."

"I remember now; I remember the air raid and the roof falling in as John was trying to get me under the table. What about the other patients?"

"Just a few minor injuries the bomb landed on the library; someone said there was nobody in there but I knew that was where you were meeting dad so I kept on until they agreed to look. I couldn't stop crying I thought I had lost you."

"Time you left;" said a nurse in a stiff white headdress. "Mrs Lloyd has had enough for one day and it is time for her medication."

"Don't leave me," Sarah cried as John bent to kiss her.

"I'll never leave you again," he said and his kiss said it all.

"We'll be back tomorrow I expect the sister will give you something to take the pain away and help you to sleep." Merryl said as she kissed her mother.

"You keep saying 'dad' does he know who you are?" Sarah whispered.

"Yes mum it is quite amazing the bump on the head brought back his memory."

The screen being pulled around her bed was enough of a hint for Merryl to take her leave.

"Love you mum; we'll see you tomorrow."

Before the last curtain was pulled around her bed she saw John turn and blow her a kiss.

"This will help you to have a good night's sleep," said the sister as she stuck, what seemed to Sarah, a huge needle in her arm.

"What injuries have I got?" she asked as she was given some tablets to take.

"The doctor will tell you tomorrow after his visit. I'll get a nurse to make you comfortable and hopefully the medication will soon take effect."

For a while she lay there in a half asleep, half-awake stupor; she could hear the distant chatter of patients and nurses but gradually the noise faded into the distance and as the lights were dimmed so she closed her eyes and slept. She dreamt that she was back in Pembrokeshire and she was dressed in white and beside her stood Betty also dressed in white; they were standing by the door of the church on the hill and looking down towards the altar she saw John dressed in his uniform and as she walked towards him he held out his arms and she ran to him. She was safe at last.

It was a good thing that she had slept through the night as the next morning she was awoken at day break with a morning cup of tea.

"Good morning Mrs Lloyd we'll be doing some more tests today and taking you to X-ray; first things first though a nice blanket bath.

'A nice blanket bath in deed', thought Sarah as she was rolled this way and that her dignity completely lost. The pain stabbing through her legs as the two nurses manhandled her.

"Why are my legs hurting?" she questioned.

"I have no idea," retorted one nurse "they are all bandaged up; I expect they'll tell you after you've been to X-ray".

"I've got to take a Mrs Lloyd to X-ray", said a youthful porter.

"Don't worry 'luv' you are safe in my hands," he said as he lifted her onto the trolley. He pushed her with great speed from the ward through the swing doors and down what seemed to her endless dreary corridors that were badly in need of a lick of paint.

"Here's your patient be back for 'er in 'alf an 'our."

She had to recite off her name and address and date of birth to three different people before she was finally pushed into the radiography department.

A pretty young nurse removed the dressings from her legs and then called to the doctor. "I don't think we should X-ray this she should have been sent to the theatre."

"There definitely appears to be a mistake Mrs Lloyd you should have been sent to the theatre."

"What film are they showing?"

Her sarcastic comment was totally ignored.

She was again transported in a dilapidated wheel chair with her legs stretched out in front down even longer corridors filled with waiting patients.

'No wonder we are called 'patients'', she thought 'we need the patience of Job'.

"Sorry about the delay Mrs Lloyd was brought to us instead of to you," the young nurse tried to explain.

Again she went through the same rigmarole as previously; name, address, date of birth, religion; "You're not from these parts then?" said the young doctor attending her.

'That's quite obvious," she was about to retort when a young nurse stuck a thermometer in her mouth.

"We'll give you an injection and you'll soon fall asleep; you'll be back on the ward before you'll know it."

"I think she's waking up", she could hear the familiar voice but it seemed so far away. "Mum it is Merryl can you hear me?"

She opened her eyes but could see very little as everything was a blur; she closed them again and decided she would go back to sleep. Her body felt numb and her head ached and then slowly she began to remember the morning's escapade. What had they done to her in the operating theatre? She couldn't feel anything in her lower extremities. "My legs," she cried out "they've taken my legs".

"Mum wake up you're all right; there's nothing wrong."

"What have they done to my legs," she screamed.

John was now by her side holding her hand; "Everything is fine my love they had to give you anaesthetic to stitch up the nasty wounds on your legs but everything will be fine now."

She could see a young man in a white coat and the sister from the previous evening standing by her bed; "I think you should leave now Mrs Lloyd needs to rest."

"I want to go home," she cried "I want to go home to Betty."

"We'll take you home as soon as we can," said Merryl as she bent to kiss her mother.

"And I'll come too," said John as he placed a lingering kiss upon her lips.

She panicked as she heard them whispering and only caught the last few words "…..it will not be for a few weeks as the wounds will have to heal."

"I'm not stopping here for a few weeks," she cried.

"If you don't calm down Mrs Lloyd we will have to give you an injection."

"You can do what you like but I'm going home tomorrow I'll not stay another day here." She had no chance to say another word as a thermometer was placed in her mouth and a needle in her arm.

Almost a week elapsed before it was agreed that she could return to her daughter's flat; the agreement had been reached as John had paid for a nurse to care for her at home.

"Remember Mrs Lloyd you must stay off your legs and do what you are told;" the sister continued talking but the words were going over Sarah's head she was just glad to be free of the regimentation of the hospital and if she wished she would now be able to sleep all day. 'Yes sister, no sister, three bags full sister,' she said to herself as the list of do's and dont's continued. 'One thing is for certain' she muttered to herself 'there will certainly be no more bed pans'.

"Did you say something mother?"

CHAPTER TWENTY ONE

"You may as well stay until after Christmas hopefully Richard will have leave and we can be a happy family together." Merryl suggested as once more Sarah had raised the question about returning to Pembrokeshire.

"The bandages are off my legs and they are healing well so there is no possible reason why I can't go home I don't like London it makes me nervous living here."

"It is too far for you to travel by train and dad said the petrol isn't available for such a long journey."

"Surely he knows a man who knows a man who can get some petrol for him?"

"Mother shame on you; saving our country is far more important than your journey home. What if we all go down to Norfolk for Christmas?"

"I'm worried about Betty."

"That's just an excuse you know she said in her last letter that she was fine and James was taking good care of her. I must get lunch ready dad will be here in ten minutes I'll leave him sort you out you can be so stubborn."

To Sarah's delight John spent most of each day with them; he brought her flowers and jewellery and any little thing that he thought would bring her pleasure.

When Merryl left them alone their passion would carry them away and they were both eagerly awaiting the time when they could once more become lovers.

"When your legs are better you don't wish to end up back in hospital."

They pleased each other in so many different ways and they both felt like naughty teenagers when Merryl returned one afternoon earlier than anticipated and caught them in a compromising situation. Sarah's thoughts were interrupted when John returned with a big bouquet of flowers.

"Hello there how are my two favourite girls?"

"Waiting for you darling," said Sarah. "I've been waiting patiently to tell you that the doctor signed me off today he told me that my legs were as good as new."

"Just what I've been waiting to hear as I have a surprise for you; and it is one that will not keep until Christmas."

"Come on dad spill the beans."

"I've bought us a house one that I hope you will share with us Merryl until Richard returns home."

Sarah kept rather quiet and John look showed his disappointment. "Cheer up Sarah my love I know what you are thinking and at the moment I'm not going to tell you any more just to cheer you up I will say that it is not in London".

Sarah laughed you are getting to know my every mood I can't keep anything from you. Come on darling do tell us where it is?"

"I've been having some work done on it and when I was away last week I arranged for it to be furnished just as I know you will like it."

"Does that mean dad that you intend two intend to marry?"

"Well I did ask her once and she accepted so I do hope she's not going to turn me down."

"I want to see you get down on one knee and propose to her properly."

"Anything you say my darling girl." The next moment John was beside Sarah's chair and taking a small box from his pocket he took her hand and kneeling on one knee he said; "Will you do me the honour of being my wife?"

Amidst the laughter Sarah said; "I will be honoured noble sir."

John opened the box and took from it an antique gold ring set with diamonds and sapphires. "I know it will fit because I took a ring from your jewellery box."

"Another of your many talents," said Merryl "I would never have guessed that my father was a thief."

After mother and daughter had admired the ring Sarah said "I can't wait to see this new house when do you intend to take us?"

"It is rather short notice but we shall be moving there next week in time for Christmas."

"You do believe in pulling out all the stops to surprise us John as that will only give us ten days to prepare for Christmas."

"Don't worry my love everything will be perfect I promise you."

"Unless Richard gets in touch soon how will he know where we are he's not due back in England until January and letters take so long to get to him."

"He already knows as he has been in on it with me from the beginning."

"Your father's a secret agent now; what will be your next occupation?"

"That will be telling; shall we go out for a meal to celebrate?"

"I'd rather stay at home," said Sarah "I hate the thought of being in the city after dark."

"Sorry sweetheart I forgot; I've got a better idea I'll get someone to bring us something here that will be better."

Sarah was beginning to get used to the life where one just snapped ones fingers and everyone jumped; John certainly had an air of superiority about him but also an endearing nature that opened many doors.

The following days were quite hectic packing up all Merryl and Richard's personal belongings and marking items that were to be taken with them.

"What are you going to do with the flat dad?"

"Keep it on for Richard and I to use or you ladies if you choose to come to London on a shopping spree after the war."

"Will you have far to travel dad from the new place you've bought?"

"If you think you'll get an answer to that you've got another think coming; I am not going to let the 'cat out of the bag, so don't try your wily ways on me. All I will tell you is that I am thinking of selling the business and opening up in a town near to where we shall be living. I've done my research and I think the area could well do with my services."

"Where's that?" Sarah asked.

"You're at it as well; what if I told you Lands' End or John O'Groats would you believe me?"

"We'll soon know when we start out on our journey so you will have to tell us then."

"I might blind fold the pair of you."

"We'll find a good lawyer and have you up for assault."

Two days later they were up at the crack of dawn ready to start their move to a destination still unknown. The hired van had been packed the previous evening and John had paid a young lad well to drive it there and back for him.

"I know what I'll do mum I'll ask Charlie where dad has instructed him to send my belongings."

John overhearing the conversation replied; "That is not going to work my love he's been paid well to work for me you'll not get a word out of him; anyhow he's gone to visit his sister; we'd better make a start because it will be after dark before we get there."

Sarah said, "Well that's one clue; if we travel at thirty miles an hour and it will be dark when we get there it must be quite a distance."

They stopped several times along the route for Merryl to 'spend a penny' and they teased her that she was going to have a footballer because she kept complaining that the baby was restless. "He'd go to sleep dad if he knew where his grandfather was taking him."

"It's a boy this week is it," teased her mother; "You were picking girl's names last week."

"Perhaps it is twins; one of each," remarked her father as he pulled into the side of the road. "The view of the River Wye would be quite splendid if it wasn't winter time; I thought we'd stop and have a few sandwiches and a warm drink."

"Have we got far to go?" questioned Sarah.

"You don't give up do you dear lady?"

They reached the town of Shrewsbury by late afternoon and as they crossed the border into Wales the heavens opened. "Well one thing I do know," said Sarah as she tried to peer out of the window we're in Wales."

"How do you know that mum?" said Merryl as she stretched out across the back seat.

"Well, you know what they say 'it always rains in Wales'".

Two hours elapsed and both women were getting restless; "I need to go again dad can't you stop?"

"Should reach a town in about ten minutes we'll see if we can get something to eat at one of the hotels."

True to his word they pulled up outside the Belle Vue Hotel; there didn't appear to be a soul in sight as they entered into the warmth of reception.

"Good evening sir how may I help?"

"Two rooms for the night and is there chance of an evening meal?"

"Will that be a double and a single sir? We have a few guests visiting their relatives for the Christmas season but I'm sure we can accommodate you. Have you got your ration books with you?"

John looked first at Merryl and then at Sarah who nodded their heads.

"In these difficult times every little helps to provide the few extras. Will you also be staying for breakfast? Dinner will be served in the dining room across the hall at seven o'clock if you would like some liquid refreshment the bar is open."

After John had signed the register and Sarah had handed over a few coupons they made their way towards the lift. "Sorry sir the lift's not working you'll have to use the stairs; you are all on the second floor."

As they slowly made their way up the stairs Merryl turned to her father and said, "I thought she was going to ask for our passports and before any arguments start I'm having the single room it is time you two had some time together."

"Our daughter is very diplomatic," said John as he turned the key to lock the door of their room. "She must know how I long to have my wicked way with you."

Sarah laughed, "Well, you'll have to wait until after dinner because we've just got time for a wash and brush up as dinner is being served at half seven."

The meal really surprised them; the soup, a concoction of mixed vegetables, was warm and appetising and the roast beef was done to perfection served with plenty of winter vegetables and rich gravy; as for the pudding John had the audacity to ask for a second helping; "The Christmas pudding was delicious," he said to the same lady who had been at reception.

"I made a few extra for my guests and I thought you looked the kind of gentleman who would enjoy some good home cooking. I pride myself with my puddings but it is hard to get the right ingredients as your misses will know only too well and before you ask I'm not going to tell you what is in the pudding all that matters is that you enjoyed it 'luv'. Have you got far to go tomorrow? You'd better make an early start 'cause my old man says it's cold enough for snow."

"I'll just go and have a glass of the local brew just be half an hour give you time to sort yourself out."

Merryl looked at her mother and smiled; "Not a very romantic place to spend your first night; I'll see you at breakfast at eight o'clock. Goodnight mum sleep well." She kissed her mother and as she entered her room Sarah could see her daughter grinning like a Cheshire cat.

'How romantic', thought Sarah as she took from her suitcase her warm wool dressing gown and her fleecy striped pyjamas. 'I'm sure I'll be a great turn on in these'.

The black-out curtains were already drawn and switching on the bedside lamps she turned back the freshly laundered bedclothes. The large radiators in the room gave out very little heat and Sarah was glad to have a very quick wash and dabbing on a little of the expensive perfume that John had bought her when she had come out of hospital she put on just the tops of her pyjamas and climbed into bed. She felt uncertain of what to do; was she to pretend to be asleep or should she get back out of bed and sit by the dressing table cleansing her face. She decided it was far too cold to get out of bed so nestled down under the bedclothes.

As she heard his key in the lock she began to shiver, not with cold but with the thought of what was about to happen. Over the last weeks since she had returned from hospital they had so often got near to the point of no return but since the time when Merryl had returned unexpected they had been ill at ease.

"Where's my gorgeous girl?" John asked as he switched on the main lights, "waiting for me I hope."

"Did you need a drink for Dutch courage," she teased.

He burst out laughing, "What the devil have you got on, your grandfather's pyjamas?"

"Hush someone will here you. I thought you would like them sexy don't you think?"

"I hope you've warmed the bed it is freezing." He said as he removed his trousers and neatly folded them, removing his shirt he hung it on a coat hanger.

"If you are freezing why are you taking so long to undress? I hope you don't think you're getting in bed with those things on it's you who has borrowed grandfather's long johns."

"I thought I might get cold if the car broke down."

She watched as he removed his underwear; "You'd better hurry up and get into bed if you are that eager for me I thought you said my pyjamas would put you off."

"I said no such thing," he said as he leaned across her and began to undo the buttons. "Slip your arms out Sarah I'm sure you will look much better without them."

She had hardly had time to disrobe before he was on top of her his mouth eagerly seeking hers and as his manhood entered her she clung to him and buried her face in his neck as she moaned with pleasure. "I love you, I love you so much" he said as he lay back on his pillow his goal achieved.

"Who is going to switch the light out?" she asked.

"No one I haven't finished with you yet; didn't our daughter say that this was our honeymoon?"

He turned over onto his side facing her and for a moment he just lay there looking at her and slowly he traced his finger across her lips and down her neck but when he reached her breasts it was with his hands that touched her; gently grasping them he then fingered her nipples until they became rigid; as his hands moved towards her secret parts he sucked like a baby at her breast. She wanted to scream out with pleasure as he brought her to the heights of ecstasy. This time when they made love the act was long and pleasurable as time and time again he brought her to such a pitch that she clawed at his back begging him not to stop. Her thoughts never wandered from the man who lay upon her; they were young and in love and not in a hotel room on a windswept street in Aberystwyth but lying on the green grass besides the water with the sun streaming down upon their naked bodies.

"I cannot begin to think what our lives would have been like if we had only been together from our youth."

"I expect we would have had a half a dozen children by now if we had spent our life time making love." She held him close and smoothed her fingers through his hair. "I love you so much John Lloyd; I've never stopped loving you and have always dreamed that one day we would meet again. Shall I turn out the light now?"

"Not yet; it is your turn to spoil me."

It was a new experience for her to do as he requested but whatever he asked of her she did with pleasure. It was he who now moaned and begged her not to stop as she teased and titillated his very being; so aroused that he could no longer stand the torment he again entered her; all her inhibitions gone she rolled over on top of him.

"You are so beautiful," he said as he pulled her towards him his lips hungrily seeking hers.

She awoke from a wonderful dream to find him still lying on top of her but his manhood now lay flaccid within her. She had no idea of the time and was afraid to reach for her watch not to disturb him. She thought she heard a tap on the bedroom door but dismissed the idea. She really must try to move as her legs had pins and needles but as tried to slide from under him he pulled her back towards him. "Where do you think you're going?"

"I've got cramp."

"I've got a cure for that," throwing back the bedclothes he began to massage her legs but it didn't stop there; forgotten was the cramp as his fingers and then his tongue took her almost to oblivion.

"I want you," she whispered; enfolding her legs around him she pulled him towards her.

"Hell, look at the time; it is almost eight thirty." His declaration put an end to their love making as they rolled apart laughing.

"That didn't take long," she teased; "by the way have we got far to travel today"?

"Thimble's End".

"At last I've got it out of you; have you bought the cottage from James?"

"That's for me to know and for you to find out; I think what happened a moment ago was John's end don't you? Come on you wanton wench it is time we got washed and dressed I wonder is there any breakfast left I'm starving I could eat a horse."

"I'll see if there's any on the menu," she said as she pranced naked across the room. Turning she saw him standing by the bed doing up his shirt and couldn't help but notice that his manhood was no longer flaccid. "You'll have to wait until tonight for satisfaction", she said as she put on her French knickers and lacy bra.

"That is if you are not too tired," she teased.

"Had a lie in did you then?" said the landlady in her delightful Welsh lilt, "travelling does take it out of you doesn't it? Your daughter has had her breakfast and she told me to tell you that she did knock your door but thought it best to let you sleep in; it is quite a nice morning so she decided to take a stroll along the front. I told her to wrap up warm especially with her in her condition now isn't it. Soon have your breakfast ready, would sir like bacon and egg? I'm afraid I've only got the powdered stuff but if madam would like a boiled egg I might be able to scrounge one from somewhere."

As the landlady returned to the kitchen Sarah whispered, "Do you think Merryl heard us?"

"Shall I ask her?" he teased. "I think I'll book us in for another night then we can stay in bed all day as well; it is very pleasurable way of making up for lost time."

"Hello you two," said their wind swept daughter as she strolled into the dining room. "Is there any tea in the pot? Did you sleep well? I slept like a log didn't hear a thing all night. I let you have a lie in thought you'd be tired after the long journey yesterday. Have we got far to go today?"

"We are going to Pembrokeshire your dad has bought the cottage where Betty and I lived."

"How did you get that out of him?"

"I have my ways and means of doing things."

"You sure have," said John as he tucked into his breakfast.

CHAPTER TWENTY TWO

The sun was shining as they left Aberystwyth but soon the sun disappeared behind a cloud and it started to rain. "Does it always rain in Wales? We'll have to make this trip again in the summer," said John as they journey took them around Cardigan Bay and over the Preseli Mountains. "On a nice day the view from here must be quite spectacular."

"Shall we stop for lunch at Fishguard?" asked Merryl "I'm starving."

"Don't you ever stop eating?" questioned her father.

"Well, I am eating for two."

"I don't think it is worth stopping it is only another fifteen miles. Betty will be worrying about us."

"I did tell not to prepare anything last evening as I guessed we might stop over and she knows we should hopefully arrive at "Thimble's End by mid-day."

"If you two hadn't slept late we would have been there by now."

The rain had stopped and a wintry sun re-appeared brightening up the day.

"How much further as travelling around these country lanes is making me feel sick?"

"Shall I stop the car? I must admit I'm not used to driving on such narrow roads."

"Shall I drive then I know my way from here? The lanes in Norfolk are no better and you should be used to these lanes as you drove here to buy the house."

"You drive? You must be joking and when I came to look over the house I came by train and I had someone to pick me up at the station."

"I'll have you know I'm a very good driver I drove Betty's car from Cardiff and I also drive a horse and cart."

"Mum you are funny you don't drive a horse and cart the horse just takes you where you want to go."

"I'll have you know it takes a lot of skill to make a horse go where you want it too and I can also drive a tractor."

"Well my love you are constantly surprising me with all your hidden talents so if you wish you can take over the driving."

191

She soon got used to John's car and as they left behind the town she began to put her foot down. "How's that for driving?"

John put his hand on her knee; "You drive really well my love but there I'm finding out that you are good at so many other things."

She turned right onto a water logged lane and to Merryl's dismay the car bumped up and down over the rocky road. "Where are you taking us mum?"

"Home," she replied.

"I think your mother might be right I'm sure it would be much better by horse and cart."

"That's the Lord of the Manor's home," Sarah pointed to the large mansion on her right and there's James' place I expect Betty will be there." As Sarah went to turn into the drive John stopped her; "Shall we go to the cottage first?"

"But Betty will be waiting for us."

"The cottage please," he tried to sound stern but a smile was creeping onto his face.

"Make up your minds you two I'm getting desperate."

Sarah pulled up outside the cottage and after putting on the brake she was about to open the door when John put a restraining hand on her arm and mouthed the word, "Wait."

"Can I get out? I can't wait for you two I'm sure I can find the bathroom." She opened the door of the car and was about to step out when the cottage door opened and Merryl stood face to face with her husband. "Richard," she almost cried "what are you doing here?"

"Shall we leave them?" said John "drive back to James' home Betty will be waiting for us there."

"Would you mind putting me in the picture? It seems to me that Richard has been sharing this secret with you as well as Betty and James. Where exactly are we all going to live?"

"I bought the cottage for Merryl and Richard and I bought the other house for us."

"Where are James and Betty going to live?"

John didn't reply and as she pulled up outside the large farm house the front door opened and a very expectant Betty came to the door to welcome them.

192

"Welcome home," said her friend hugging her, "the bulge prevents me from getting to close."

"You are looking beautiful, pregnancy really suits you; where's James?"

"Just putting the finishing touches to lunch; I've set places for the six of us do you think the young ones will join us?"

"I'm sure they will as Merryl is constantly hungry." Taking her friend's hand Sarah said "I thought you were my friend yet you have kept this secret from me you never even dropped a hint in any of your letters."

"I was sworn to secrecy," Betty laughed.

"Is there room for us all here? I thought John had bought the cottage for us."

Betty turned to John; "Shame on you Major not telling your good lady what you have been up to,"

"What's all this 'Major' nonsense his name is John."

"I know dear it is just a shared joke. When John first got in touch with us he spoke in his superior voice and said 'Major John Lloyd-Smythe is Mrs Betty Johnson available?' That's why James and I refer to him as the 'Major'."

"Neither of you have answered my question."

"We'll tell you after lunch as I think it is almost ready." Betty returned to the front door and pulled the cord that hung from a large bell. "That will bring them hurrying for lunch."

"We used to call the cattle like that," teased Sarah as she sat next to John at the dining table. "Do you think you can tell me how Richard got leave to be here or is that another secret?"

"I don't know if I should tell you," teased John "one doesn't know who could be listening 'walls have ears'."

"Well I'm not a German spy so perhaps you can tell me."

"He's stationed down here."

"That wasn't too difficult was it now how about telling me where we are going to live?"

"This woman is like Polly Parrot keeping on and on do you think I'd better tell her?" He put the question to Betty.

"When the other two arrive; I can see them with their arms around each other crossing the yard."

Everyone was happy as they settled down to a steaming bowl of vegetable soup and warm crusty bread. "All home grown," James boasted "They tell us to 'Dig for Victory' I'm definitely doing that. Do you think we'll make a landowner out of John?" He questioned but refrained from saying any more as Betty's frown warned him off. "Sorry; I wasn't aware that Sarah hasn't been told."

"Sarah hasn't been told anything; I'm completely in the dark all I know is that the cottage is for Merryl and Richard and this is your home so I would like someone to tell me where we are going to live; can I assume that you've converted a barn?"

"Now that's an idea I haven't thought about; is it all right for us to stay here until the cow shed has been converted."

"I'm sure you are all getting great pleasure out of teasing me but until I get a sensible answer I'm not going to eat any more." Sarah put her spoon on the plate and folding her arms she sat back in her chair.

"We can't let such a lovely lunch go to waste so perhaps it will be a good idea if we tell mum," said Merryl tucking in to her second bowl of soup.

"So you're in it as well," laughed her mother.

"Honestly mum I've only just found out Richard told me."

"Shall I tell her?" asked Betty.

"If you wish," replied John moving his chair so that he could put his arm around Sarah.

"How do you fancy being the Lady of the Manor?"

"What Manor?" Sarah was tingling with excitement.

"The Manor here at 'Thimble's End; John read about it in a London newspaper and phoned us to ask what it was all about. It was only then that we found out that all three properties were classed as 'Thimble's End'; he asked us were we interested in buying 'The Manor' or any other of the properties. So after a meeting when you were still in hospital we decided we'd buy the farm house and John The Manor for you and the cottage for Merryl and Richard we both paid half for the land."

Sarah could hardly speak with excitement; "Are you telling me that we are all going to live here and work the land together?"

"Yes my love we are all going to live here but as for working the land Betty and I will leave that to you and James. I'm going into business in town and hopefully after the war Richard will join me."

"Shall we drink a toast?" said James 'popping' open a bottle of champagne.

The glasses filled everyone stood to their feet and John raising his glass said "to us all and 'Thimble's End'."

"This is all very nice", said Sarah holding her glass for a refill "but when do I see our new home?"

"If you go on drinking 'bubbly' like that you'll not be able to walk there and back."

"I'm afraid you might be disappointed as only half the work has been done; there's a new kitchen and laundry room, the dining room, lounge and my study and a smaller sitting room have all been decorated and furnished and three of the five bedrooms have also been refurbished with an en suite to one of the bedrooms and the builders have just finished tiling the family bathroom I had to give them a Christmas bonus to get the work done."

"It all sounds wonderful but can we all hurry up and finish as I want to see our home. How did you manage to get men to do the work with so many away in the forces?"

"Two elderly brothers and their grandsons and they managed to subcontract to men they knew would be glad of the work. If you are satisfied with everything the men will recommence work after Christmas.

'Satisfied' wasn't the word that Sarah would have used she was absolutely enchanted with the house as she walked from room to room. "Betty dear you know me better than I know myself," she said hugging her the furnishings are just what I would have picked. We'll have great fun doing up the rest of the house."

"I don't know about that I think I might have my hands full when the baby arrives; people look at me with amazement when they see someone my age having a baby."

"I'll look after the baby you can do the decorating," Sarah teased.

"The place is well aired and your love nest is ready for you."

Sarah felt a bit 'hot under the collar' when she thought of the previous night's activities and she thought she saw a smirk upon her daughter's face.

That night Sarah and John lay in their bed with the curtains open.

"Just the perfect night for love," said John as he hungrily kissed her.

"We'd better draw the curtains you don't know who could be watching us."

"Only the man in the moon my love."

"The same moon that shines down on my brothers wherever they are; do you think we'll ever meet up again?"

"Make a wish upon that star that is shining more brilliantly than the others and I promise your wish will come true."

"You are so romantic," she said kissing him, "goodnight my darling sleep well."

"What do you mean 'goodnight' I have no intention of going to sleep this is going to be a night of love."

Dawn was breaking in the eastern sky before they fell asleep in each other's arms.

"Breakfast is served madam". John stood before her holding her breakfast tray with only his bath robe covering his naked body.

"You are really spoiling me; what are you having?" She said as she put some homemade preserve on her toast.

"You and two slices of toast."

Even after their night of passion she noticed that he was ready for more love making. "Are you coming back to bed I've nearly finished."

"Is that an invitation because as you can see I haven't finished I have only got to look at you and you turn me on."

She was getting used to and enjoying the foreplay as he teased and tormented her; she was quickly learning the things that he liked having done to him and after the final act of love they lay nestled together both almost falling asleep when a familiar voice called; "Is there anyone around? Betty wants us all to go to lunch at their place."

"We're making the beds," shouted John quickly pulling on his trousers and then throwing Sarah's robe to her.

"I'm glad someone has some initiative," said a very flushed Sarah. "She'll know what we've been up too."

"So what we're a couple aren't we?"

During lunch Sarah was rather quiet, John's words lingering on her mind. 'Yes,' she thought 'they were a couple but not a married couple'; suddenly she brightened up when realisation dawned upon her as she arrived at a solution. It would have to wait until after Christmas but plans could be made now.

"Don't any of you take offence but I'm going for a walk with the dogs and I'd like to go alone.

"No offence taken my love I'm exhausted after such a delicious meal."

Merryl coughed; "You should see a doctor nasty cough that," said her father with a glint of humour in his eye.

As she walked the dogs down the country lanes Sarah had one goal in mind and the results of which she would not confide in anyone until all arrangements had been made. The afternoon was bright but there was quite a keen wind that James had said might bring snow. Thoughts of a white Christmas filled her with joy and also the anticipation that for the first time in many a long year she would be catering for a large family as it had already been arranged that Betty and James would supply the food and they would all dine at The Manor. She returned home, her mission accomplished, feeling quite excited as her plan had been set into motion.

"Where have you been? We were about to send a search party to look for you."

"I walked further than I realised and of course then I had to walk back," was all she said.

Christmas Eve the 'two fat ladies' as they now referred to themselves sat each side of the kitchen table sampling the mince pies and sausage rolls as Sarah baked batch after batch of delicious savouries. Neither questioned how she had managed to get all the ingredients; 'a good thing really' thought Sarah as she stuffed the turkey that had been raised on the farm especially for Christmas.

"Is there carrot in these mince pies?" questioned her daughter.

"That's for me to know and you to find out; I've had years of experience in making do."

"Can I have my Christmas present now?" asked John as a very weary Sarah fell into bed beside him.

"You know I can never say 'no' to you but don't forget my love I have to be up at the crack of dawn as I have a busy day in front of me."

"I've have a busy night," was his reply as he began to caress her weary body. Forgotten was her weariness as his kisses and caresses filled her with eagerness for love making; also forgotten was the coldness of the night as they lay naked upon each other.

"That's the best Christmas present I've ever had," he said playing with her nipples.

"You keep doing that Major and I will be wanting my Christmas present too."

"Naughty, naughty making fun of your friends but there you are a naughty girl enticing me like that."

"I just love the way they call you 'Major'," she said as she kissed him 'goodnight'. "I really must get some shut eye as I should be up before seven and it is now three o'clock."

"Goodnight Mother Christmas I love you."

Sarah was happy that she had made it the 'best Christmas ever' for her family and friends and together they welcomed in the New Year of 1944 with the hope that peace would soon come with hope for the future for the two babies that would soon arrive and Sarah added an extra wish that the plans she had made would all work out perfectly.

CHAPTER TWENTY THREE

"Are either of you two ladies able to come shopping with me I need some advice?"

"I'd love a day in town but what if……" Sarah didn't give Betty time to finish.

"If baby decides to make its appearance I can always take you to the hospital and the same goes for you Merryl. You've both got at least six weeks to go so I can count on you both; I'll ask John if there's enough petrol to get us to town and back or it will be the horse and trap for us."

"No way," said Merryl as she settled back in one of her mother's comfortable chairs, "you'd need a crane to get us two up in the cart and what about the poor horse."

"I'll pick you both up about ten o'clock and perhaps we can find somewhere to have a bite to eat in town."

"Did you say you'll pick us up?"

"Yes; why?"

"I'd feel safer if dad was driving."

"Saturday is his day off he's been working hard building up his clientele so he deserves his week-end to relax."

"Sarah Ann Lloyd I know you better than you think and I believe you are up to something."

"Let you know tomorrow but in the meantime can you ask James to pop around when he has five minutes preferable when John isn't here."

"What are you up to mother?"

"Tomorrow," was all she said as she ushered them to the door.

"Hello there, Betty said you wished to see me; what can I do for you?"

"Two things; firstly how good are you at keeping a secret and secondly how clever are you in persuading someone to leave work and come to a special meeting with you?"

"Betty said you were up to something and can I assume this 'someone' you are referring to is John?"

"I want you to persuade him to wear his uniform as you have been invited to an old comrades regimental fund raiser or whatever you can think up on Monday at two o'clock."

"I'm sure that will be easy enough but the question is why?"

"Betty will tell you tomorrow as long as you can arrange to get John dressed up in his uniform on Monday."

The following morning Sarah awoke early and slipped out of bed hoping not to disturb John; "Come back to bed the bed's cold without you; it's my day off and I thought we could make whoopee all the morning."

"You and your making whoopee you know I'm taking the girls to town to shop for baby clothes."

"Sorry, I forgot I'll just have to wait until tonight but remember it will be early to bed for us."

As Sarah bent to kiss him he tried to grab her but she picked up the pillow and threw it at him and quickly left the room calling back; "Have a nice day."

"How can I without you," was his retort.

An hour later as she called to say she was going to pick up Merryl and Betty there was no reply so she guessed he had gone back to sleep. The two ladies were waiting outside Merryl's cottage; "Glad it's fine I hate going shopping when it is raining," said Betty as she clamoured into the back of the car and was joined by Merryl.

"Now that we are out of ear shot are you going to tell us what you are up too?" asked Betty as they were driving into town.

"I'm getting married and we are going to town to buy some finery for my wedding day."

"When did Dad arrange this?"

"Dad hasn't arranged it, I have and as yet he doesn't know a thing about it."

"But what about the wedding rings?"

"I bought one for John last time I was in town and I've got my grandmothers; she had a long and happy marriage and I just hope her ring will bring me good luck. Grancha gave them to me when nana died; he had them in a box as the rings kept slipping off her fingers."

"When did you arrange all this?"

"Remember the afternoon I went for a long walk; well I walked as far as the church on the hill and asked my friend the vicar when could he marry us and so the 14th February was booked at 2 o'clock. John had surprised me about the house and I wanted to give him a lovely surprise."

"You are romantic mother picking Valentine's Day how are you going to get John there?"

"I've left that to James; he's has to get him to wear his uniform for an old comrades' do or something or other."

"I believe he has done that because I heard him telling James he's hasn't worn his uniform in over twelve months so he'll have to give it a good press and he hoped it still fitted."

"What about the wedding breakfast?"

"We'll have a special dinner in the evening."

"Who is going to cook that?"

"James is cooking the turkey and the soup for starters and I'm sorry to have to tell you but you two will have to do the vegetables and I was lucky enough to get some tin fruit when I was in town so all in all it should be a jolly good feast and I've also told James where to find a few bottles of something special that John has stashed away!"

"Your mother is a great one to organise things; she did all the arranging for our move to Pembrokeshire and as it has turned out it was the best thing I've ever done. James and I are waiting to get married until after the baby is born I'd look well walking down the aisle like this."

"Well you'll have to do it on my wedding day because one of you can give me away and the other can be my matron-of-honour; a good word to use to describe both of you. You can discuss that with each other or draw straws."

They were all laughing as they parked the car in town and together headed for the finest dress shop the town had to offer.

"I'm afraid we don't stock baby clothes," said the elderly assistant.

"I'm looking for a wedding outfit," said Sarah beaming from ear to ear.

"I don't think we have anything in stock that will er um….." the assistant coughed, "fit your daughter in her condition."

"My daughter is married," Sarah replied "the wedding outfit if for me."

"We have very few bridal dresses as they take so many coupons but we do have a nice range of utility costumes. What exactly is madam looking for?"

"What have you got in evening wear; something in a pretty blue."

"This is nice mum dad loves you in blue," Merryl pointed to a long silk dress with a lace overlay.

"How lovely renewing your marriage vows; it is lovely to hear something nice with all the suffering we have around us."

Sarah couldn't help but say, "We haven't been married before this is for our wedding day I don't think I should wear white, do you?"

A very red faced assistant ushered Sarah to a changing room whilst Betty and Merryl hid their giggles by looking at suitable maternity wear to camouflage their bumps. "Perhaps we can wear white," Betty teased.

"When are you James planning to marry?" Merryl questioned and was glad that she wasn't overheard.

"We are thinking sometime in May; if we don't make it then we'll have to wait until after the harvest."

Sarah viewed herself in the mirror; "What do you two think I've tried on two others but I think it will have to be the blue one."

"What are you going to wear with it mum it will be too cold to go out without a coat?"

"You can wear my mink stole and hat."

"That's a good idea Betty; something old, something new, something borrowed, something blue. I have grandmother's old rings, I'll borrow your stole and hat and I have a new dress that is blue. Now I'm sorted out what about you two?"

"I rather fancy this long dress; the rich shade of violet will suit me and it is nice and loose and I have just the shoes and hat to go with it. By the way, we have decided that I will be your matron-of-honour and Merryl, as your daughter, will give you away."

"What do you think of this lilac two piece mum? It has a long skirt and a smock top and I have that lovely navy pill box hat and navy shoes and bag that will be just perfect."

As the three satisfied customers left the shop they noticed that their assistant was deep in conversation with two others. "I bet she's telling them that I have a grown up daughter and now I'm marrying the father."

"Well, it is the truth isn't it mum?"

"How are we going to keep all these packages hidden from John and how are you going to get readt?"

"I'll tell him I'm spending the day with Betty as he's off gallivanting with James. We can prepare a lot of the food in the morning and everything should be organised in time for us to dine at six o'clock."

Merryl laughed, "We will not have to keep that from dad for long because once James gets him to the church he'll smell a rat."

Sarah pulled the car into Betty's drive and unloaded the boot keeping a sharp look out that John wasn't about. James came to help them and said "I think John is walking the dogs I saw him going by about ten minutes ago."

"If you're going to church in the morning mum Richard and I will join you if you don't mind going in the jeep."

"One thing I didn't think about is getting to the church; John will say he needs the car to take him and James to town."

204

"If I ask Richard perhaps he can come home in one of their cars instead of the jeep, he can say it a matter of great urgency; I hope so anyhow or we will definitely be going by horse and cart."

"See you in the morning," said Sarah as she saw John coming up the lane the dogs bounding in front of him.

"Have a good day shopping? Did you get what you wanted?"

"We bought some napkins and some baby nightdresses and nightdresses for Betty and Merryl," she was telling the truth because after they had left the dress shop they had gone in search of some necessary items for the two expectant mums to be.

The day of the wedding dawned bright and Sarah could hardly hide her excitement.

"I forgot to ask; where are you and James off to today?"

"Some fund raising do or other that's why I was up at the crack of dawn ironing my uniform."

"I can't wait to see you in your uniform it will remind me of when we met."

"Both myself and my uniform have changed since those days. I'd rather spend the day in bed with you than go to this old comrades' gathering."

"If you weren't going there you'd have been in work by now."

"I have plenty of time before I pick James up at one thirty; how about an hour on the bed?"

"Sorry, I have to decline your very tempting suggestion as I've promised Merryl I'd help with the baby's room and I should have been there ten minutes ago." Placing a kiss on his cheek she said, "Don't you think you'd better have another shave you don't know who you'll meet at one of these occasions?"

"No one as lovely as you; I expect we'll be late home as we'll most likely go for a couple of beers."

She dashed off down the drive, up the lane and across the yard to Betty's home; "What a lovely smell" she said as she entered the kitchen "I hope John doesn't catch a whiff of the turkey cooking when he comes to pick you up James."

"I'm meeting him at your place; everything is organised for dinner now we got to get John away in time for you ladies to get into your finery."

"I must say you are looking very smart James I love to see a man in uniform."

"I'm proud to wear the uniform of the Royal Welch Fusiliers."

"I will be well protected today with three men all in uniform; what tactics are you going to use to get John to the church?" Sarah asked.

"I can pretend I've got the venue wrong and get him to drive down different lanes until we stop at the church."

"Don't be late because I will be waiting in the church."

"I thought it was the bride who kept the groom waiting not the other way around," teased Merryl. "I hope you don't pass Richard on your way or dad will be wondering why Richard is on his way home."

The three women leaving James to keep an eye on the turkey went to the cottage to begin preparing themselves for the afternoon's big event. At one o'clock all that was left to do was to slip on their dresses so the three sat by the kitchen table drinking a cup of freshly brewed tea and discussing what John would say when he found out that he had been hoodwinked. "Talking of John," said Sarah what if he decides to come over for me to see him in his uniform or check on how the decorating is going."

"I never thought of that," replied Merryl, "don't worry mum he'll never twig if he sees us sitting at the kitchen table in our dressing gowns."

"I'm off," shouted James as he passed the window, "see you in church."

By one thirty they were all dressed and waiting for Richard to arrive, "What if he's been called to duty."

"Don't panic mum he's not on duty today."

206

"What if John doesn't want to marry me?"

"Now you are being stupid that's all he's been talking about is fixing a date for your wedding. He was thinking you'd make a lovely June bride."

"I know what I forgot to do."

"What's wrong now?"

"I haven't got a bouquet."

"Will this do," said Betty as she returned from the bathroom with a posy of snowdrops and wild daffodils, "That's all I could find in the garden."

"It is beautiful and just like you my dear friend to remember that I love the little snowdrops the herald of spring."

"Do you remember me saying that when I got married I would have the church filled with daffodils?"

"Come on you two not time for reminiscing; get your wraps, Richard is here."

"What a posh limousine," Sarah said as she lifted her skirt to get into the back with Betty.

"Where to ladies I'm your chauffer for the afternoon?"

"To the church on the hill please," said his wife leaning over and giving him a kiss.

"I thought I was going to the maternity hospital."

"Don't tease," Merryl replied the way his lordship is playing up that wouldn't surprise me."

There didn't appear to be a soul in sight as they drove through the village and following the little white road that led up hill and down dale until the final hill brought them to the church. "What a lovely view," said Richard as he opened the doors for the ladies to alight. "I so glad the sun is shining for you." He bent and kissed Sarah on the cheek; "dad will fall in love with you all over again when he sees how beautiful you look. I had better put the car round the back or there will be questions asked."

The vicar had suggested that they wait in the vestry; carefully picking their way along the cobbled path they saw him waiting for them. "I'm sorry it is rather cold in there so let's hope John will arrive on time am I to assume he still doesn't know he's getting married today."

Sarah nodded; suddenly she was feeling rather nervous and all kinds of thoughts were flooding through her mind.

"You will hear the organ and that will be your cue to make your entrance."

"I think I can see dad's car coming up the hill; I'll make myself scarce," said Richard as he followed the vicar through the door; the vicars robes flowing behind him.

"How is James going to get John into the church?" Merryl asked.

"He said he would tell John that the church door is open so he'll go and see if there is someone there who will tell him the way and hoping that if he is long winded about it John will come to look for him."

Sarah kept pacing up and down and kept asking Betty the time; "Only two minutes have gone since you last asked." Her friend replied.

Sarah was about to ask the time yet again when she heard the familiar chords of the Bridal March being played on the organ. 'Thank you God,' she prayed silently 'Thank you God for everything.' She hooked her arm into her daughters and with Betty following behind they walked through the open church doors. Her eyes met those of John's as he stood at the altar steps with Richard by his side. Both men smartly dressed in uniform but her eyes were only for the man who would soon be her husband. It was only then that she noticed that the church wasn't empty and she looked at Merryl and smiled. How kind the vicar was to rope in his congregation for her special day. Slowly she made her way down the aisle until she was by his side. His eyes said it all as he mouthed the words "I love you."

His voice was so deep and masculine and filled her heart with joy as he repeated after the vicar the vows to love and to cherish her till death they do part; unlike her own sensitive, soft tone as she promised to love and obey him. She was trembling with excitement as he placed her grandmother's gold band on her finger and as she held his hand she came over all hot as her thoughts wandered, just for a fleeting moment, back to the bedroom and the remembrance of his hands caressing her body. As they knelt together by the altar she said a silent prayer for her absent brothers and their safe return.

"Well Mrs Lloyd-Smythe you have really had one up on me," John said as they signed the register. He whispered in her ear, "just wait until I get you home."

"What are you two whispering about?" Betty questioned.

"Our honeymoon; that I will have to arrange."

As they walked back down the aisle to the airs of the Wedding March Sarah thought; all in all their wedding had been perfect. James had read the lesson from Corinthians with the words 'Faith, Hope and Love but the greatest of these is Love,' and the congregation had sung 'Love Divine' and at her request Jerusalem. She was the one to be surprised as a guard of honour from Richard's air force base were waiting outside the church.

"I love you all for making our wedding day a day we will never forget."

James with his box Brownie took photos of the happy couple and then the vicar took photos of them all together.

"Your carriage awaits," said Richard and she stood and stared in amazement as one of the farm workers arrived with the horse and trap. The horse wearing an old straw hat and a bow of ribbon in his neatly plaited tail.

"You said if there wasn't a car available you would go to church in a horse and cart so that gave me the idea that if the weather was fine I'd arrange for you to travel home that way; with you at the reins being you arranged everything." Merryl kissed her mother and then her father. "We'll see you at home don't get lost."

"Before we leave I must say something to the congregation"; turning she went back into the church. "I just wish to thank you all for making my wedding day so pleasurable and when this terrible war is over my husband and I will invite you to a garden party at our home; thank you all and God Bless." The words 'my husband and I' lingered on her mind it was a lovely thought that at last they were one.

Arm in arm they walked down the path through the guard of honour and were greeted with a shower of rice; and lifting the skirt of her dress, to the applause of those gathered to see them off, she took John's hand as he helped her step up and taking the reins she said "Home boy, home to 'Thimble's End'.

CHAPTER TWENTY FOUR

The war was over; the end of six long years of misery for the people of Britain but those that were gathered with Sarah today were there to thank God that they were there to tell the tale.

On the 14th February 1944 John and Sarah had been married in the pretty little church on the hill it had been the realization of a dream that had begun way back in the summer of 1917.

It was a beautiful August day and as she sat on the garden bench nursing a baby she looked out at the people of the village who had gathered that day for her garden party; the party that she had promised them on her wedding day.

Two toddlers; a boy and a girl played at her feet and a small group of older children were trying to fly a kite over the far end of the garden and playing with them was a bearded gentleman. Admiring the flower beds were her husband and another slender man in his early forties. Her daughter Merryl and her friend Betty were busy in the kitchen keeping a constant flower of cups of tea and soft drinks whilst Richard and James kept the men happy as they poured out glasses of larger and handed out bottles of beer. It was just as she had planned and everything was running smoothly.

Victory in Europe had been declared on the 8th May when the people of Britain had celebrated with street parties and London had gathered outside Buckingham Palace as the King and Queen joined by the Prime Minister Winston Churchill had come out onto the balcony time after time to the cheers of the crowds whilst the two young Princesses had mingled with the crowds. War with Japan had only just ended on 15th August.

Sarah had had many a reason for the delay in holding her garden party one being that she had wanted her two brothers and their families to celebrate with her. It had been easy to get in touch with Emlyn as he had been home in Portsmouth with his family since the beginning of May but it had taken her almost two months for Dewi to make arrangements to come home. She was so proud of the two 'boys' who had left the valley with nothing and now were respected citizens; Emlyn had risen in the ranks and had decided that the navy in peace time would still be his career. His pretty little wife Carol and their three children; two boys and a girl were an added bonus to Sarah's ever increasing family and as she had welcomed Dewi and his Spanish wife Marguerite and their young daughter Marie who was the living image of her dark sensual mother she had wept as all the old memories came flooding back. Dewi had revealed that his 'hush hush' war time work had entailed working with the French Resistance getting British soldiers, air men and resistance workers out of occupied France. The first words he had said when they had met at the station were, "Hello sis you haven't forgotten your promise to come to listen to me sing at the Albert Hall; I'll get to do it one day."

Her sister Wendy and her husband Glyn had arrived the previous evening making the family reunion complete. The war years had worked magic on Wendy and the elegant black dress that she now wore did justice to her sylph like figure and brought many an admiring glances. Both parents of the two sisters, they had taken as evacuees, had been killed during the air raids on London in the summer of '44 of the V2 rocket (an invisible weapon that the first the people knew of its existence was when it exploded) and wheels were now in motion for Glyn and Wendy to legally adopt the two girls as it seemed they had no other relatives that would take them into their home.

Poor Millie, Morgan's daughter, hadn't made it through the last winter; the harsh weather conditions had been the breaking point for the fragile young woman and she developed pneumonia and had died in hospital. Sarah hadn't been able to go to the funeral that Wendy had arranged, as she had taken to her bed, not because of ill health but for a far more pleasurable reason, the baby that she now held in her arms. Almost a year to the day of their wedding Thomas John Lloyd arrived in the world weighing in at seven pounds twelve ounces. She had chosen his name in memory of her beloved grandfather and hoped that he would grow into a strong and upright man just like his father and great-great-grandfather. The birth of their son, under very difficult conditions, had brought Sarah and John even closer together; a child they never thought, at Sarah's late age, they would ever have. Her doctor had kept her in bed for the last three months and Thomas John had surprised them all by making uncomplicated, early arrival into the world.

Knowing that there would definitely be no more children and that Thomas John was a precious gift, an added bonus to their now perfect life their love making grew more intense and their need to please each other never ebbed. They took the opportunity, at times when baby slept, to make love and John would take it all as part of their family life when baby cried at the most inopportune moment.

Here gathered on the lawn of The Manor at Thimble's End were her family: Merryl, Richard and their little boy Edward Richard Lloyd; Dewi, his wife Marguerite and their daughter Marie; Emlyn, his wife Carol and their children Michael, Allison and her name sake Sarah Anne; Wendy, Glyn and the twins Alice and Kate and still very close to her heart her friend Betty; now Mrs James Brown who had just celebrated their first wedding anniversary with their beautiful seventeen month old little girl Elizabeth Sarah Anne.

Someone turned up the volume of the radio and Miss Lynne's words filled Sarah's eyes with tears; *"We'll meet again don't know where, don't know when…"*

She felt her husband's strong hand on her shoulder and she looked up at him the love in her eyes driving away the tears.

"They are playing our song," he said kissing her on the top of her head, "I told you darling that the blue skies would drive the dark clouds away. It has taken a long time but here we are my love, here to tell the tale, of the fire of the love in your heart that kept you hoping and dreaming that one day we would meet again."

"I loved you then and I never stopped loving you and now my darling I love you more than ever."

A cork 'popped' behind them and James called out "I hope you've all got a glass of something never mind if it is lemonade or beer shall we raise our glasses and toast our hosts." Betty handed them both a glass of champagne as James continued "To John and Sarah may they have a long and happy life."

"Three cheers for Mr and Mrs Lloyd," someone called from the throng of people who had gathered in front of the house; "Hip, hip hooray".

"Thank you all," said John "and now I will raise my glass to you all and to our country; to us the people who made Britain Great."

All characters are fictitious –

Grammatically errors are all part of typical Welsh conversation.

Text Copyright©2014
Val Baker Addicott
All Rights Reserved.

Made in the USA
Charleston, SC
11 March 2014